TWO INCHES TALLER

AN ARMY WIFE'S JOURNEY FROM CHAOS TO CALM

NANDITA WARRIER

Readomania

Readomania
An imprint of Kurious Kind Media Private Limited
readomania.com
email: contact@readomania.com
Facebook: facebook.com/iamreadomania
Twitter: twitter.com/iamreadomania
Instagram: iamreadomania

First Published in 2023 by Readomania

Edited by Indrani Ganguly (Managing Editor, Readomania)

ISBN: 978-93-91800-32-1

Typeset in Palatino Linotype by Shine Graphics
Printed in Delhi

To my little Pihu, who completes me…

PROLOGUE

Ladakh Sector, 1995

'Life can change in a split second.'

I experienced this on that sunny morning when the world seemed more than perfect—a glorious expanse of the Himalayas at a distance, a sparkling tributary of the Dras barely a hundred feet away, and a valley showing off a fresh, new carpet of wildflowers!

After months of bitter winter, when temperatures dropped to minus 30 degrees Celsius, I was soaking in the warm, toasty feel to the air. That wasn't all! Breaking the long spell of solitude, I had the pleasure of some interesting company—Capt. Gautam, my senior from the unit, who had come visiting from his forward post. "You lucky bastard! We deal with gunfire, and you get to live in this heaven!" he slapped my back hard.

"You're right, sir, this place is something else! But don't forget, just a few weeks back, the snow was ready to eat us up!"

We were standing on the edge of a cliff, overseeing the colourful valley fenced by tall mountains. Capt. Gautam looked around, "What a sexy view, man! Wish I had my camera." He had climbed up to my post, straight after a night patrol in the neighbouring valley. I gave him a mock salute, "No sign of fatigue, sir, can't make out that you were up all night!"

"*Oye! Maska mat lagaa, chai-shai pila,*" he rubbished my compliment.

"Right, sir," I turned to instruct the cook to arrange for our breakfast.

Barely had I moved 20–30 steps when I heard a loud bang—artillery shelling! Even before we could take positions, there was another explosion and a shell landed pretty close to Capt. Gautam. As the splinters flew around, he heaped up on the spot. I lay on the ground, stunned. Being a newly commissioned officer, I had heard of the terror of artillery, but never experienced it. I took a while to recover from the daze. In the meantime, some of our sentries jumped into action. Literally putting their lives on the line, they rushed towards Capt. Gautam and moved him to the safety of a bunker.

I can never forget the sight—how in one instant, that cheerful, smiling man was reduced to a blood-soaked limp body, matted with debris; barely breathing. Through all the blood and gore, I noticed that he had lost a portion of his right leg.

Gathering all my courage, I took charge, and requested the Battalion Headquarters for an urgent air evacuation. I was asked to wait for an update.

Suddenly, the world around us started to change, as if the weather was somehow connected with our sagging spirits. Thick, dark clouds appeared from nowhere, increasing our anxiety manifold. Even in clear weather, air access was difficult given the tall mountains on all sides.

Now with poor visibility, the task seemed impossible.

The shelling had stopped, but it could restart any moment. After ensuring that our troops were safe and bunkered in, I focused on helping Capt. Gautam, whose erratic breathing was making me breathless. We were doing everything possible to stop the bleeding, which honestly didn't add up to much. Time was running out and if he didn't get help fast, he wouldn't be able to make it.

Just then we heard the rumble of a helicopter. We peeked into the sky, but it was too hazy to spot anything, even though the chopper seemed to hover somewhere close. Hope lit up our faces and I started assuring my knocked-out senior that everything was going to be fine.

"The sound seems stationary, they're not able to approach us," someone whispered. "How can they fly between the mountains in this haze and rain?"

The pilot hung on for a while before making a retreat, as though he wanted us to know that he tried. As the rumble went down and finally died out, I had a pit in my stomach. Despite the field dressing, Capt. Gautam had lost a lot of blood and chances of saving this good man seemed bleak. In desperation, I even considered moving him down the mountain on a stretcher. But the weather and the distance ruled it out. Helplessness was killing me!

Even though I had trained hard to be an army officer, at 23, I was just a youngster. I tried to project courage and positivity to my troops, but in reality, I felt like a five-year-old: lost and terrified.

Capt. Gautam's happy face, beaming in the morning sun kept flashing before my eyes. Why did he have to visit my post at all? Why couldn't he have come a day prior? Why didn't I ask him to walk along with me? What kind of wicked fun explains such attacks?

Suddenly, we heard the rumble again. Our people hadn't given up on us! I got emotional just listening to the operator: "Adverse conditions. But pilot trying to access the valley from another side." After a few moments, the precious update we were all praying for: "Chopper approaching in seven minutes."

My heart burst with pride! One man was risking himself to save another life—that of a brother officer who in fact, was an absolute stranger.

Even after two years, memory of the incident gives me the chills!

That day, through sheer determination and skill, the pilot airlifted Capt. Gautam and deposited him at the Base Hospital at Srinagar—a place legendary for saving lives. Thankfully, the tradition continued with Capt. Gautam. Despite losing a foot and some part of his intestines, he battled it out at the hospital, making a full recovery in three months. I couldn't speak to him during this period, but I got a letter from him with a 'Thank You' note! He believed that it was our exemplary care that saved him despite such grievous wounds. I wrote back: "*Chai Shai* is waiting for you, sir. This time, bring along your camera."

After a few months, I was moved to the Kashmir Valley—the world of Counter-Insurgency. Unlike the isolated post, life here was busy and dynamic. We were constantly on our toes adapting to the unsteady socio-political mood.

Six months later, I was back in the mountains. This time, higher up in Bimbat, where the winter was unforgiving, with temperatures dipping below minus sixty! No artillery shelling this time, but we braved an avalanche, which unfortunately took two of our men. The rest of us escaped narrowly, with some 'chilling' memories of survival.

Overall, my field tenure was quite action-packed. But through this bumpy ride, I became the soldier I wanted to be!

After two rugged years, replete with violence, injuries, disruption, and death, I was about to start a brand-new chapter of my life; one that would be filled with love, laughter, and peace.

Or so I thought!

My unit was moving to a family station—Namkum, a remote cantonment in Bihar (now Jharkhand). While everyone was excited about the new place, I was obsessed with just one thought—what's the point of a family posting if one is single! I know, 25 is rather early for marriage, but for me and my girl, it had already been a long wait. And so, ignoring factors like peak summers and little preparation time, an impromptu wedding was planned.

Finally, it was time to proceed on my annual leave. Moving out of the valley into the plains of Jammu, I started comparing my life with the terrain—just like the Zojila Pass, I was leaving behind all the twists and turns of life.

Here onwards, it would be a smooth sail...with the most special person in my life—Mohana!

1

Mo in Soldierland

Namkum, 22nd of May 1997

Mohana hoped for the journey to end soon. Sitting cramped for hours in a jam-packed, smelly bus had made her stiff.

When they had boarded the bus at Tatanagar, it was packed to capacity, or so she thought. But during the next few hours, the bus kept stopping every now and then, allowing more and more people into its ever-expanding folds.

After a point, all hopes of a comfortable journey were quashed, breathing having remained the only function under one's control, much like peak-hour travel in Mumbai's suburban trains. She was lucky to have a window seat; the ones on the aisle were crushed under the weight of the standing crowd, pressure shifting with every turn of the bus. Suraj, her poor husband, was pressed against the enormous paunch of a jovial man, laughing hard and sending belly-tremors all around.

They were travelling through one of the poorest states of India with fellow passengers reeking of country-made liquor and staring at them non-stop. Finally, when they reached the much-awaited Namkum, Mohana and Suraj tumbled out of the bus, which screeched ahead creating clouds of dust. "How will they pass time, now that the zoo exhibits are out?" Mohana chuckled.

It was a muggy summer evening with no breeze. Wearing a full sleeve kameez with salwar (dupatta and all) was a mistake she was not going to forgive herself for. Still, she had to live up to the image of a new bride which, apart from donning traditional attire, also involved not making a fuss. Her sparkling new husband had no such benchmarks to live up to! Suraj was effortlessly cool and completely unaffected by the heat, dust or the crowd—an ability that would both help and hurt, in their life together.

"Welcome home, *yaara,*" said the husband, once the dust had settled down.

Mohana looked around hoping to see a perfectly manicured army cantonment—wide roads lined with grand oak trees, sentry posts, troops marching in a single file, smart salutes, crisp uniforms. Instead, all she saw was a few small shops on their side of the road and a lane of yellow, double-storeyed houses across.

'Where is home, did I hear him right?' She looked at the clean-shaven face of the husband who was a delightful combination of ruggedness and chocolate boy looks. His tall, lean built and the tan acquired from the outdoor army life gave him a rough and tough appearance. However, his smooth complexion, and a ready smile made him look more like a student than a Lieutenant in the Indian Army, though the short crop was a clear give away.

"Did you say home?" Mohana clarified.

"Oh yes," Suraj replied looking around.

"Really! Where?" Had she lost peripheral vision or something?

"Well, this is home Mo—Namkum, where our unit is posted. Most of our unit officers live in those houses across the lane. Let's try and meet some of them later today." She was still grappling with the reality—a quaint lane of houses right next to a highway was not quite her idea of a cantonment.

"Are we going to live in one of those?" Mohana eyed the yellow houses.

"Ummm...I don't think so. Those are for senior officers. And you'll be happy to know that yours truly is the junior-most married officer of the unit." He winked and took a bow at his achievement. He was 25; she six months younger, immensely proud of the advantage of youth she had over him. The twinkle in his eye and the bow made her miss a beat and her sweaty face broke into a smile.

"Actually, I don't even know if they have any accommodation for Lieutenants. Usually, people don't hitch up before getting at least the Captain's rank. *Koi na,* we'll pitch a tent," he grinned.

God, this was a double whammy. First, to not like the unglamorous look of the houses, and to then be told that one doesn't even qualify for them! The realization suddenly made the yellow houses very attractive! Though plain and boring, they seemed neat with well-maintained gardens. Some of the roses and sunflowers called out to her and she was clearly disappointed that this was home, but not quite!

"Hey Suraj, hello ma'am!" said a baritone voice and the newlyweds turned around to see a pleasant face looking at them with excitement.

"Good evening, sir! What are you doing in the Namkum market?" asked Suraj, hugging the pleasant-faced man who looked like an army officer given his short crop and an almost flat belly.

"*Arrey yaar,* wife sent me on some errands: jobs for which the *sahaayak* is not quite eligible and she is certainly overqualified. Now that you're married, you'll figure these things fast," he winked at a beaming Suraj.

"Sir, we just landed here from Tatanagar. You're the first person from the unit to meet Mo...I mean Mohana. Mo, this is Major Asif, my Company Commander." Ah, so this was Major Asif, she had heard great things about him.

"Hi ma'am, welcome to the unit! You must be tired. Why don't you come home and freshen up? We have a welcome party for you in the Mess at 1930 hours. You'll get to meet everyone from the unit."

Even before she could consider the invitation, the decision was made and they were already marching towards the yellow houses. Brand new husband and 'pleasant-face' walked ahead with suitcases in both hands, while Mohana dragged herself behind them, holding a small purse and a huge sense of uselessness.

'What was that about ladies not being allowed to carry bags? I've lugged suitcases all my life, what can be wrong with it all of a sudden? Why are we going to somebody's house when all I want is to spend a relaxed evening with the husband? It's almost five and there's a party in just a few hours! Why didn't anyone think that I may not want to jump into a party right after hopping off a goddamn bus!' She was wading through a web of thoughts, her signature frown firmly controlling her sweet face. Sight of her over the moon husband catching up with his senior, totally forgetting her, wasn't helping matters!

Like always, a part of her started arguing with the other. This had been an old habit and as a kid, Mohana had nicknamed the conflicting voices in her head 'Chika & Mika'—Chika, being the sane voice who always knew the right thing to say or do; the 'teacher's pet' variety. Mika, on the other hand, was a rebel—strongly opinionated and fiercely protective of Mohana, her main life motto was 'self before others'. While Mohana would have loved to favour Mika, she was often badgered by the nagging Chika who didn't easily give in. Both these voices ensured that her head was in a state of constant flux.

Chika was ready with her dose: 'What is so upsetting about this friendly gesture of "pleasant-face"? The poor guy is lugging your heavy bags while you're free to prance around, and yet you're cribbing. How cool is it to have a welcome party! In fact, tell me something, how many welcome parties have you had in your happening life?' Mohana was almost muttering out the dialogues complete with bouncing eyebrows and tiny gestures. Thankfully, there was no audience.

Oblivious to the action under her thick curls, both the officers ambled towards Major Asif's house. Another pleasant-face opened the door and welcomed Mohana with a hug. "Wow, Mohana! So good to finally meet you! This Suraj has been telling me *hajjar* stories about his Mo!" Major Asif put an arm around 'pleasant-face-no-2' and said, "Meet Shaheen, my lord and master."

Shaheen rolled her eyes and said, "Don't believe any of his nonsense. *Ye sab haathi ke dikhane wale daant hain.*" It was Major Asif's turn to roll his eyes and push the laughing Shaheen away.

Shaheen promptly got into the hostess avatar. "Please sit. Today is unusually hot. Some fruits and chilled nimbu soda should cool you down."

When people fall in love, they start seeing things in slow motion, at least that's what the movies tell us. Mohana's moment came as soon as she laid eyes on that tall glass of divinity! The effervescent liquid with ice cubes dancing at the top, the coolness on her fingers when she touched the thin film of mist lining the glass and the ethereal taste of the first sip!

Though this scene seemed to play out in slow motion in Mohana's head, in reality she had finished the glass in a few big gulps. Walking up with a big smile, Shaheen patted her cheek fondly, "Come, Mo. Let me show you the guest room, freshen up and lie down for some time." Enough for Mohana to instantly fall in love with Shaheen's effortless warmth!

She was then escorted to a neat room which had an AC! After having travelled through 44 degrees Celsius the entire afternoon, this was heaven! The moment Shaheen left the room, Mohana flung herself on the inviting bed.

"Mo...get up." The husband was shaking her shoulder. Dazed, Mohana sat up and saw the wall clock—6:30 pm. She'd been lost to the world for almost an hour. Damn, the welcome party! "Can't we go a bit later?" she pleaded.

"*Yeh fauj hai, koi mauj nahi!*" declared the husband. Pulling her out of the bed, he elaborated, "Forget late, dear lady, in the army, we go before time. It's a five-minute drive from here, so please make sure you're ready by 7:15... SHARP."

Mohana pressed the fast forward button to get ready. Her curly mop was so dusty from the travel that it simply had to be washed, even though that would eat up all the time! As expected, after the shower, she had barely five minutes to put herself together. Some kohl, gloss and...the 'jonga's' arrival was announced! The poor girl was forced to step out in damp hair, her only consolation being a fresh face (thanks to the quick beauty nap) and well-behaved curls.

As a kid, she had travelled quite often on a tonga; but never in her life had she heard of a 'jonga'. So, there was this excitement of an aristocratic vehicle ferrying them to her welcome party. High hopes! The jonga was just a bigger version of the jeep, painted olive green. No match to its stylish name which, she later learnt was an acronym for **J**abalpur **O**rdnance a**N**d **G**uncarriage **A**ssembly.

A tall sardar in army uniform stood next to it. A sharp salute to Lt. Suraj, a polite '*Sat Sri Akal, memsahab*' to a curious Mohana, while holding open the door for her to climb in. This was a first for her. Back home, it was auto rickshaws that she mostly travelled in, when she couldn't get her hands on her dad's car. Amused at the chivalry and also the reverential feel to the word '*memsahab*', she sat with an air of royalty. "Where's Shaheen?" she looked around.

"Asif sir and ma'am left for the Mess some time back. They must be ready to welcome you!"

The Mess was, well unlike the name, quite a magnificent place. Washed in yellow light with huge paintings and potted plants, the lobby looked captivating. Smiling at his pretty wife, Suraj walked her into the big hall right next to the lobby. Lo and behold, the room was already full of people!

Perfectly dressed, good-looking humans flashing broad smiles to welcome the newlyweds. Biting her lip, Mohana walked in. Though accustomed to both gatherings and good looks, she felt nervous. Smiling self-consciously, she wanted to cling to Suraj for support. Luckily, Shaheen appeared from a corner, resplendent in a red and black sari. 'Wow! Did she go to a salon while I slept like a log!' wondered a wide-eyed Mohana.

Her simple peach salwar suit with golden embroidery was too dull for the occasion. Plus with no time to unpack, she wore the same flat sandals she had travelled in. And all eyes were on her! A huge tidal wave of diffidence engulfed her as she slowly crawled towards Shaheen. "Wow, Mo, you look so fresh after some rest! Come, let's meet the ladies of our unit."

They started with a short lady in an exquisite midnight blue sari. "This is Mrs. Pratap, our first lady."

"Hello, ma'am," Mohana said with a smile and extended her hand. Mrs. Pratap instead offered a hug. Oops, handshakes worked in the corporate world she'd happily left behind. A quick learner, she earnestly hugged every woman she was introduced to. There were nine of them—dazzling sari-clad women, a formidable force of make-up, chiffon, and pearls!

Introductions done, it was time for polite talk. Mrs. Pratap led the conversation by telling her a bit about the unit and then checking on Mohana's background.

"We also want to meet the new member of the unit," said a short, bespectacled man with Suraj in tow.

"Mohana, meet Colonel Pratap, the CO (Commanding Officer) of our unit." Ah, the big boss! Hand-shake or hug? Undecided, she waited for him to take the lead. He opted for a nod instead. Mohana promptly copied him. His tiny smile got a bit bigger. Hers followed and then froze when she heard his abrupt question, "So, Mohana, what do you know about Namkum?" Huh? Where did that come from! All she knew was a few shops and the yellow houses.

"Umm, well…not much. We just came in a few hours ago," she mumbled.

"That's fine, but you must have found out about the place you would be living in. Didn't you?" Truth be told, she had been so busy dreaming about the man she would be living with, that nothing else had mattered. Not even the budding career she had thrown away without a thought! In fact, when Mohana had put in her papers, her boss had asked about her plans and was clearly displeased with her blissful ignorance.

Now Suraj's boss was asking the exact same questions!

"Well, no. I just wanted to be with Suraj and the place didn't matter," she blurted the truth. "Hmm, good for you because there isn't much except the three army units stationed here. I hear you are a management professional?" he enquired with a raised eyebrow.

"Yes, I was working with a technology company after finishing my MBA," she was matter of fact.

"Great, some of us are doing correspondence MBA. You can help with our assignments," he said with a laugh that felt sarcastic. "Right then, you enjoy the evening." Col. Pratap nodded and walked away.

Suraj, who had been a mute spectator, then introduced her to the other officers of the unit: suave, polished gentlemen. Their polite but confident body language, their chivalry, their physique...everything set them apart from... well, the non-*faujis* or civilians. All of them joked around over drinks, making fun of Suraj's decision to get married so young. Enjoying their camaraderie and positive energy, Mohana began to relax.

Admiring the mammoth chandelier hung in the centre, and taking in the fascinating people, Mohana felt like 'Alice in Wonderland'.

Just then, a sardar appeared, perfection personified: Olive-Green uniform (OG), crisp turban, shiny black shoes. Marching across the hall towards the group of officers, he announced in a thunderous voice, "*Sat Sri Akal, Saab!*

Shriman, bhojan prastut hai." Mohana was so startled at the loud announcement, that her heart started pounding. One of the ladies gently tapped her shoulder and whispered, "I had the same reaction when I saw this the first time. Don't look so shocked, or these guys won't let you forget your expression." Glancing around, Mohana did find people watching her with amused smiles.

Promptly picking up her dropped jaw, she whispered back, "What was that?"

"*Mess Hawaldar* announcing that the food has been served. It's a part of the army tradition."

Mohana confessed, "Sorry, I'm already confused with names."

The young lady grinned, "Anu. I am so glad to have someone my age in the unit. We're going to have a blast." Mohana beamed.

Back from the party, when Mohana lay in Shaheen's guest room, the world felt beautiful. She was an absolute outsider knowing nothing about the place. Yet, the people she met were so warm, that Mohana felt she belonged.

She couldn't have been further from the truth!

2

Clouds on the Horizon

Hey! This is my story. So why don't I narrate it. Here goes…

Namkum, 23rd of May 1997

The next morning, Suraj told me that we would be shifting to a temporary accommodation in the Officers' Mess, since housing allotment could be a long-drawn process.

As we approached the Officers' Mess, I started peeping out with eager eyes. Huge trees lined both sides of a narrow road that led to the main building, which looked quite different in daylight. Belying the splendour of the previous evening, there stood a drab, single-storeyed structure, painted white with brick red borders.

As we crossed it and moved further, the foliage thickened, giving the feel of a forest. A row of tiny, grey structures appeared and the jonga stopped in front of one of them. It felt like early morning because the sun was blocked out by trees. Another thing that caught my attention was the silence, as if only birds had a permit to speak. The sweet fragrance of greenery reminded me of a jungle safari I'd been on during my childhood. I jokingly asked the driver if there was any wildlife around. Just some foxes, I was told.

As the jonga disappeared, the place suddenly felt eerie. I was glad my hero was around. He opened the door and we stepped into a dark, musty room. Suraj spotted an old-fashioned switch with push down levers. Not having seen such a switch in ages, I dreaded a shock or a spark when Suraj touched it.

His command was obeyed by a bulb hiding under a peeling, aluminium lamp shade. A hint of pale-yellow light was all it could manage to throw around. I laughed, "Does that fellow lack confidence?"

Ignoring my splendid joke, Suraj simply said, "Voltage. It lacks voltage. That is often a problem in this area. We are lucky that the electricity is intact."

I should've been cautioned by those words. Instead, the lovelorn me put my arms around his neck, "How will I handle this hottie without a fan spinning on my head?" Before Suraj could respond to the invitation, there was a knock on the door.

"*Sat Sri Akal,* sir, CO *saab yaad kitta hai.*" This also was an indication of what lay in store. Oblivious to the divine warning, I watched Suraj get into blistering action.

"The CO knows I'm on leave; so there must be something urgent."

Noticing him change was like watching a movie in fast forward mode! Never knew someone could get ready in two minutes flat—uniform, shoes, beret et al.

That was the first time I saw Suraj in his army attire—it had meant so much to him right since childhood. Boy! Didn't he look dashing in that perfectly fitting OG. I felt respect and pride for the uniform, love for our nation and lust for my husband, all at once. The handsome man, who should be walking the ramp, was instead wading through a maze of open suitcases. "Listen, Mo, I'll get the Mess staff to serve lunch here itself. No idea when I'll be back, so don't wait for me. Relax and have fun." Like Jim Carrey in *The Mask*, he whizzed past me and disappeared behind the trees while I stood dazed at the door.

My first instinct was to just lock the door and curl up till Suraj returned. But as soon as I closed the door, the room became so dark and the lone bulb so inadequate, that I wanted to bolt out. Darkness and I had never been friends. Not knowing what to do, I walked towards the window that opened to the backside and moved the curtain.

Wow! What a breath-taking sight—wild flowers in purple, orange and yellow sprinkled all over the dense bushes. Without too many trees this side, the Sun God had managed to slip in. Rays of the sun and the glowing flowers immediately uplifted my slump spirit. I stood there charging my batteries until I was ready to operate.

There was a sofa set with a small centre table, a study table with a chair and...a table lamp. I switched it on and hurrah! The world looked a tad brighter. With an instant spring in my walk, I went about my inspection duty and walked into the other room.

As expected, this was the bedroom with a nice, big double bed in the centre and two wooden wardrobes of different sizes on either side. Not bad. There was an attached toilet which I stepped in to examine. Most fixtures were regular; but something stood out, a wooden *patiya* or a bath stool. At some point in time, it must've been painted white, but now the paint was visible only in patches, which did not make for a good visual. Not a big problem, one could live with it. But the disturbing sight was the wear and tear of the wood, exposing poky shards. How the hell does one sit on it for a bath? 'There must be a bum helmet,' I chuckled!

Over the next few hours, I unpacked and put the stuff neatly in the wardrobes, empty suitcases on the top. I occupied the bigger wardrobe and generously assigned three fourth of the smaller one to Suraj. The man hardly had any belongings, what was the point of empty cabinets.

Hearing a knock on the door, I ran with a smile to welcome Suraj. Alas! It was the Mess staff with my lunch. 'Room service...that too without ordering!' Chika cheered me up.

I've always detested eating alone. Growing up in a close-knit family, I seldom had a chance to eat by myself. And on a rare occasion when I was alone, the TV would keep me company. Without any of those luxuries, swallowing food was not easy. The thought of my family and our bright home formed a lump in my throat. The man for whom I'd left it all behind was nowhere to be seen. Before the painstakingly built spirit would dissolve, Chika sprung in and took me to task, 'You are an army officer's wife now. Stop being a cry baby, will you?'

The food was neatly arranged on a lovely silver tray. Picking up the heavy porcelain plate, I enjoyed the awesome aroma before serving myself some *aloo gobhi masala, daal tadka*, cucumber salad, and roti. Then I saw it—a bowl with *semiya kheer* and squealed with joy! The food was delicious and I had not realized how hungry I was until I started eating. Enjoying every morsel, I wolfed down everything and then wondered if I should've waited for Suraj.

It was 2:30 and there was still no sign of him. Having nothing else to do, I decided to lie down for a while. As I sat on the bed, it creaked loudly. I carefully spread myself on it and without warning, rolled into the centre. What was that...an earthquake? Gathering my heartbeat, I tried making sense of what had just happened. There was a depression in the mattress and I was piled up in the centre. Closer observation revealed that the bed was in fact a charpoy, a bedstead with a web of jute ropes for a base. Just like the bathroom stool, the charpoy had seen a long, arduous life with significant wear and tear. The sagging, loose ropes would succumb to gravity at the slightest hint of weight.

Feeling sorry for the poor charpoy, I lay huddled in the centre. The mattress seemed to be from the same generation—lumpy. Just like unequal distribution of wealth, some parts were puffed up with excess cotton while some were completely bereft.

Suraj and I were capable of some heavy duty action in bed and I wondered how anything would be possible on this *Laxman Jhula*? Was this some kind of a practical joke on us newlyweds?

I woke up groggy. Afternoon naps are as it is saddening; waking up in that dark, musty room was positively depressing. I stepped out and stood in the small garden in the front. There was no sign of human life and the trees felt even more daunting, now that the sun had gone west.

Just 24 hours ago, I had set foot in Namkum. The place had felt so different with Suraj by my side and people around. Now, all alone in this dreary place, I had nothing to do and nobody for company. I was gazing at the trees when I heard someone approaching. Suraj! No, the Mess staff again, this time with evening tea. Hey, wait! The tray had two cups! Could it mean…?

And there he was, the king of my heart, walking towards me with his trademark smile. I yelped like a puppy and wished I could transform into one. Then I could bark happily, jump over him, wag my tail and lick him nonstop. As a human being, all I could manage was tears...big, embarrassing tears which surprised Suraj. "Hey, what's wrong, Mo? I was away just for a few hours," he said holding me close. Incapable of speech, I just clung to him. He patted my back and soothed my hair. But I still held on. Once my lachrymal glands are set in action, they don't stop easily. Being well aware of this phenomenon, Suraj quickly employed a trick that always works with me. Cupping my face, he leaned in to kiss me. A tender, lingering kiss was all I needed to wipe away the blues.

With Suraj around, the evening turned bright and promising. When I showed off my day's labour of arranging the wardrobes, Suraj did not mind my trespassing into his territory. He quickly changed into shorts and we went out for a walk in the main Mess area. I wanted to hold hands but he strictly warned against any PDA. "The army is a traditional and conservative organization and one needs to be careful in these matters," said their spokesperson. Sulking, I walked along. Mika instigated me to question the whole point of getting married, if one couldn't lock hands with the officially wedded partner, that too in a secluded forested land! "What you're saying is correct, Mo, but not here. The army operates quite differently from the civilian world you and I come from. Now that we are here, we must follow the law of the land."

Suraj was the first one from his family to join the services. It was amazing how quickly he had adapted to this new life. "Wow, you seem well marinated in the army culture," I observed. I meant it as a compliment but was not sure if it had landed well.

"Marinated!" Suraj laughed. "I'm not as well marinated as you think, Mo. After getting commissioned, I went straight to J&K and spent all my time on remote posts. So I understand 'rugged field soldiering' because that's what I've seen so far. But life in a peace station is unique and we both will figure it out together," he smiled. "One thing we must be clear about is that the army has a strong culture of tradition and conformity."

The very mention of these words was enough for Mika to raise her head, but Suraj smartly silenced her by talking about hierarchy in the *fauj* and the numerous levels and ranks, making it clear that we were heaped at the very bottom of the pyramid. "I am a Lieutenant and the junior most officer in the unit. Don't expect me to question the system." The tone of finality ensured that there was no further discussion.

Trying to cheer myself, I asked him about the next day's plan. In response, Suraj rubbed his palms together, "Let me tell you about something really interesting…it's called *Ghaatak.*" I perked up for the story like a child. And he started…

"True to its name, Ghaatak is a deadly platoon with every infantry unit. They specialize in infiltrating deep inside the enemy territory, carrying out surgical strikes during night, and returning before sunrise. Naturally, there is immense pride and esteem associated with these platoons. During peace time, keeping them engaged, fit, and battle ready is ensured through the Ghaatak competition, held annually. All the Ghaatak platoons under a division (some 8 to 12 teams) fiercely compete with each other for the prestigious Ghaatak trophy. The fact that this is a battle to identify the 'best among the best', makes Ghaatak one of the most arduous and challenging competitions for infantry soldiers.

Usually, units select their toughest and fittest officers to lead the team."

That was an awe-inspiring preamble and I was curious to know where this was headed.

"From our unit, Capt. Gulshan Bagga was selected this year and he had been training hard with his team. He is two years senior to me, strong like a rock. Things were moving fine until yesterday, when Capt. Bagga came down with some stomach ailment. He had to be admitted to the Military Hospital this morning, which is why the CO called me. The competition is just a month away and the momentum has to be maintained...and hence the CO has instructed me to take over with immediate effect."

Zor ka jhatka, dheere se lage!

"This means your leave would be cancelled, right?" I tried to hide my disappointment.

"Well yes, for starters. This also means I'll have no set schedule or routine till the competition. The good part is that I had trained this team for some time, so there is mutual comfort. The problem is my own fitness, which has gone for a six; I haven't worked out once in *chhutti*."

I didn't quite agree. Doesn't all the action between the sheets qualify as working out? And who could vouch for his fitness levels better than me? I ogled with a naughty smile but he wore a faraway, pensive look. "These boys are competent and have trained hard for months. This is the last lap and I cannot let them down, *yaara*."

Abruptly, he turned towards me and looking deep in my eyes, said, "I need your support, baby." *Baby*? Coming from a man incapable of such endearments, it almost sounded like foreboding.

Which...is...exactly...what...it...was.

"You now know about Ghaatak platoon and how it operates. For exact simulation, the competition is held during night. There are multiple challenges spread over an area of 25–30 kilometres, ensuring we run with our weapons and *pitthu* through the night. Our boys have developed superb stamina, we just need to focus on night navigation. Starting tomorrow, we will practise after dark and I may return only in the mornings."

I had a sinking feeling. "I will also need to resume office duty from tomorrow Mo…so it's going to be terribly busy now onwards." He stopped to take a quick peek at me and then added, "I know how you feel right now. But you'll get used to the place and it won't feel so difficult."

No response…both Chika and Mika refused to speak.

Suraj said encouragingly, "Come, let me take you to the Mess library. It may not be great, but I'm sure you will find something to keep you company."

Just a nod with pursed lips.

"You have to do this for me, Mo! I promise to make up after the competition." Left with no choice, I had to act sane.

"Yeah, I'm a bit shocked because it's all too sudden. But don't worry, Suraj, I can handle this."

What an effortless liar I was! Suraj beamed and paced up excitedly. "Now, that's my girl! Let's get you some books."

Dinner was a bleak affair with just Suraj and me in that huge place. The hall was dimly lit; just enough for the two of us. The magnificent chandelier that had mesmerized me the previous night now hung dark and listless.

More than anything else, I was weighed down by the thought of living all alone in that gloomy room. Just one day had been tough enough, how would I survive a month? Suraj seemed preoccupied. . .and quiet. . .and distant, thanks to this sudden responsibility.

Both of us sat trapped in our own webs of thoughts. We did attempt helping each other: I tried to act cheerful and Suraj tried to act interested.

That night, when we made love on the sagging, lumpy bed, my need was emotional. . .and Suraj's response was mechanical.

The Ghaatak Platoon had struck!

3

WHAT A MESS!

Namkum, 28th of May 1997

It had been five days since Suraj had got *'Ghaatakized'* and I had barely seen him since. He would leave before 8 am and return for lunch which, to save time was served in our room itself. He would gobble up the food and head straight for *Laxman Jhula* while I would still be eating. And they say *faujis* are chivalrous! To be fair to Suraj, I am a slow eater...he would be snoring away by the time I finished. After a couple of hours, he would change into the combat uniform, wear those heavy boots, sling a *Pitthu* on his back, and walk out. His parting line would always be, "Not sure when I'll be back. No waiting, no worrying. *Theek hai, yaara*?" And true to his words, there was no fixed time for his return.

Today, after being away the whole night, he came back at 8 am—hair all messed up, uniform embellished with blades of grass and mud. And filthy, soaking wet shoes!

Suraj's flushed, sweaty face broke into a smile as soon as he saw me, "One hell of a night, Mo...lemme shower up before I fill you in." Chika reminded me of my promise to support him. Suraj and I had barely had a conversation in all these days and he hadn't once asked how I was doing. Guess he just assumed that I was doing fine, which was a fact, wasn't it? I had a decent place to stay in, *Laxman Jhula* to sleep in, ready meals, and a few books for company. What more could one ask for?

The bitter tone of these thoughts made it obvious that Mika was spewing small doses of sarcastic venom. To distract myself, I started laying the breakfast—fresh, aromatic poha (with a slice of lemon) and some toast, butter, jam. Before I knew, I got lost in the delightful combination of butter and toast—holding a crispy toast in one hand and spreading a dollop of soft, creamy butter on it with the other! The consistency of butter is critical—the melted variety is no fun to work with and the cold, hard type just destroys the toast's crusty, golden surface. However, this one was just perfect...without resistance, it glided along as I pushed it right up to the edges, filling in every pore, every crack. Unable to resist the temptation, I dug into the heavenly treat. Ummm...crunchy toast and the salty, velvety spread on top!

Munching on my favourite comfort food, I listened to the sound of running water, assured of Suraj's presence. Even though I could not see him, had not managed to speak to him and was unable to cut through the barrier between us, I was deeply comforted by his mere presence. Satiated from the buttery toast, I felt the warmth of happiness—like snuggling up in a comforter on a cold, winter night.

God! Just please let my comforter stay with me....

"Wow, Mo! You look nice in the sun!"

"Like a fat cat, right?" I laughed and opened my eyes to a delightful Suraj—nicely scrubbed and shaven.

"Well, cat you are and fat you'll become if you continue to polish off butter like this." He was so right, the amount of butter I'd consumed in the name of catharsis!

"I was getting bored waiting for you…anyway tell me about your night safari." I poured him some tea.

"The night was fun, *yaara.*" *Yaara* was a special term of friendship between us. Suraj used it when he wanted to chat up the way he would with his guy friends.

"Yesterday was a complicated night navigation exercise. We were practising in a tough, unknown terrain, some 40 kilometres away. Things were fine till midnight, which is when it started raining, and how! One moment we were running on dry land and the next, we were struggling on slippery mud," Suraj dug into the impoverished toast with just a hint of butter. With the kitchen in a separate building and no phone in our room, I couldn't ask for replenishment.

"We slowed down but then I felt that we might not be able to finish in time."

"What happens if it rains on D-day?" I spoke out my worry.

"Exactly! Monsoons are around, and in all probability, the competition will be held in thick rains. So we better got used to it."

"So?" I butted in.

"So…" Suraj teased me with an intense expression. He knew that I loved stories and liked them delivered fast. I had to slap his arm to get him started, "So we continued, what else, Mo? We still had about 15 kilometres to cover but the rains had made things difficult—our uniforms, *pitthus,* boots…everything was drenched and heavier. The soil in this region is almost like silt—no sand or grainy pieces. Unbelievably slippery, we all learnt it the hard way," he calmly showed me the bruises on his palms, elbows and knees.

"Ouch!" I winced.

"At about 0200 hours, we hit a hilly patch, full of vegetation. It was pitch dark, but since the hill wasn't slippery, we automatically gathered pace. Satnam and I were in the lead, he a bit ahead of me. All of a sudden, he disappeared into thin air and I heard a loud thud." My eyes popped out and my hand involuntarily cupped my mouth. Suraj continued, "It was a sharp cliff, and he ran straight off it… Both his legs broke on the spot… I think the right one is pretty bad."

Oh my God! Never thought such things could happen during a regular exercise. "Luckily, I could break my momentum and stop just in time. Poor Satnam…he was screaming like a child before the pain knocked him out. The boys quickly made a stretcher and I instructed a few of them to carry Satnam to the jonga."

"You didn't go with them?"

"No, I assigned the strongest guys to this task. In any case, our team had still not achieved the target…we couldn't have ignored that either. Right?"

I still believed that as the leader, Suraj's responsibility was more towards an injured team-mate than the task at hand. He perhaps sensed my dilemma, "Listen Mo, Satnam was in good hands. The camaraderie among the troops is very strong, and I trust this bond. I had other things at hand…the team was clearly shaken. I couldn't have allowed this incident to break their spirit, because such accidents do happen sometimes. One has to learn and move on. So we regrouped, rested our fears and pulled on. Despite losing so much time, we finished the exercise 10 minutes before time," he closed with pride.

I took my time to understand his perspective, but when I did, I was impressed with Suraj's approach. At such a young age, he was so clear about handling such situations.

I wondered if quick and spot on decision-making is a part of the military training.

I watched him in admiration while he focused on the poha. But I had lost all will to complain. I felt so small and insignificant in the scheme of things...it felt stupid to harp about myself. Suraj hadn't had a minute to himself, had been missing dinner and had barely slept for 4–5 hours the past few days. Last night, his team had zero sleep, bad bruises, major injuries and yet no one was complaining.

And here I was, creating imaginary challenges for myself!

A knock at the door disturbed our chat. This time the Mess staff announced, "Adjutant *saab yaad kitta hai*." What? Who is this adjutant now? If CO *saab* wasn't enough to make my life miserable, now there's this adjutant *saab* snatching away my comforter!

Why does everyone need to speak to my husband who, incidentally, has returned after 15 hours? Don't they do any other work in this unit? And why does this Suraj start behaving like a slave as soon as he gets their message? Is it like some *aakaashvani* from the Gods that he simply has to comply? Doesn't he have a say, a choice? Why can't he just tell them that he will speak to them later?

And why the hell is he changing into the uniform once again? Didn't he just get out of one? What is this nonsense about not entering the Mess in casuals? What is wrong with a nice T-shirt and a pair of shorts...especially when there is nobody apart from kitchen staff in that darned old building? What kind of a primitive set up is this, with no phones in these dilapidated rooms? And they call it the Officers' Mess. Nothing Officer like, but mess this surely is. Ha!

Mika was firing a Heavy Machine Gun but Suraj had already left. All the admiration for him had disappeared in a flash.

I learnt something big about emotions that day—between loneliness and anger, the latter is easier to deal with. So I embraced it tighter, allowing Mika a field day.

Back soon, Suraj was unaware of my mental gymnastics. He simply told me that the adjutant wanted a report on the Satnam incident, and congratulated him on handling the crisis well. Satnam was now lying in the same hospital as Capt. Bagga, with three major fractures. The guy was heartbroken to not participate in the Ghaatak competition. Suraj feared much worse—would Satnam ever be able to run?

Hmm. The information ensured that the anger monster loosened up a bit. In 30 seconds, Suraj was back in his shorts. "I'm crashing out, *yaara*. The adjutant has exempted me from the office today but has asked me to be present for games. So I'll leave at 3:30. Can I sleep for a few hours now?" Without waiting for a response, he climbed into *Laxman Jhula*.

I kept sitting on the sofa, brooding and reading alternately. By lunch time, I was done with the fourth book and the prospect of the last one, wasn't too attractive. I wanted to step out of the room and interact with someone. I remembered Shaheen. Why hadn't she checked on me? In fact, where were all the ladies? Had they taken up jobs as mannequins in sari shops? More targets for anger meant less chance of attacking Suraj!

Lunch got served but Suraj refused to budge. He was so deep in sleep that I hoped he would forget about the adjutant, games...and that Ghaatak team—the bane of my life. Wishful thinking! By 3 pm, the man was fresh as a daisy, gobbling up cold lunch, changing into a new attire—the 'games' uniform.

White half-sleeve shirt, white shorts, white socks, and white canvas shoes! Two things about this new getup stood out—first, the oversupply of white reminded me of Jumping Jack aka Jeetendra. Second, the shorts had taken their name rather seriously—they were really short! Suraj seemed to have gotten into the uniform of a school kid. All he needed was a school bag and a water bottle!

Despite the anger monster, I burst out laughing. "What happened?" asked the overgrown kid. But I'd gotten into a laughter attack—flapping nostrils, teared up eyes, air strapped lungs. Suraj stared in exasperation, unbothered by the trigger. Guess he had guessed.

He was all set, waiting for the jonga. "I'm heading for games, and after that I will visit Satnam at the hospital."

'Games' got my goat. "With so much else going on, is there really a need to play games dressed like school children?"

Though I'd said it in exasperation, Suraj seemed to be tickled by what I said. He laughed aloud, "You need an army induction programme, Mo, so you know about life in the services. Hey, why don't we ask Shaheen ma'am to help you? Would you like to meet her?" I jumped with joy and immediately threw my arms around his neck. "Ok, ok. Don't crumple my clothes now. Narayan won't approve," he winked. Narayan, his *sahaayak,* took great pride in ironing Suraj's uniform to perfection.

Just then, the jonga drove in, "If ma'am is available, you'll get a message through the Mess staff. Don't keep the jonga waiting. Ok?"

Clicking my heels, I threw a salute.

4

Life is a Lemon

Namkum, 30th of May 1997

I waited for the jonga with excitement. As we went out from the Mess gates, I felt as if I was stepping out of a small cage, that had trapped me for a week. The evening sun was breathtaking and I wanted to go for a nice, long drive. Alas! We reached the yellow houses within no time. Thanking the driver, I pressed the doorbell and stood with a wide smile, expecting Shaheen.

Instead, the *sahaayak* opened the door and ushered me in the beautifully decorated living room. One entire wall had a display of harpoons and *khukhris* in silver. Maj. Asif seemed to have a collector's eye for all war related stuff because I could also spot miniature canons, life-size swords and even a nunchaku! Apart from this battle paraphernalia, there were handicrafts made of bamboo, jute and brass, earthen pots, indoor plants and a beautiful embroidered umbrella in a corner. An eclectic mix, but it all came together pretty well.

Shaheen made an entry, looking a mere shade of her radiant self. She gave me a hug and patted my cheeks; her warmth intact if not her smile. Playing safe, I started with the customary, "How are you?"

She gave a weak smile. "Forget about me, how have you been?"

Something was clearly amiss and I kept glancing at Shaheen to find out. Finally, letting go of tact, I held her hand, and asked, "Are you all right?" She avoided looking at me for some time and then burst into tears. "What happened, are you not well?" She nodded her head in a way that I couldn't make anything of it. Deciding against any more questions, I allowed her to sob into her dupatta while my mind raced in all directions.

Could this be a case of domestic abuse? God, there were so many weapons on display in this room itself. Does Maj. Asif beat her with that nunchaku? He seems incredibly sweet for such a thing but who knows, looks can be deceptive!

The *sahaayak* served us water and left without a word. He seemed to know. I encouraged Shaheen to sip some water. She did as asked, wiped her face and whispered, "I had a miscarriage, Mo…four days ago." Too shocked to respond, I listened. "My third…in 12 years of marriage. I've been under treatment for five years…everything seemed perfect this time." She broke down while I sat numb. The situation was rather odd. One, I barely knew her. Also, my knowledge of such issues was almost non-existent. She told me about the medical complications, the prolonged treatment she had been undergoing…how they were on top of the world when she conceived…how this tiny life had become the centre of their world in the last few months…and how she had lost all hopes of a joyful life now. "Maybe I am a bad person…maybe *Allah Miyan* is punishing me for something…maybe He thinks I won't be a good mother… God, if only I knew."

Pained to see her condition, my tears offered company to hers, mourning the loss of Shaheen's unborn baby.

Just then, Maj. Asif walked in and we hurriedly wiped our tears. He looked far more collected, though not his cheerful self. He wished me and walked straight up to Shaheen and gave her a gentle hug. She looked at him with a feeble smile and they seemed to speak through their eyes. Keeping an arm around Shaheen, Maj. Asif assured me, "Don't look so worried, ma'am, she'll be fine. We will fight this out together."

What a lovely couple! Throwing a guilty glance at the nunchaku, I said a silent prayer for them.

Despite her situation, Shaheen insisted that I stay over for dinner. She said I was her responsibility since Suraj was part of Maj. Asif's company. While she felt guilty that she hadn't been able to look after me, I was amazed that she was even thinking about me in all this!

Over dinner, I assured my hosts that I was quite comfortable in the Mess—the food was awesome and I had some great books for company. I was getting proficient at lying.

Maj. Asif was all praises for Suraj's ability to win the team's respect. He warned me that the last few weeks of preparation would be the most rigorous. Shaheen was immediately concerned, since she was going to her mother's place for a few months. I assured her that I could always meet Anu, if I got too bored. That's when I learnt that Anu and her husband Capt. Niranjan had left for a two-month-long course.

Loneliness was written on the wall…in BOLD.

Back in my cage, I slumped on the sofa, gaping at the ceiling. Witnessing the tough side of life, had set off a churn; compared to Shaheen, my void and loneliness seemed paltry. My life would start in a few weeks; but her painful wait could be endless.

Why was God being so cruel to her? Maj. Asif and Shaheen would make the most loving parents. Why were they being denied this experience when countless unwanted kids are either killed in the womb or are destined to a life of poverty and neglect! Why couldn't God send just one of those kids to Shaheen? Why is life so unfair…so tough?

Suddenly, I felt intimidated by life and the challenges it could throw at us. I wanted to go back to being a kid…to the safety of my mother's embrace.

I cried myself to sleep snuggling a pillow, imagining it was Maa's lap.

5

A Raw Deal

Namkum, 5th of June 1997

Life was akin to the backstage of a fashion show, with the model constantly getting out of one costume into another! Some days, it would be the classy OG (Olive Green) with the ranks, stars, leather shoes, leather belt, and a beret or a peak cap. On others, it would be the combat or camouflage uniform or *chitri bitri* as Narayan called it—heavy duty ankle boots, a broad rugged belt, and a cap.

Using my sharp ability of observation and analysis, I deduced that the OG was the formal office attire, whereas *chitri bitri* was for outdoors. In the corporate world, whether you're in a conference room or out in the field, your attire doesn't change. Companies with a conventional culture make their sales guys sweat it out in the field with ties around their necks. On the other hand, new age firms don't mind denims in the board room!

Not the army. They have a discrete dress code and a good part of Narayan's day would be spent keeping all the uniforms ready. He would meticulously polish the ranks with Brasso, tirelessly shine every shoe to perfection. The whites from the 'overgrown kid' look had to be immaculate and crisply ironed just like other uniforms. While I claimed that nobody could love Suraj the way I did, I doubt if I could do Narayan's job half as good!

He put his heart and soul in taking care of his *'saab'*. No wonder he would guard Suraj's wardrobe like the LoC (Line of Control) and thwart all my attempts to get into his territory with pre-emptive strikes. It started with glances...then hard glares...followed by threatening stares...then warning the enemy that trespassing was prohibited and when the defiant enemy didn't stop, making an official complaint to the high command! Suraj tried to make me understand Narayan's displeasure, "He has his own arrangement you know...and doesn't like any interference." What? Managing uniforms was Narayan's job, I got that...but wasn't this fellow taking things a bit too far? He was the orderly and I was the wife. How could he miss this simple fact?

Turf war with an orderly—clearly, I needed to get a life. The turf, in any case, was totally indifferent, so what was the point?

I soon realized that apart from the guest visits from Suraj, Narayan Singh was the only other human presence in my life. So calling a truce, I assured him that the wardrobe would be out of bounds for me. The move was wise indeed; I had a fellow human to interact with, and an interesting one at that!

Narayan Singh was a fourth generation *fauji*. The unwritten rule in his family was for the eldest son to join the army. The tradition had inspired many a family in his village aka *'pind'* to follow suit. Today, his entire village was serving the nation and Narayan was hugely proud. Rightly so!

All of 19, he had joined the army a few months ago. Apart from his sincerity, what stood out was his enviable ability to see things through a positive lens. For Narayan

Singh, living in the barracks was fun and serving his officer was a joy. Food was *changa*, outdoor exercises were *changa*, sentry duties were *changa*, even the discipline was *changa*... in short, everything about the army was *changa*.

Was he a chronic liar?

Once, I pointedly asked if there was any problem at all and he shared that friends in the barracks made fun of him and asked if he had joined the army to wash his officer's underwear. I got upset because this was demeaning and factually incorrect. Surprisingly, Narayan, much younger and less educated, had a very different response. He said it was all part of the army life. Troops in the barracks were away from families and evenings often got lonely. So they would crack jokes at each other...harmless banter, just to stay happy. He never took offence, because none was meant.

What wisdom, what maturity!

Narayan became a friend and I started enjoying our small chit-chats, whenever he came to the room. Both of us being new to the army were unaware of the sacrilege we were committing.

One afternoon, I decided to venture out in the garden, a fairly big space covered in thick vegetation. I asked Narayan if he knew the area and if he could show me around. He readily agreed and we went out on a tour gazing at trees, bushes and...a dance floor! Right in front of the Mess hall, hiding behind thick shrubbery was a beautiful dance floor. Narayan said he had heard stories of dance parties in the garden, leaving me thrilled at the prospect.

The next evening, when Narayan came to serve me tea, I asked if he could play badminton. He was a bit hesitant because he had to carry some papers to the office. But when I suggested a short game, he agreed. The game was fun and after sitting around for so long, a little exercise felt wonderful. The decision to include badminton in my daily schedule was made and I excitedly got my sports shoes ready for the next day.

However, this was not to be. Suraj returned from the office with a strange expression. "Did you play badminton with Narayan?" he asked point blank.

"Yeah, he plays quite well. Wonder why I didn't think about it earlier." Suraj just kept staring at me and breathing heavily. As if he wanted to say something but was not sure. Finally I asked, "What? Why are you so restless?"

"Well, Mo, he is my orderly. You shouldn't be doing such things."

"What things? We just had a quick game of badminton. What's wrong with that?" I asked, incredulously. There was a long pause...and some more heavy breathing.

"Well, someone from the Mess has complained. The adjutant spoke to me about this."

Mika emerged—well armed. "Complaint? What complaint? How can this be anybody's business? For the last two weeks, I'm rotting here and nobody gives a damn. When I try to break the boredom with a simple game of badminton, there's an official complaint!"

Suraj looked exasperated. "It's not an official complaint against you, Mo. Narayan should have known better."

"*Arrey,* how does that change anything? What was his mistake?" I was livid.

"His mistake was that he played badminton with an officer's wife." Suraj said in a measured voice, as if this statement was enough to answer my question. Since

I remained unconvinced, he was forced to elaborate, "He is supposed to be *my sahaayak.* He has a certain responsibility to help me. For the remaining part of the day, some other duties get assigned to him. Instead of doing those jobs, if he starts playing badminton with you in the Mess area, it is bound to get reported."

I sat stiff—neither liking what was being said nor the man who was saying it. Suraj persisted, "Look, Mo, I told you that the army is quite conservative. Back home, you could be playing badminton with your friends, neighbours, domestic help or whoever you wished to play with. It wouldn't matter. But things are not the same here. We ought to maintain protocol at all times."

I cut him short. "So, is there a rule book that will tell me about my protocol?"

Suraj threw an irritated glance. "Of course not! This is common sense."

Awesome! So now, apart from conduct unbecoming an officer's wife, I was also being charged of lack of common sense. Mika insisted on resisting this non-sense, so I glared at Suraj and said defiantly, "I'll tell you what my common sense says. It says I can play badminton with anybody. That person has to be interested, that's all. My common sense also says that I did no wrong by playing a game with Narayan."

"You're right. It's not your fault, Mo. I just dumped you here without giving any context about the army." Even though his stance had become more empathetic, Mika remained furious.

"Forget the army, you tell me, Lt. Suraj Shastri. Do *you* also have a problem if I play badminton with Narayan Singh?"

His face softened a bit and he reached out to me and said, "No, *baba*. Personally, I have no issue with this. But I am a tiny cog in the wheel and can't take on a system which doesn't approve of such behaviour."

I was still stuck with 'baba'. One, it felt immensely nice... with a touch of romance that was completely missing from our relationship. Two, it didn't augur well....

"Actually, rookies like Narayan shouldn't get assigned as *sahaayaks* because even they are clueless about such sensitivities. Anyway, they have already assigned a tenured jawan in his place. I just hope Narayan doesn't get bullied in the barracks."

Suraj gone...

Anu gone...

Shaheen gone...

and now, Narayan gone too.

I never saw my friend again.

6

Down in the Dumps

Namkum, 6th of June 1997

Not sure if it was bitterness from the Narayan episode or something in the food, but I felt unwell after dinner. Usually, once Suraj was back, I would be happily asleep till the morning tea arrived. Not today. After tossing and turning for a few hours, the stomach cramps came knocking... followed by nausea. Both kept building up while a tired Suraj slept peacefully.

I tried sitting on the bed, the chair, the sofa...different positions. Nothing worked. Pacing around didn't help either. The room felt hot and suffocating. Had Suraj been awake, we could have stepped out for some fresh air. By myself, the task was impossible. It was pitch-dark and the trees seemed sinister. Plus, the eerie noise of insects and croaking frogs reminded me of horror movies.

I missed my family and imagined how things would be if I were home. Maa would give some *ajwain* with warm water, sit with me, pat my back and soothe my hair...comfort me with her mere presence!

And here I was, not just in this Mess...but in absolute MESS...where even basics like medicine, warm water, herbs or a caring companion were unavailable! Suraj was sleeping like a log and I didn't have the heart to wake him up.

Without warning, the bile rose and I made it to the washroom just in time. I hoped to feel better after throwing up. Secretly, I was also hopeful of Suraj waking up because of the noise.

Sadly, neither happened.

By the time the Mess staff brought the morning tea, I had thrown up six times and was lying listless on the sofa. Suraj was still asleep. I wasn't even sure if he had slept through the episode, or had simply chosen to ignore! Agreed, he was exhausted, but how can one not hear the horrible retching noises just a few feet away? Despite Chika's protest, I felt let down by him.

The new *sahaayak* had taken over and I refused to even look at him. Suraj got ready and only then did he notice that something was wrong. By now, I was in the 'I can manage without you' mode. When he asked me if I was ok, I played down the problem…told him that I had thrown up a few times and would be fine with some rest. How I would have loved being fussed over! Instead, he just bought the story and finished his breakfast. Before leaving, he did mention something about visiting the unit doctor if I didn't feel better by the evening.

I chose to not respond.

I was miserable over the next few hours—physically and emotionally. Difficult to say which was worse! Cramps twisted my gut, emotions twisted my soul. The body was adamant to throw out anything I had…the heart, firmly held on to despair.

Where the hell had I landed? I had left behind not just my family and friends, but also my education, job, and ambition. What for? Why had I been so blinded by love? Why didn't I really think about the life I was opting for? And why didn't anyone advise me to think about myself and take my own dreams seriously? Maybe they did, but I had paid no heed!

I had walked out on everything that I had created for myself. The amount of hard work I had put in to get into an MBA program was not small. After two years of slogging, I had bagged one of the best jobs on campus—a great company, growth opportunities, and some wonderful colleagues. Like a fool, I had given it all up... for LOVE!

What is Love in any case? Is it giving preference to others while you blend in the background...kill your own aspirations? Simply waste all your talents? Pretty unfair, considering there is just one life, after all!

The churn had turned me into a philosopher of Mika's liking.

The day was spent wading through emotions ranging from anger and regret to loneliness, worthlessness, and gloom. By evening, my condition had deteriorated enough for Suraj to take me to the MI (Medical Investigation) room. It was interesting to see a doctor in army fatigues. Sadly, the difference ended here. He was as unfriendly as any other member of his fraternity. Or maybe I was a grouch! Anyway, he said it was a stomach infection and prescribed antibiotics and some diet restrictions.

Back in the room, there was no communication between Suraj and me; partly because of fatigue, partly because there was nothing to say. I didn't feel like sharing any of my inner turmoil with him. Not that he was keen to find out. The man hadn't once asked me why I was so quiet. Ego bigger than the Everest!

He got the Mess staff to serve me some khichdi with curd. I had my dinner in silence, took my medicines and closed the door after Suraj went for his night practice.

While I had left behind my entire world for this guy, he couldn't even change his schedule knowing well that there was nobody to help me in sickness.

And we were supposed to be partners for life!

The next morning, my tummy felt better. No cramps. My heart still hurt though.

I glanced around to find Suraj all dressed up, looking bright in the OGs. He came and sat on the bedside next to me and touched my forehead. "I don't have fever, in case you didn't know," I snapped.

"Yeah, this was just to get a reaction from you. Haven't heard your voice in ages," he teased with a naughty smile. Neither willing to forgive him, nor having the energy to fight, shutting my eyes was a smart solution—Ostrich syndrome!

When his hand started soothing my hair, my eyes jerked open. Suraj was observing my face with such tenderness! His whole face—eyes, that soft expression, a delicate smile... everything was talking to me and I felt so loved in that moment. "You've been so strong, Mo. I plucked you from your world and dumped you here. Trust me, this wasn't the plan. Without warning, I got sucked into Ghaatak and now...the competition is just round the corner. However much I might hate leaving you behind like this, I don't have a choice. You do trust me, right?"

Mika wouldn't allow me to respond. Suraj took my hand, "You know, firing practice was planned for last night. It's a big logistical affair that requires approval for weapons, ammunition, sanctioning of a vehicle, out pass for the troops etc. Everything was done—the boys were ready and firing gear had already been loaded in the vehicle by the time I reached. But you were in such a bad shape that I wasn't sure about leaving you here all alone. So I called off the exercise and explained the situation to the boys, who were very understanding. But such decisions need to be explained to the Adjutant, the Quarter Master, and the Company Commander. Though everyone was supportive, the CO will still want to know why a planned activity was called off at the last minute. I'll also be questioned on plans to make up for it." Taking a deep breath, he added, "I'm not complaining, Mo, don't get me wrong. I just want you to understand my position. When I say I'm stuck, I want you to trust me."

He was gently rubbing my hand now. Though his fingers felt hard and rough, I loved the softness of the gesture. Holding hands can be the most soothing gesture known to humans, isn't it? Suraj held my fingers and pressed them against his lips. I could feel his emotions building. On impulse, he tried to kiss me and I instinctively pulled up the bed-sheet. I had strict rules for hygiene. Kissing was allowed only when the breath was mint-fresh. Suraj wasn't surprised because he had suffered this many a morning. Diverting his kiss to my forehead, he held a bunch of my hair and shook my head affectionately. "You and your dumb fetish! No one has killed such moments more than you. Hey, you know what, Mo? They should make you in-charge of population control. Under your rules, there will be no time for romance. People will be so busy brushing, flossing, rinsing and whatever else you strongly prescribe!"

I kept holding the sheet over my face such that only my eyes were seen. This also helped me hide my expression which was melting faster than butter on a hot pan. I wanted to stay angry and not allow Suraj to get away so easily. But what he said made sense. Also, that look on his face…boy, hadn't it healed me in an instant?

After Suraj zoomed off on a bike borrowed from a fellow officer, I dragged myself out of the bed and forced some *daliya* down my throat. Instead of tea, they had served buttermilk and I wondered whom to thank—Suraj or the Mess staff.

Either way, it was thoughtful!

A long day stretched ahead. I alternated between dozing, some reading, and a whole lot of thinking. Suraj's explanation did help matters, and Chika decided to straighten out the remaining tangles.

Chika: You're upset because Suraj is not giving you time. Tell me something, can an army man think of his family during war or riots or rescue operations?

I: No

Chika: So is it wise to expect a simulation be any different?

I: Umm, maybe not.

Chika: By marrying an army officer, you've also married the army way of life. So adapt.

I: What if I don't want to?

Chika: Then forget about Suraj. Go back and start afresh.

I: I love him too much to do that. I want to be happy and make him happy.

Chika: Then the only way is to adjust to this life.

This little tête-à-tête revealed something important—while I had fancied the romantic notion of being an army wife, I had no clue what it really entailed! As an outsider, I only knew of travel and the glamour of parties; but the real deal was unfolding now. Chika said something that ran a chill down my spine, "You are cribbing and complaining during mere practice. Someday, Suraj may be out for a real strike."

I thought about the other army wives. Wasn't this their story as well? Each of them must be battling loneliness and longing. And while the soldiers enjoy immense pride and respect, there is no glory for the struggles of their families!

My lone, unsung battle had started....

7

Suraj Walks Down the Memory Lane

Ratlam, 1st of July 1986

I still remember the day I saw Mohana for the first time.

School had just reopened after the summer break and we were exchanging hugs and high fives when the bell rang. It was raining, which meant 'no assembly'. The bell was a signal for us to settle down, which we grudgingly did, even though it made us feel like trained animals of a circus. After all, we had finished middle school and were in that strange age of being neither kids nor adults.

Just then, a frail girl with a huge school bag walked into the class and changed our world forever....

I believe any new girl can create havoc among the boys... but when you are in class IX, the impact is nothing short of a catastrophe! Especially in our sleepy town, where such occurrences were rare. So when a new student...that too a girl like Mohana should walk in one fine morning, all hell is bound to break loose.

She had strikingly sharp features and the loveliest curls. She looked around with bewildered eyes as everyone sat on their seats staring at her. Visibly scared, she stood unsure for some time before mustering the courage to check if it was class IX A. She took a seat in a corner while we all sat transfixed. Through the corner of our eyes, we observed her nervousness and all the half grown men immediately wanted to help the damsel in distress…reach out to her, hold her hand, bring her to sit right next to us and assure her that she was safe.

Alas! We couldn't manage more than some furtive glances.

Mohana soon became everyone's heart-throb and the school had an added element of excitement. Her delicate frame, her smile, and of course her curls became the hot topics of discussion and everyone started making efforts to get to know her. Turned out, she was quite chirpy and made friends easily.

Amidst all this, I was one confused soul—affected by her presence, but too proud to admit. Least of all, indulge in loose talk about how I felt. My friends were brazenly competing for Mohana's attention and every chance eye contact was openly celebrated. I somehow never partook in such frivolous fun. Agreed, her initial image of a scared little bird stayed with me and kindled some sort of warmth towards her. But I did not like the brouhaha around her and the more attention Mohana received, the more I stepped away.

This created an awkward situation. Soon, she was friends with most people…except me. Everyone started visiting her house on some pretext or the other and I firmly avoided being included in all such plans. Perhaps I was different. Or I just wanted to prove that I was different. Whatever the case, it created a wall of ice between us and as some common friends shared, Mohana thought I was snobbish. She had judged me too soon but I chose to do nothing about it.

The initial euphoria around Mohana eventually settled down but the awkwardness between us never did. We studied in the same class without as much as exchanging a smile. The fact that she had a lot of friends and most spoke of her as a simple, down to earth person sometimes made me wonder if I was missing out on a good friend for no reason.

Guess Mohana was right after all—I was a stuck up, proud asshole, trapped in my own doings.

When we were in grade X, the school organized a picnic to a river resort and we all bundled up in a bus and sang our way to the spot. Everyone jumped in the sparkling water, losing track of time until the teachers started calling us for lunch. Their pleas were suitably ignored, till the whistles came out—the shrill noise ensuring quick compliance.

I had walked a bit deeper into the river and while wading back, something pierced my foot and I winced in pain. Limping out as fast as I could, I noticed a deep gash. I looked around for help but everyone had gone to the lunch area. Not knowing what to do, I just sat down on the riverbed pressing the wound, hoping for the blood flow to stop. Suddenly, I heard footsteps and saw Mohana looking for something. "Oh," she said with a startled expression on spotting me.

For a few seconds, we just looked at each other, forgetting the world around us.

Mohana had tied up her hair in a pink scarf but some of her curls had managed to slip out and were flying with the breeze. I couldn't take my eyes off her innocent, little face. Recovering first, she blurted, "I dropped my pocket torch somewhere", and started looking around. Then she noticed that I was bent in an awkward position holding my foot. She came closer to examine and was shocked to see all the blood. "Oh my God! This is bad. Let me get you some help," she gasped and ran back, forgetting all about her pocket torch.

Help arrived. First aid happened. Lunch followed. Good time with friends continued. But those eyes! They just wouldn't leave me alone. I can never explain what happened in those few moments…it was such a powerful experience, as though we were connected in some way. It was a first for me and I stayed impacted through the day. On the way back, some students dozed off while some fooled around. I sat in my cocoon, silently watching the setting sun and trying to make sense of the 'encounter'. When my friends celebrated an eye contact with Mohana, is 'this' what they also experienced? How could they joke about it? What I felt was so profound and so personal that I knew I would never share it with anyone.

The next morning, taking myself to task, I decided to get the surreal experience out of my system, since it was nothing but distraction.

Mohana never asked me about my foot nor did I ever thank her for the help. And the second year also went by… walking our own separate paths.

Papa's transfer orders brought commotion in our quiet household—after all, the entire family was to move with him to Mumbai. The thought made me excited and sad—shifting to the fanciest metropolis of India was super thrilling. But leaving behind all my childhood buddies was not easy; and I even shed a few embarrassing tears in the safety of the school toilet.

It was the last day of school and everyone was busy planning meet ups during the summer break. Only my closest friends knew about our move, I had to break it to the rest—gathered under the big Peepal tree in the school playground. Determined to stay in touch, I approached them with a diary to note down their address, so I could send letters. There was a cacophony of reactions—some were visibly shocked and disappointed that I was going away; while some started cracking jokes about Mumbai and how smart I would become now. Curiosity drew more students to our convention, filling the diary with more and more addresses.

"Hey! What's happening here?" I turned to find Mohana peeping into the diary.

"Suraj's dad got transferred to Mumbai. We are giving our address so he can write to us." The diary reached Mohana's hands and she looked puzzled. How awkward; we hadn't said 'hi' in all these years and here she was, holding my diary with a questioning look. Just to avoid social embarrassment, I smiled, "Yeah please! Do share your address. I'll send interesting stories about my life in Mumbai." My best friend who knew about the icy vibes I shared with Mohana giggled and I threw a nasty stare at the prick.

Without a word, Mohana scribbled her address and passed on the diary.

In Mumbai, after the initial running around, I started missing my friends and pulled the diary out. It had 19 addresses; many just got caught in that moment. But rather than dismissing anyone, I chose to be polite and sent postcards to all.

Writing 'Dear Mohana' felt odd and I hesitated before dropping the letter in the post box. At the most, she would feel weird receiving a note from me and would throw it away. Not much to lose...just a little pride.

In less than a week, replies started coming in. Perhaps my friends were missing me terribly, or maybe the buggers had nothing better to do! Either way, it was a blessing. Just the handwriting of my childhood buddies triggered emotions. Everyone complained that life was not the same without me and that I should visit them soon. Every letter helped me heal from the pain of separation and I sent long, detailed responses to all.

And then came the letter I had least expected and secretly hoped for—a nice one pager from Mohana, which started with 'Hi Suraj' (instead of 'Dear Suraj'), making me feel instantly snubbed. She apologized for the delay in responding, explaining that it took her a while to find someone who could decipher the Harappan script. The girl was openly making fun of my handwriting and I was beaming like a moron! Taking offence was futile because many a time, even I couldn't read my own scribble. Taking the joke further, Mohana added that finally when she found a person who could read the script, he turned out to be a rogue. Cheating her of her precious belonging, he sold the letter to the Archaeological Society of India to be showcased in their museum. After winning a long drawn legal battle, she finally got the letter and was applying her skills of guesswork to respond to me.

The cheeky girl! She did have a funny bone. And I thought I was the king of poker-faced humour.

Changing tracks, she wrote in the most straightforward tone that she understood the circumstances which compelled me to write the first time. There was no need to be polite and no compulsions to respond to this one. I was beginning to wonder if she was smartly signalling me to back off, but before closing she wrote something really sweet. She said that my friends truly missed me and there must be something special to have this effect on people. She shared her regret at having missed the opportunity to get to know me face to face, but wondered if letters could be a medium of friendship. She signed off with 'Best, Mo'.

I was blown. What a fascinating read and what an interesting person—this Mo. Now I truly regretted being on the high horse without reason. Letters sure were a wonderful medium to undo the damage.

And this is how it started...my friendship with Mohana...Mo.

We started writing regularly, and the number of pages kept increasing. Letters from other friends gradually waned, but to my delight, Mo maintained an unblemished consistency.

I loved the unhurried, unpretentious process of getting to know each other. We had no idea where this would lead or how long it would continue. So we chose to be totally honest about whatever we shared and boy! Didn't we share the world? Stories from childhood, issues with siblings, challenges with subjects (math for her, physics for me), favourite teachers, least liked teachers, families, extended families, problems with our looks (acne for her, uneven moustache for me), first crush (neighbour in her case, English teacher in mine), faith (yes in her case, no in mine), favourite sports, sports stars (Kapil Dev for her, Steffi Graf for me), friends, food...

The list just went on and on and on.

Mo once asked about my aspiration and that was the first time I let out my secret—the Indian Army. I was quite lanky and fearing ridicule around my fitness, I kept this to myself. But with Mo, there was no fear of being judged. Sure enough, in the next letter she asked me about the selection process of the armed forces and if I had already started preparing.

About her aspiration, she said she was flirting with a few options. Entrepreneurship was the most compelling one on her list; though she had no clue about the line of business or the way to get there. Mo was neither afraid of dreaming big, nor ashamed of doing small jobs! I would be amazed to read about the odd jobs she would take up during summer breaks. This, along with the home tuitions she gave to neighbourhood kids. Once I checked if her family was under financial stress and she reasoned: "Is money the only reason to take up work?"

Her thinking was so unique and unconventional. And all the while I thought I was different.

We had been pen-friends for almost two years but hadn't spoken even once, though I was often tempted. Apart from the exorbitant STD call rates, my own insecurities were a big deterrent. But Mo's upcoming birthday demanded something special—a surprise phone call! However, we'd never exchanged phone numbers. Our common friends were ruled out because they could give away the secret. I had to device a smart game plan. Finally, after much thinking, plans A, B, and C were chalked out. Plan A involved calling up my father's colleague who also knew Mo's family. Unfortunately, he didn't have their number and I couldn't request him to get it for me. Plan B involved confiding in my sister who knew Mo's cousin. Didn't work either. She flatly refused because I had apparently not helped her with something earlier that week. Sisters are blisters, period.

I reached Plan C real fast—a rather convoluted plan that involved approaching Mo's neighbour Mr. Pai, who happened to be a distant relative of ours. I didn't want anyone to know about my interest in calling a girl, so I had to hide my identity from him. The risk of getting caught was huge, but throwing caution to the wind, I dialled Pai uncle.

From the small cubicle of a telephone booth, I feigned a voice that I thought would be harsh enough to represent the income tax department. In a flat, unhurried tone, I told him that his name had appeared in the department's random check and I needed to verify basic information like his address, place of work, names of other earning members of his family etc. He was a bit taken aback but went ahead with the probe where I gave information and he verified it.

Then I asked him for three references who knew him. He asked me why this was required and in a practiced tone, I said, "Routine procedure." The strategy worked and how! The very first name he shared was of Mohana's father's. I asked for his address and phone number. Grinning ear to ear, I noted the residence phone number, and then needed a truckload of patience to keep up the act, as poor Pai uncle struggled with the other names. As soon as he was done, I thanked him and disconnected the line.

The tiny pang of guilt for having tricked a simple, honest man vanished the moment I dialled Mohana's number. Instead, a sudden wave of nervousness gripped me as if I were gate-crashing a party. What if she doesn't like surprises? What if she's cold and distant? Battling self-doubt, I held on till she chirped, "Good evening, birthday girl here. How may I help you?"

I burst out laughing, "Who talks like this?"

"Is that you, Suraj?" To my surprise and absolute delight, she had recognized me instantly.

"Wow! I'm so glad you called. What an awesome gift!"

Mo and I spoke without any awkwardness...as though we were used to calling each other. I loved her voice, her carefree banter and her ability to constantly pull out silly jokes from nowhere. When we finally disconnected, I felt disappointed and wanted to call her right back.

On my way home, I bought an ice cream...Mo's favourite flavour! Silly, I know, but I just wanted to stay connected with her somehow. By now, I couldn't deny that we did share something special.

Whatever it was, I wasn't rushing into giving it a name or doing anything stupid that could spoil things.

Over the next three years, both of us completed our graduation. She opted for commerce because it was 'easy' (Mo's authenticity bordered on buffoonery sometimes). Also, it gave her the freedom to take up a part-time job and small assignments like door-to-door selling. Mo didn't shy away from these supposedly petty jobs since they taught more about life than a college course. Without any such fundamental belief system, I opted for science because it was a respectable option.

College life witnessed the birth of new friendships while some old associations withered away. But Mo and I stayed rock solid. By now, we were so much a part of each other's lives, that there was a sense of permanence in our relationship. My friends in Mumbai had heard a lot about her and couldn't believe that we had not met in five years. Phone calls were also far and few.

Letters continued to keep us steadily anchored.

Life moved on. I got selected in the Short Service Commission of the Indian Army and left for the Officers Training Academy (OTA) in Chennai. Mo got into an MBA program and finished her first year while I completed my training and got commissioned.

Before joining my unit at Dras in J&K, I headed to Mumbai for some family time. Gods were watching. The same week, Mo was coming to Mumbai for a summer internship. She was to stay with a relative who lived an hour from my place.

Early morning when I reached Mumbai, the 'city that never sleeps' was opening its eyes, local trains gearing up for another gruelling day. Coming back to the familiarity of one's home town is so soothing. Mo's presence made it even more special. We were in the same city after seven years and even the atheist in me thanked the Lord for the timing. Had I come just one week prior, we would have missed meeting each other.

At the first opportunity, I called her and we decided to meet on Friday, two days away. The plan worked well for me—after months of brutal training, sleep was all I wanted. Which is exactly what I did...apart from savouring '*ghar ka khaana*' since I knew I would be away from such luxuries for an indefinite period.

We decided to meet post work, on the terrace outside her office cafeteria. The army culture of 'better early than late' had been drilled into every cell of my *fauji* body and I reached the place well before time. Buzzing with excitement, I kept imagining how we would react seeing each other after so many years. Would Mo look the same—simple and frail, or would she have transformed into a stylish professional?

Lost in thought, I had downed a few cups of tea before the curly head appeared on the terrace. Mo looked simply ethereal! In my memory drive, she was still a lanky girl in school uniform. What I saw instead was a lovely, young woman in an off-white shirt, tucked into a pair of well-fitted jeans. Nothing fancy, and yet I was swept off my feet!

Taking in the glow on her face and the dance of her signature curls, I realized that my breath had quickened. Mo was looking around but had obviously failed to recognize me, thanks to my transformation in the military academy. My hair was super short. Plus, outdoor life in the blazing Chennai sun had rendered me suitable for a night offensive. Secretly, I was happy to join the 'tall, dark, and handsome' brigade—the first two being facts and the last one, my unbiased opinion. I sported several bruises and scars from the training; with skin peeling off from my face, neck, and hands. Convinced this ruggedness added to my sex appeal, I got up…and with the swagger of Clint Eastwood in *The Good, The Bad and The Ugly*, I stepped out on the terrace.

Having pictured this rendezvous in my head, I had decided that I'll walk towards her with a warm smile, shake her hand like an officer, take her out for a coffee and drop her back home like a gentleman. All this preparation was good to just boost my confidence; for when Mo and I actually came face to face, I forgot all about the script!

Standing just a few feet from Mo, I tried suppressing a smile even though I was grinning ear to ear in my heart. Mo was staring at me with an unsure frown. I removed my sunglasses to help her get a good look and slowly walked towards her. For a few seconds, we just kept looking at each other with ever growing smiles. Tears started twinkling in Mo's eyes and even I felt a sudden lump in my throat. She just said, "Oh my God, Suraj!" and ran towards me. We held each other in a tight embrace forgetting the fact that it was her office building and there were a few curious onlookers.

Hugging her was the most natural thing to do and that one warm embrace spoke way more than all our letters put together. In that emotional moment, while I remained tongue tied, Mo was more forthcoming, "I'm letting my tears tell you how happy I am!"

As I looked into her moist eyes, I felt the same connect that I'd felt nine years ago, on the day of the picnic.

Only more powerful!

During that one week in Mumbai, we met every evening, either in the cafeteria or some coffee shop nearby. Once, even at a railway canteen. The place really didn't matter because we would have a great time everywhere...even on the crowded 'locals'. Being new to Mumbai, Mo didn't understand the local trains. So, instead of the compartment exclusive for ladies, I would make her travel with me, which was an event in itself because Mo never left home without her charm and effervescence. There was always an admiring audience and I felt that my army training was being put to good use protecting her!

Standing close to Mo on the train also meant fighting my own self. I was hopelessly attracted to her and felt like touching her all the time. I had refused to admit that I was infatuated right from the moment she had walked into the class. There was no denying the truth now. Also undeniable was the sexual tension between us—strong, urgent, and demanding. Often, I found her looking at me longingly, but then I was not sure if I was playing it up in my head.

It was time to find out.

Before I knew, it was Thursday and I was to leave for Srinagar the next morning. With just one more evening together, it was time to get off that stupid high horse.

We had decided to meet at a coffee shop near her office and go straight to the Juhu beach for a stroll. As luck might have it, Mo came two hours late, profusely apologizing for the delay. Apparently, there was some important presentation that just wouldn't get over. She looked super sexy in high heels but I wondered how the idea of a 'stroll on the beach' would work out. Plus, it was quite late already. But Mo wouldn't have any of it.

"Oh come on now, Suraj! I have already told my aunt that I would be late and a friend would drop me back. This is Mumbai. And, I'm with an army officer, mind you!"

We reached the beach when most people were leaving. Without a care, madam took off her heels, stuffed them in her bag, rolled up her trousers, tied her hair into a bouncy bun on top of her head, and ran straight into the waves.

We started walking, taking in the cool, salty breeze and the sound of the splashing waves. My heart was prodding me to speak and my mind wanted me to wait for the right moment. During this internal tussle, I suddenly developed cold feet—what if Mo didn't feel the same way? It would be terrible to break the magical spell just before going on my first posting. Wouldn't it be better to sit on a post, dream about Mo and wait for her letters, than get turned down now and deal with the disappointment all alone? 'Chicken heart *fauji*!' I mocked myself.

We kept walking in silence with a few dogs who had taken it upon themselves to guard us and wouldn't have it any other way.

Our arms brushed and I tried my best to not grab her hand instantly. But it was impossible to resist the temptation and after a while, displaying a total lack of self-control, I reached out and held her hand, half expecting her to pull away. Instead, she opened her palm against mine and we locked fingers tightly. It seemed like the most natural thing to do.

We ambled amidst the gentle waves. Suddenly, the dogs got agitated about something and created a ruckus right behind us. A startled Mo immediately clung to me and there was no way I could let go of her after that.

I put my hand around her waist and brought her closer to me. No resistance, just a gasp of surprise. I wished it wasn't so dark...I wanted to see her expressions...but had to make do with a silhouette with bright, shining eyes. Looking straight in my eyes, Mo held my shoulder and then almost in unison, we just reached out and kissed. I think both of us were equally startled at what was happening because we just lingered tentatively for a while. Soon, emotions took over...followed by need. Tentative brushing of lips turned into tender nibbling and before long, we were consumed by passion. I lifted Mo against my body as our kisses grew deeper and more demanding.

I wanted to explore her body but suddenly remembered that we were in full public eye. A siren went off in my head jerking me out of the trance. I deposited her back on the sand and quickly tore myself away and looked around.

Thankfully, the audience consisted only of canines, who were not interested in moral policing.

In between our uneven breaths, we stole glances and laughed. Mo clung back to me and I had to do the exact opposite of what I wanted. I just held her close, kissed her hair and helped her relax. Standing still, we held each other, neither of us speaking. The moment was too intense and we didn't feel like breaking the spell. A part of me was torn by raw want while the other was filled with a sense of peace.

Without a single word, we had professed our love and how!

The memory of our first kiss became a part of me. It would make me lonely in a crowd, lonelier on isolated posts. And on the toughest days, when my spirit would be down in the dumps, it would keep me company and give me the strength to hang on...just so I could hold Mohana tight, and kiss her again.

8

REALITY CHECK

Namkum, 7th of June 1997

The whirring sound of the engine snapped Suraj out of his reverie. He checked his wristwatch—1:30 am. He had been enjoying a flashback while his Ghaatak boys struggled to solve a problem. Their loud cheers announced success! "These boys don't give up. Do they?" he muttered with a smile, relieved that the night was saved.

Things had seemed quite bleak just an hour back. They had come to a firing range and after practice, when everyone was seated in the 3 ton, the old dragon refused to wake up. All tricks were tried, but the vehicle remained dead as a rock. Some youngsters, just back from a course on 'Mechanical Transport', were keen to open it up. Giving them half an hour to try out their skills, Suraj had settled under a tree, dreading the long night ahead.

Fortunately, the newbie mechanics were able to fix the problem and everyone happily awaited a few hours of sleep. The prospect of some rest felt delicious to Suraj as well. But the flashback had stirred his emotions and got him concerned about Mohana's well-being. 'My happy, chirpy Mo is wilting...as if she has lost a grip on herself,' he thought, sadly. And the challenge was not Ghaatak, it was army life. How would a fiercely independent girl like Mohana adjust to life in Namkum?

Ever since she was a little girl, Mo had been trying to gather experiences that would strengthen her wings. And just when she had taken a flight, he had whisked her away and cooped her up in a small place. Agreed, she was more than eager to start a life with him, but instead of checking her readiness for this massive change, he had gladly accepted her choice made in absolute naiveté.

Suraj felt terrible about being so selfish, ready to make amends right away. First thing in the morning, he would speak to Mo about going back to Mumbai and finding a job. They could meet during his annual leave; she could also visit him sometimes. It would not be easy to stay away from each other, but this was important. He should have thought earlier.

Never mind. Better late than never!

What Suraj didn't know was that Mohana had woken up to the reality of being an army wife. So when he apologized for being selfish, and asked her to go back and be happy, she surprised him by plonking on his lap. "Lieutenant Suraj Shastri, I am staying right here, creating happiness with you."

The tension between them melted away as they caressed and kissed, over and over. With tenderness adding strength to their bond, Suraj and Mohana decided to stay together and make the most of what life had to offer.

And boy! How blissfully unaware were they of what lay ahead!

9

Initiation by Fire

Namkum, 12th of June 1997

My resolve to live up to the role of an army wife was tough to execute without a JD (Job Description) or clarity from the husband. Would the entire journey be trial and error? Just like always, Gods were watching…

One afternoon, Suraj brought the news—some Major Rana had been posted back to the unit. He along with his family would be putting up in the quarter next to us.

Human beings! I won't be rotting alone now. Being an ardent lover of kids, I was overjoyed that the Ranas had two small children. Sensing my excitement, Suraj warned me against piling on them as soon as they arrived. How could he always guess what I was likely to do?

When I heard a chatter of kids, I tried my best to obey Suraj's instruction but it was too much to just sit inside when people were moving in next door. I went out and stood in the small garden waiting to spot someone 'just by chance'. Sure enough, a little girl saw me. I smiled and waved at her. In response, she ran inside, and dragged her mom out. A pretty woman with a flawless, creamy complexion, perfectly straight hair, honey-coloured eyes, and a glistening diamond nose stud. Wearing a light blue salwar kameez with a soft, hand embroidered white dupatta, she was elegance personified.

Perfection can be so unnerving! Plus there is something peculiar about curly hair. The moment they come face to face with the silky straight variety, they run into self doubt! "Well, you score over her in the weight department" Mika observed with wicked satisfaction. Gathering my wits, I walked up to her and introduced myself. She gave me a warm hug, "Lovely meeting you, Mohana. I am Neelam Rana."

I beamed and spoke from my heart, "Hi Neelam, you have no idea how happy I am to see you!"

Her expression stiffened, "You can call me Mrs. Rana." I was taken aback because normally, people encourage you to address them by their first name.

I acted unaffected, "Sure, if you prefer it that way."

She held my hand and smiled, "Yes, I do prefer it that way, dear. Let me introduce you to my brats." She called out their names and both the kids came running and stood next to their mother. "Don't stand staring at me like that, say hello to aunty." *Aunty!* I was simply not ready to embrace the aunty status! Numb with shock, I heard the kids politely wish me "Good morning, aunty" and managed to mumble "Hey, good morning buddy!" Just then, a jonga full of luggage arrived and everyone got busy with it. Taking advantage of the chaos, I slipped out with a 'see you soon' to come back to my den…and lick my wounds.

Aunty—what a caustic, stinging word! How mean to use it for someone who was just a little over 23…ok 24! It made me feel old and haggard. When I told Suraj about this disastrous experience, he couldn't stop laughing.

However, he did have an opinion on the 'call me Mrs. Rana' comment. "Major Rana is quite senior to me. Perhaps ma'am prefers to maintain the seniority." To make sure that I got him, Suraj elaborated, "Addressing her as Mrs. Rana is a mark of respect, for her and her husband. Isn't it?"

"What's that supposed to mean? I don't even know them, so where does the question of respect or disrespect arise?" Ignoring Suraj's 'How can you be so dumb' look, I clarified, "You know, 'Mrs. Rana' sounds so formal…it's like a barrier between us."

Suraj jumped in, "Exactly! She wants that barrier, Mo. She doesn't want you to treat her like a friend. She wants to be treated like a senior…which she is."

It was my turn to cut him short, "Her husband is your senior, I get that. But how is she my senior?"

Suraj wore an exasperated smile, "Mrs. Rana is your senior by virtue of being married to someone who is senior to your husband. In fact, every lady in our unit is your senior. Mo, please understand, this is how it works. In fact, there is a saying in the services: The wife always wears one rank higher than the officer. By that logic, Mrs. Rana is a Lt. Colonel and you are a Captain, get it, kiddo?" he pulled my cheeks.

I wasn't amused one bit, "But Shaheen is fine being called Shaheen. So is Anu." Suraj's expression changed and he said in a flat tone, "Well, you should check their comfort. Perhaps they don't mind…or maybe they do and haven't managed to tell you."

This was new to me. I didn't expect this kind of hierarchy among the women. Mika immediately protested, 'A system where you are defined by your husband's rank does not feel right.'

The next morning, Mrs. Rana invited me for lunch. Tired of the Mess food, I excitedly looked forward to this change. I was expecting an apartment similar to ours; but this layout was bigger and better. There was a small kitchen, up and running in one day, while I had been living like a parasite for weeks. How could she turn the place around so quick? Mrs. Rana didn't seem to think much of it though, "After so many experiences of packing and unpacking, one naturally learns all this. You will also become an expert, just you wait and watch." I wasn't as sure!

Mrs. Rana started the conversation, "Since we may have to stay here for a few months, might as well make ourselves comfortable. Sam (I guessed this must be her husband Maj. Samrat Singh Rana) was told that Major's accommodation is not available right away, at Namkum. There is another neighbouring cantonment called Khojatoli…15 minutes from here. But it's quite cut off and I like to be in the thick of action," she announced. Offering me some starters, she continued, "Our first lady, Mrs. Pratap is very active… just like me. It's better to be close by to help her whenever required. Even Sam prefers being around the CO. The senior lot should stick together, I feel."

I munched on, controlling an impulse to say 'Sure, but why do you keep flashing the seniority card?'

Mrs. Rana continued, "Mo..ha..na—that's a unique name. A bit old fashioned…but I like it. You remind me so much of my early days after marriage and how lost I used to feel. Sam could hardly keep his hands off me and that part of my life was great," she winked. Barely had we met and she was already sharing bedroom stories!

"But getting used to this *fauji* life took time," she seemed to go into a flashback. I perked up for some of her experiences and how she coped. Instead, she said, "You must understand one thing, Mohana. You will contribute to your husband's success in a big way. In the services, wives play a huge role in shaping the careers of their husbands." I raised my eyebrows in surprise. "I'm not kidding. Nobody explains this to a new wife and the poor girl has to figure everything out on her own. I think we senior ladies must share our experience with junior ladies like you."

Her middle name should be 'Senior'—Mrs. Neelam Senior Rana!

"Army life is peculiar with our bases usually at far off locations, just like Namkum. Cut off from friends, family, and all local civilian contacts, our social life exists within the boundaries of the cantonment. Life in an infantry unit is even more unique. We spend several years together and move as a flock from one posting to another. Like one big family, and women play a big role in keeping everyone together and happy."

Hmm. That explained Shaheen's warmth and also her concern for my well being…just like an elder sister. I thought about Shaheen wistfully and hoped that she was feeling better.

Just then, the kids appeared and bombed me with the 'A' word! Patting their heads, Mrs. Rana sent them out to play. "Don't disturb us. Mamma is discussing something important with aunty."

A full-blown induction session was on the cards.

Neelam Senior Rana (hereafter referred to as NSR) opened her session, "Norms of socializing are a big part of the army life. People call on each other all the time; plus there are Mess parties and formal get togethers. Can you cook?" I mumbled a yes with more confidence than I felt. "What?" came a more pointed question.

"Well, the usual stuff. Everyday food I guess."

Before I could elaborate, NSR passed her judgement, "Then you will need to learn. Anyone can cook regular stuff, Mohana. If you want to stand out, you have to be an exemplary cook. Serve your specialities to guests and never repeat your menu. Just see how fast people begin to know you."

I frowned, almost in disbelief. "Most people don't understand this. Food can be a great medium to win people over and keep them happy. Ask officers of this unit, who used to eat more at my house than in the Mess. And they can't stop praising me even today. As a matter of fact, wherever I go, stories of my cooking reach beforehand!"

Wow! This woman was something—loving herself so unconditionally!

"In the army, we take care of the bachelors as if they're our little brothers. Sam would be so strict but I would baby them, especially Gulshan."

"Is there anything else?" Oops! The question jerked out before I could stop myself. I was still struggling to understand how I could shape Suraj's career; obviously there would be more than cooking well and feeding the bachelors.

"You need to show more respect and patience when you're with your seniors," pat came her barbed response. "You're new to the unit, Mohana...you need to blend in... behave gently, so people accept you," she said in an agitated voice. Couldn't blame her, I had asked for this.

Two wonderful things happened over lunch. One, I got to know NSR's kids—Aseem and Asmi aged nine and six. Chubby, cute, and extremely well behaved. Two, I enjoyed a heavenly meal! NSR was every bit the exemplary cook she claimed to be. Never before had stuffed *karela* tasted so good—crunchy and crispy on the outside, soft and smooth on the inside. A perfect blend of spices that tasted delicious with the steaming hot paranthas. Showstopper was the divine *rabdi*—NSR said she'd spent three hours making it because my first visit had to be special. I was touched.

Food is indeed a powerful medium to win people.

Over the next few days, NSR and I bonded really well. She introduced me to the AWWA (Army Wives Welfare Association) and spoke about their work to care for the troops and their families.

I also learnt that 'support' is big in the *fauji* culture. "But let's be clear—while people are always there, we must ask for help only when things are beyond us. We must be strong enough to handle challenges without complaining. That is the true spirit of an army wife."

Despite her habit of stuffing a suppository of *gyan* up my backside, NSR was a sweet soul.

One afternoon, NSR summoned me. I thought she wanted to teach one of her magic recipes. Instead, she asked me to sit down for a chat. Without any preamble, she complained, "You have not been behaving well, Mohana." Huh? "I saw you run in the Mess garden." She looked at me as though this was sufficient for me to render an apology. My blank look prodded her on, "You are an officer's wife, a lady. You should behave like one."

I tried defending myself, "But I was playing with Aseem and Asmi. How can one play an outdoor sport without running?"

"Then don't play games that require you to run. This is the Mess, Mohana. These things get noticed."

Mika was furious, 'Who are these people observing you all the time? Are there defence satellites hovering over to catch unladylike behaviour of army wives, especially Mohana Shastri?' But with NSR, you never knew how long a leash you had, so it was best to keep mum. My silence was mistaken for a penny dropping moment, and she decided to hammer when the iron was hot. "One more thing, the other day when we were having tea in the garden, your *bhaiyya* (Suraj's *sahaayak*) came to give you the keys. I observed that you took it directly from him."

Now what in the world is that supposed to mean! "So? What's wrong with that?" I couldn't mask my irritation.

"Well, you never take things directly from these men. You should have asked him to leave it on the table instead."

Either I was dumber than the dumbest, or NSR was crazy. Because I just couldn't make sense of what she said.

Just then, Major Rana walked in and much to my embarrassment, NSR pulled him into the conversation. He gave me a patronizing look and thundered in his heavy voice, "Neelu is absolutely right."

So it was two against one now. Before I could concede defeat, Mika took charge. "Can someone help me understand this—what is wrong in taking keys directly from *bhaiyya*? Is he some untouchable or what?" I asked in the most irreverent tone.

Major Rana shook his head disapprovingly, "Ma'am, I don't think you meant what you just said. Still, let me clarify—there is no such divide in the army. Yes, we are quite hierarchical as an organization, and for a good reason. The troops, however, remain our key asset and also a big part of our lives. Hence you must appreciate the sensitivities around them."

He paused and NSR cut to the chase, "These men are mostly away from their families...their wives, you know.

If accidentally, they happen to touch you, they might get ideas, right? They are also human after all. And hence we never give or take things directly from them!" Looking at my shock, Major Rana added, "Don't worry, ma'am, such things are very rare. Our boys are very well behaved and respectful towards the ladies. Still, it's best to be careful and maintain a distance. Hope we answered your question."

Holy Moses! Was this the general thought process? And here I was, playing badminton with Narayan! No wonder it had warranted immediate action. Memory of that unpleasant experience must've played on my face, because NSR immediately noticed, "What's bothering you, Mohana? You still look upset."

I didn't want to embarrass myself by narrating the Narayan Singh story, but this was a good opportunity to get some clarity. "Not upset, Mrs. Rana, I was just wondering about the role of *bhaiyya* in our lives. What exactly is his job?"

Pin-drop silence, as if I'd stepped into some forbidden territory. For once, NSR seemed tongue-tied, leaving the heavy lifting for Major Rana. "This is not an easy question, ma'am, and let me admit—there may be no straight answers. As I see it, the tradition of assigning a dedicated soldier to an officer goes back to colonial times when every officer used to move around with an 'orderly'—responsible not just for the officer's comfort, but also for ensuring work efficiencies. The system has continued since, but the word 'orderly' has been replaced with '*sahaayak*' or 'batty'—short for battle companion or buddy in battle. As the word suggests, he is the most trusted companion of an officer, during war and peace. His exact job is often at the discretion of the officer and hence you'll see *sahaayaks* doing different tasks to support the officer and his family in a peace station. But at the end of the day, they are trained soldiers like all of us, proud to serve the nation."

Hmm. This explained Suraj's statement about Narayan being 'his' *sahaayak*. I had found his anger unjustified back then, but I could see his point of view now! Dear God, this world and its ways were so unique. My education and all my life experiences had hardly prepared me for this.

Why is there no SOP (Standard Operating Procedure) for army wives?

One afternoon, NSR was away. The kids and I decided to explore the area behind our room and asked Suraj's helper to caution us if anyone was around.

Calling ourselves the three musketeers, we ventured into a territory, bursting with wild mushrooms. Warning the kids not to touch them, I looked around and a gorgeous *Jaamun* tree laden with fresh fruit caught my eye! I immediately wanted to chomp on them. But how? The tree was pretty tall; the bark wet and slippery.

After a failed hunt for a long stick, we made an idiotic attempt at throwing stones only to risk hurting each other. The juicy, ripe *jaamuns* were making me insane! If I could somehow climb atop our bathroom, I could reach the branches near the parapet.

Blinded by lust, I started climbing the window grille and quickly reached the top. The asbestos roof was covered with decaying leaves, fallen fruit etc. As I walked along the edge and reached the branches, a sweet fragrance filled my nostrils. Relying on my childhood experience of climbing trees, I reached the main body, full of ripe fruit. I stuffed my mouth and oooooh...each one was filled with nectar! Aseem spread out his jacket and I dropped a nice, big bunch for them. Squealing with delight, they attacked the sweetmeats created by Lord Almighty.

Our party was in full glory when I saw them—Suraj, NSR, Major Rana, and *bhaiyya* (who by the way, was supposed to watch out for us) standing below, shell shocked! I was caught red handed—arm stretched out; legs sprawled at an unbecoming angle to maximize my reach. A part of me still wanted to pluck the bunch now that I was that close...but the looks from the delegation below warned otherwise.

Suraj watched in amusement, NSR in disgust, Major Rana in disbelief, and *bhaiyya* in awe as I walked over the asbestos sheet, got on the cement frame protruding over the window, hung on it with the support of my elbow, got on the window, climbed down, and jumped off to the ground. Much like a kid caught with her hand in a cookie jar, I stood awkwardly—a breath-taking sight with grimy elbows and *jaamun* stains.

Suraj's straight face made it difficult to guess the emotion beneath the intrepid exterior. NSR recovered from the shock and started doing tch tch glancing at Major Rana who looked more embarrassed than me. She dismissed *bhaiyya,* looked at Suraj and made a gesture of hopelessness, "So much for educating her on lady like behaviour. I step out for a bit and she goes climbing trees like a monkey and stands here looking like a street urchin." I kept examining my filthy shoes. She finally addressed me, "Mohana, next time you feel like having *jaamuns,* just tell me. I will send *bhaiyya* to the market to get you some." Then ignoring their excitement around purple tongues, NSR grabbed the kids, instructing them to clean up right away.

Suraj and I walked towards our room without a word, opened the lock, got inside, closed the door behind us, looked at each other, and burst out laughing. We shushed each other, lest the sound waves travelled straight to NSR's dignified, ladylike ears!

"Street urchin, you need a shower," Suraj said scooping me up and walking towards the mouldy bathroom.

10

Ants in Pants!

Namkum, 18th of June 1997

D day, finally! The back breaking practice for Ghaatak was at test. The competition was spread over a week, with teams competing each night to finish a series of tasks, assessed on speed and precision. Suraj's team was among the last two to compete. It was early evening when Suraj left for the competition, with clear instructions to not expect him before noon. By night, I was restless—what would be happening right now? How would our team be performing?

'Our' team? Had I begun to belong?

Early next morning, I awaited some news. Finally, unable to hold back, I went to check if Major Rana had any update.

He was having breakfast, dapper as always—moustache crisp and fresh, just like the rest of him. He was quite surprised with my anxiety, "Relax, ma'am. Are you going to lose sleep every time Suraj participates in a competition? Come, have some tea."

Rain had drummed down all night and a nice cup of ginger tea was just what I needed. NSR was packing tiffins and she slipped in a piping hot aloo parantha along with my tea. Biting into the divinity, I dreamt—what if the Ranas adopt me. Lifelong supply of NSR's cooking. While some people think through their gut, my tastebuds were incharge!

After Major Rana left, I happily downed another parantha and returned to our room.

In less than an hour, there was a knock and I ran to welcome Suraj. Instead, I found Major Rana and NSR outside our humble abode. How come Major Rana was back from office? Unsure, I invited them in. They occupied the sofas, and ignoring the anticipation in my eyes, got busy complaining about the shoddy upkeep of the quarter. Great! Finally, someone saw my point. But wasn't it irrelevant? All I cared for was some news on Ghaatak.

Finally, Major Rana said, "I reached office and got the news on Ghaatak. So, I immediately started back to let you know." Avoiding eye contact, he said, "Our boys tried very hard. In fact, considering the level of complexity, they did really well."

NSR chimed in nodding vigorously, "Yes, they get full marks for effort. In all these weeks, I've hardly seen Suraj—always away for practice. Hardworking fellow."

'Cut the crap and come to the point,' Mika was muttering in my head. Somehow, I managed to hold her back and keep a straight face. "Well," Major Rana continued evasively, "It's not really what we had hoped for..." Why stretch the conversation like a rubber band...knowing well that patience was what I lacked more than any other virtue?

"Can you just tell me what happened?" I jumped in.

"We came fifth. Suraj's team lost their way in the jungle. They couldn't complete the task." Jesus Christ! This was just not expected. Suraj had mentioned that they were a bit weak in night navigation. But getting lost...and unable to complete the task? He must be crushed!

"But they did cover up in firing despite such a rough time through the night. Most people would have given up under duress, but Suraj and his boys hardly missed a mark!" Major Rana tried to cheer me up. I did feel better...but it was sad that despite so much hard work, Suraj couldn't achieve what he wanted to.

Another knock and in walked a tall, well-built officer. I had not seen him earlier. He quickly wished NSR and Major Rana and then addressed me, "Good morning, ma'am. I am Capt. Gulshan Bagga. I couldn't meet you earlier because of some health challenges." He had a charming, friendly personality but wore a look of worry. Turning to Major Rana, he said, "Sir, the CO is asking for you. He is quite upset."

Major Rana quipped, "About what—the Ghaatak boys getting lost? These things happen, *yaar*, he needs to relax!"

"No, sir, there is a problem...Suraj goofed up. After the firing competition, our team returned two rifles short."

Major Rana's face changed, "What are you saying? How can this happen? Where is Suraj?"

"Major Asif is questioning him, sir. Suraj seems disoriented...unable to recall anything."

Major Rana looked at him incredulously. "This has never happened in our unit. First, this idiot gets lost in the jungle, and then he loses weapons!"

That didn't sound good at all. NSR sat with her head in her hands. Capt. Bagga stood fidgeting—his worried expression much deeper now. Major Rana paced around radiating anger.

"So what does this mean? What will happen to Suraj now?" I stammered. No response. People kept looking away, lost in their thoughts.

I repeated and Major Rana snapped in an irritated tone, "Who knows, ma'am? If the weapons are found, perhaps he might get away with some light punishment. God forbid, if the weapons don't get traced, there could be a court martial. He could even be jailed."

My heart stopped beating. I went up to Major Rana and asked in a trembling voice, "Can I meet Suraj?"

"Didn't you hear what Gulshan just said? A court of enquiry is going on…Suraj is being interrogated in the CO's office. How can you meet him now?" He was clearly annoyed with my request.

Still, I persisted, "Suraj cannot be careless. The fatigue must've taken a toll. Let me meet him please, perhaps I can help him relax and recall things."

Major Rana seemed unsure. "Well, I can take you to the office, ma'am, but the CO has to agree. Court of enquiry is an extremely serious matter and I doubt if he will allow any disruption."

I remembered Col Pratap's solemn personality and knew that Major Rana was right. "But we don't need to let him know. The interrogation is being done by Major Asif, right? I'm sure he will understand and agree," I beamed with confidence.

"Then you don't know Major Asif," chuckled Capt. Bagga. "He is tough like hell and by now, Suraj must be regretting having Major Asif as his company commander."

I was livid with this Capt. Bagga! How could he have a laugh at Suraj's expense when he was to blame for everything. Had he taken better care of his health, Ghaatak wouldn't have landed on Suraj's head! Throwing him a disgusted look, I resumed pleading and finally, Major Rana agreed. NSR, bless the noble soul, volunteered to come along just in case I needed help.

Sitting in Capt. Bagga's small car, we drove towards the office in silence.

A rise in the number of men in uniforms indicated that the office was not far. After completing the security checks, we crossed an immaculately maintained ground, the size of a football field. The car stopped in front of a plain, single storied building, which, I was told was the office.

Despite my harried state, I noticed that unlike my swanky office in Mumbai, this was plain and run down. However, the place had character. Beautiful plants and flowers added colour and life. The pathway to the office building was marked with bright red bricks, each half buried in grass, pointing the sky at the exact same angle. Ashoka trees stood erect in a row, like soldiers in attention, signifying discipline and order.

I had often wondered what actually goes on in the army offices and had once asked Suraj about it. "I don't know about others, but after the heavy breakfast you stuff me with, I generally doze through the most part." His response seemed even more ridiculous now, as I studied the stern looking corridor. Men in uniform moved in and out of various rooms. The sound of typewriters added to the serious feel of the place.

We walked towards an adjoining building where we were ushered into a small room. The officers deposited me and NSR there and went ahead to speak to the CO. We were sitting twiddling our thumbs when we heard some commotion in the next room—someone shouting in a harsh voice. Oh my God, Major Asif! And then I heard a weak, tired voice...mumbling incoherently. Suraj!

I sprang up and NSR immediately blocked my way. "Don't be stupid, Mohana," she warned. "Sam has already taken a big risk by getting us here without the CO's permission. Let him figure things out." Major Asif continued to roar loudly and after a while, Suraj almost stopped responding. Suddenly gripped by fear, ignoring NSR's warnings, I pushed into the interrogation room. Suraj sat slumped on a small chair, while Major Asif paced around, face flushed. Surprised at the barging in, he immediately shifted his wrath towards me, "Who gave you the permission to come here? Can't you see we are in the middle of an interrogation?"

Moved by Suraj's pitiful condition, I sprung in his defence and shouted back equally hard, "Can't YOU see what your interrogation has done to him? Does he look like he is any condition to remember things? And why are you interrogating him as if he is a criminal? Is it a crime to lose a competition or to succumb to fatigue? Do you have any idea about how much effort he has put in the last month? Just because he couldn't get you some trophy, is THIS how you are going to treat him? Allow him some sleep and he will tell you about those darned rifles! Are they more precious than somebody's life? All that sham about unit being a family and Suraj being a brother officer! Is this how you would treat your brother? Tell me, Major Asif!" I thundered back, forgetting everything Suraj had ever told me about hierarchy.

Stunned, Major Asif stared at me in disbelief. Suraj had been sitting in that sagging position all this while, his head hanging in shame. Suddenly, his slouching shoulders began to shake. Gosh! He was crying, I'd never seen Suraj cry and I immediately rushed to his side. He was trembling and only when I bent down to see his face did I realize that he, in fact was laughing! I couldn't comprehend anything and looked at Major Asif who also had cracked up. I gawked at both of them, looking my dumbest best.

Just then, Major Rana, NSR, and Capt. Bagga came in laughing hysterically. NSR ran towards me and held me close. "Mohana...you Jhansi ki Rani. Even Shaheen couldn't have given Asif this tongue-lashing!" Then she asked Suraj, "Are you sure she is above 18? What a feisty kid!" Everyone was in splits while I stayed dazed.

Major Asif slapped Suraj's back and said, "*Moonh meetha karao,* ma'am, *apna hero pehla aaya hai.*" Dumb me, I still didn't get it. "Suraj won the Ghaatak, ma'am! Our team came first! They were outstanding in all departments."

Capt. Gulshan chimed in, "Sir, these guys sped through the night challenges as if they knew the placement of targets—superb planning and co-ordination!" He too thumped Suraj's back with pride and affection.

Amidst all this, stood my hero...smiling. Not wanting to add anything, not wanting to boast, not wanting to act special in his moment of glory.

I was delirious with joy and anger—Suraj had ganged up with these people to make an ass out of me. NSR sensed my displeasure and said in a soft voice, "Don't get mad at him, Mohana. It was Sam's idea...mean fellow. When you came to us in the morning, Sam knew that our team had won! But your anxiety triggered this devious plan. And of course this Gulshan had to join in—always ready for pranks." She slapped Capt. Bagga's arm fondly while he grinned, their camaraderie obvious.

"You guys should be in a drama company!" I said, trying to be a sport. More laughs.

"I know! Our officers can easily be in movies. They have good physiques, can act well and know real action. Sadly, I might be a bit late in switching careers," Major Rana sighed, rubbing the slight bulge of his belly. Capt. Bagga and Suraj showed sympathy with exaggerated tch tchs.

I let out a deep breath to relieve the knots in my system. Major Asif gave me a friendly smile, "*Kya karein,* ma'am? Life is so stressful for us *faujis*. We do these silly things to have fun and enjoy our time together. New ladies joining the unit are often soft targets for such pranks."

NSR added, "Mohana, you still got away with very little, because this was impromptu. I was not so fortunate...they ragged me for hours, you know. I was told that Sam had killed a civilian in some stray firing and had been beaten up by the locals. He was brought in black and blue, blood on his clothes!"

Wow! This place was incredible. And these people were so much fun. Major Rana winked, "Next time, we will include you also...if we have a role of an angry young woman."

All is well that ends well...my lonely days seemed to be over.

Well, at least for some time.

I was so proud of Suraj but a little drama was only fair. Soon after reaching our room, I opened fire, "I feel cheated, Suraj. After this, how will I ever trust you again?"

Suraj was taking off his shoes, "Come on, Mo! You make it sound as if instead of Ghaatak, I was busy elsewhere. Ok. Let me make it up to you. For the next two days, I am your slave. I am not going out anywhere." Whoa! How did this happen? "Happy with our performance, the CO has excused the team from all duties."

After landing in Namkum, we had not spent a single day together. I squealed with joy and gave him a tight hug.

He winced and told me that he had sprained his back last night. Since we didn't have any muscle relaxant, I thought of borrowing it from NSR. But Suraj stopped me, "Don't go anywhere. A hot shower should help. If it doesn't, maybe you could give me a nice, relaxing massage. Or perhaps an arousing one!"

I loved his suggestive smile. Hiding my excitement, I pushed him, "First get a shower, you stinking reptile!"

Yay! The goddamn Ghaatak competition was over and I had my husband back. While Suraj cleansed off the dirt and grime, I wondered how to make it special for him.

For starters, he was going to get a memorable massage... that too from the best masseuse in the world. So what if there was no oil? Talcum powder could always come handy. I spread a soft, white dupatta on *Laxman Jhula* to create the ambience. And I drew the curtains. And I lit a candle in a corner. And I wore my most seductive smile. And I waited.

Wrapped in a towel, the man arrived...freshly scrubbed... squeaky clean...smelling nice and looking irresistible in his damp, dishevelled hair. Was he always this handsome or did the glow of victory make him even more attractive? My plans of giving a massage almost dissolved at this appetizing sight. But with the elaborate arrangements in place, there was no turning back now.

Controlling desire, I invited him for a massage. "Are you also going to hum an instrumental track now...for a complete spa effect?" Suraj teased.

"Anything for you, my love," I said softly, making him lie on his stomach and splashing his body with talcum powder. The cool fragrance enhanced the relaxing feel of the room.

"Sir, would you like me to start with your back or legs?" asked the masseuse in a flirtatious tone.

"Shoulders," replied the client.

"Sure." Sprinkling some talc around the neck, the masseuse got into action.

"Ummm...this feels nice," said the happy guest. The masseuse continued to work in circular movements before getting tempted by the back muscles. Not sure if the massage had any impact on the muscles...but those taut muscles had certainly impacted the masseuse!

Just then, a strange noise jerked me out of the trance. Snoring! Sprawled on the bed, coated with talcum powder, Suraj was sending vibrations and sound waves into the pillow.

My poor husband! How tired he must be. Those shoulders must've carried so much weight...and those legs must have climbed hills and crossed jungles...all in one night! Let my hero enjoy a well-deserved rest....

Covering him with a bed-sheet, I went to the other room to calm down my hormones and pick up something to read.

11

THE PECKING ORDER

Namkum, 21st of June 1997

The Ghaatak victory was celebrated with a fantastic Mess party. NSR predicted that days of active socializing were round the corner. "Just you watch, the first invite would be from the CO and after that, invitations from others would start pouring in." Sure enough, Mrs. Pratap invited us for a lunch on the following Sunday.

This was going to be my first formal invite. Unsure of the etiquette for such occasions, I felt unsettled. Husband dear was relaxed, "Col. Pratap loves to enlighten lives, you will be taken care of," he winked through the mirror we were sharing.

Ignoring the newer options in my wardrobe, I chose a well-worn silk salwar kameez. It was a soft pink beauty with exquisite silver-white embroidery and a flattering fit. A little make-up worked wonders to accentuate the look. Now came the challenging part—hair! Wish it didn't have a mind of its own. My rebellious curls perfectly suited for a rock concert, were killing the demure persona I was trying to create. I finally secured them in a high pony and sealed the deal with some pearl jewellery. Phew! Suraj, on the other hand, had spent all of 30 seconds to slip into his favourite attire—white shirt and a pair of denims, and still looked as good, if not better!

Colonel Pratap's orderly welcomed us into a nice, classy room. As soon as Mrs. Pratap walked in, Suraj sprung up to wish her and so did I. She praised the Ghaatak team once again and told us that congratulatory calls were still pouring in.

No sooner had we descended on the plush sofa than the CO appeared. Once again, Suraj sprang up and so did I. Col Pratap, in his peculiar way, ignored Suraj and enquired with a straight face, "Why are you standing, ma'am?" I stammered at this unexpected question and thought it was best to let it pass, not knowing that such tactics didn't work with Col Pratap. He requested me to sit, before doing so himself and then asked the same question, "Why did you stand up?"

I was reminded of the serious faced, external examiners during viva-voce and practicals. And I tried to hide behind the same silly smile one wears, when one can't answer their tricky questions. "Umm…well, you are the CO of the unit. Everyone respects you. I've seen everyone get up to greet you…so…" I shared my analysis.

"Your facts are partly right. Yes, I am the CO and everyone respects me. But only the officers get up to greet me. Not the ladies. Ladies never get up for the officers; it's always the other way round."

My lame smile deepened. Colonel Pratap had this odd impact on me; he made me unsure. After a while, he started off again on why I had left my job without finding out anything about the army life. For Heaven's sake! Didn't he have anything else to talk about? Either he had forgotten that we had already discussed this or he was trying to find out something.

Thankfully, Mrs. Pratap invited us to the dining room. The South Indian cuisine was a welcome change from the Mess food and I happily dug into the steaming hot idlis and sambhar. Col. Pratap seemed to have an opinion on this too.

"Why are you dipping the idli in the sambhar so lightly?" I threw an exasperated glance and wondered if anything at all would meet his approval. "You're nibbling on dry idlis, ma'am, that's not the right way. If you really want to relish the taste, drown the idlis in the sambhar."

'This is how five-year-olds must feel on constantly being corrected by their parents,' Mika grumbled as Col. Pratap poured me sambhar in a separate bowl. "Come, put your idlis in this," he insisted and I obeyed. I ate my lunch under his hawkish watch and he was visibly happy when I asked for a few more helpings. "Great! I like people who enjoy good food. Welcome to the hearty eater's club!" he flashed a broad smile. I hadn't seen him smile before and it was amazing how it completely transformed his face. The twinkle in his eyes and the glowing red cheeks made him look like a toddler with a fat moustache. The amusing thought made me break into my first relaxed smile of the afternoon.

Back in the living room, Mrs. Pratap served her special fruit cream. I enjoyed two helpings while Col. Pratap sat back with a satisfied smile. He sure loved to feed his guests.

After dessert, Col. Pratap enquired if I liked paan and asked his helper to arrange some from the Namkum market. Sitting back, he started, "Ma'am, there is a reason why I've been asking about your move to Namkum. Ever since Suraj told us about your educational background and former job, I've been worried about how you will adjust in this place. And if you are not happy, Suraj won't be happy either. You see, I give enough grief to my officers. They should be happy at home at least." He said with a poker face but when I grinned at his joke, he also gave in, giving me another glimpse of the toddler.

So this is what had been bothering him. I didn't have the best response ready but I tried, "Thank you for being so concerned about us. I know it's not going to be easy to adjust to this new life, but trust me, sir, I'll do my best. Suraj is precious, which is why I am sitting here today. I'll try my best to stay happy and keep him happy."

He listened with a straight face and then said, "That was nice. By the way, you will not call me sir. Only my officers have that privilege."

"What about my privileges?" Mrs. Pratap protested. "You have not allowed me to have any conversation with Mohana at all!"

Col. Pratap rubbished her complaint, "Oh, you'll get enough opportunities to interact with her at AWWA meets."

"You're right," Mrs. Pratap nodded. Then turning towards me, she asked, "What are you doing tomorrow?"

An honest response would've been, 'Waiting for Suraj to return from work. That's all I do and I do it rather well.' Instead, I said, "Well, nothing much, Mrs. Pratap."

"Then come with me to Ranchi for an event at the Division Headquarters. You will get to meet ladies from the entire division. Make sure you wear a nice sari, it will be a formal event and a lot of senior officers and ladies will be present."

I returned with much more than I'd hoped for.

The next morning, our tiny abode crackled with excitement created by one woman, thrilled with the idea of going out. And going out where—New York, Paris or London? Come on, Ranchi is no less!

Preparation for the event started the previous night, with oiling my hair. Before going to bed, I also pondered over what to wear and selected a turquoise blue chiffon sari with a sleeveless blouse. Chika woke me up early so that I had sufficient time to get dressed. The army culture of being ready 'before time' had caught on with her as well!

Suraj had been sane enough to stay out of my way while I hummed and went about the delightful task of getting ready. I had practised sari draping for my job interviews and thankfully, the skill was not forgotten. The pretty sari wrapped perfectly around my frame, and I celebrated with a small jig. Then I shifted the focus to my face which was perfectly smooth for a change (normally, God ensures at least a scar if not acne to fend off *buri nazar*). I wore a peachy pink lipstick, a hint of kohl and finished with a brand-new neckpiece. "Alluring," I complimented myself with a smile. It was my day. Forget 'looking' pretty, I 'felt' pretty that morning!

I cleared my throat to grab Suraj's attention. He blew a whistle and I grinned. My pick-up arrived and with Suraj in tow, I walked towards it with child-like excitement, reminded myself mid way to move like a lady, climbed on demurely and waved at Suraj like a queen!

After reaching Col. Pratap's house, I was told that CO *memsahab* will travel in the Number 1 jonga. What in the world was that? Just then, a shiny vehicle, painted cream and green arrived and I climbed inside this new animal.

The interiors were significantly different. Instead of green rexine, the seats had plush cushions covered in red velvet and there was a mini carpet on the floor. White, sheer curtains lined with delicate lace gave it a stately feel. Just then the door opened and Mrs. Pratap was escorted in, looking like royalty in her peacock blue silk saree. "Nice! I like your sari. I was not sure you could drape it so well!"

I beamed and spoke my heart out, "Mrs. Pratap, this is so basic. Compared to your stunning look, I feel underdressed."

"You're such an open book, Mohana! Now let me take a good look at your lovely curls."

On our way, she enquired, "So what have you learnt about the army so far?" NSR's induction sessions had helped me build a good understanding of the unit life. Happy with my clarity, Mrs. Pratap started briefing me about the bigger ecosystem—how different units add up to form a brigade, brigades add up to form a division…so on and so forth. Soaking in the information, I didn't realize that we had reached Ranchi.

And a completely new universe!

The jonga entered the massive gates of a magnificent building, boasting of colonial architecture. As soon as we entered the breathtaking lobby, a young officer walked up to escort us to the auditorium. Early birds had taken the front rows, but there were plenty of good seats. We settled in and Mrs. Pratap started whispering, pointing out the who's who sitting in the front. She kept saying GOC but I had no clue what it meant. "GOC means General Officer Commanding—a Major General or a Lieutenant General, who is in charge of the Division. I hope you know about these ranks?" she raised an eyebrow. Thankfully, Suraj had drilled this in my civilian head and I knew that these ranks were stacked at the top of the pyramid. I started observing the GOC and his stylish wife with glazed eyes and wondered how many challenges and hardships they must have seen in their army tenure before reaching this place of prominence, travelling together and alone on so many paths. What a treasure trove of experiences their lives must be!

The chain of thought was broken by an announcement about the event—a presentation by a retired General on army's role in environment protection. The delivery was short and engaging and the event was wrapped up with a formal vote of thanks.

We were ushered to the beautiful lawns and that is when I felt the full force of the army's glamour. Sure, officers looked swashbuckling in their formal uniforms—medals and all, but it was the ladies who took the cake. In their best attire and finest jewellery, each was more charming than the other. Most wore sunglasses, as if to protect their eyes from the collective dazzle!

I wished I had a friend along to analyze the variety of make-up, hair, and attires. Alas! I had to tag along with Mrs. Pratap who was busy meeting friends from other units. She would introduce me to each of them but there were so many, that I didn't get a chance to go beyond a cursory hello. Also, they had so much to catch up on...about things and people alien to me, that I soon started feeling lost. Everyone wanted to talk to each other. Except me! Nobody was interested in me and all my effort around hair and sari was in absolute vain.

Never having experienced social awkwardness, I wasn't sure how to deal with it. Should I wear a mask of confidence, break away from Mrs. Pratap and just introduce myself to people? Paralyzed by the word 'protocol', I couldn't decide and simply followed Mary like a little lamb.

Thankfully, refreshments were announced and a wave of joy ran through my body! I had a friend after all—food! An inviting spread welcomed us. I quickly grabbed plates for both of us from a separate table and handed one to

Mrs. Pratap. She thanked me and stood in a queue and I waited right behind her. The long wait finally ended and after Mrs. Pratap was done filling her plate, it was my turn.

Just when my hand stretched out to pick a samosa, the server said, "This queue is for senior ladies." I wasn't sure if I heard him right or understood him. So I just gaped for a bit and then pointed at Mrs. Pratap to clarify that I hadn't gate crashed. Mrs. Pratap was merrily chatting with the woman ahead of her, oblivious to the confusion behind. The server helplessly peeked at the grey-haired woman behind me, who had been silently observing the situation. She pressed my shoulder and whispered in a gentle voice, "My dear, you are in the wrong queue. This table is for the senior ladies. You should go to the other table that side."

Choosing to be a sport, I thanked her with a broad smile, apologized to the server for my ignorance and walked towards the 'correct' table. It had a much longer queue, which I joined cheerfully, as if nothing had happened. Inside, I was crushed. Distracting myself with the task of examining the empty plate, I smiled at the small talk around. Unable to spot Mrs. Pratap, I just stood by myself and focused on the food which tasted like ash.

After what felt like eternity, it was time to leave. On our way back, Mrs. Pratap asked about my experience and I mostly spoke about what I liked in the presentation. She asked if I liked the snacks and I nodded my very heavy head.

Entering the Mess gates, I hoped Suraj was late because I didn't want him to know how deeply I was impacted. Thankfully, neither he nor NSR or the kids were around. By the time I pulled out the keys and opened the lock, moisture had started building in my eyes. Collapsing on the sofa, I finally set my tears free. Hot tears of humiliation and anger…the 'strong and silent' type, they operate without supporting actions like nostril flaring, shoulder shaking, or even erratic breathing. They just flow down the face noiselessly, draining your soul.

I was sitting in that tired state when Chika, the good natured, stupid soul sprung into action. Why the hell can't she let me be!

Chika: Come on now, Mohana! This is a bit of an overreaction. Why take things personally? Why take offence when none was intended?

Mika couldn't be held back and I braced for a face off.

Mika: What do you mean overreaction? In front of everyone, Mo was asked to go to another table. What for, a samosa?

Chika: It's not about the samosa. And it's not about Mo either. It's about rules.

Mika: Oh please, Miss Goody two shoes! I have nothing against rules which are logical. Not this—this is discrimination basis social status.

Chika: So what is wrong with that? Do you fight with airlines when they discriminate between business class and economy class passengers? Isn't that divide also based on social status?

Mika: There is a difference. When Mo buys an economy ticket, it's her decision to spend within her means, or maybe a business class ticket is out of her reach. Either way, she knows what she is entitled to.

Chika: So isn't it the same here? Aren't the senior ladies entitled to certain privileges?

Mika: Why?

Chika: Well, their husbands have served more and picked their ranks…not without the support of these ladies. These women have sacrificed a lot and seen way more hardships than young girls like Mo. So they deserve respect and these small privileges. Won't you agree?

Mika: If caste/colour/gender-based discrimination is wrong, then this cannot be right. Shooing her away like some untouchable—Shudras cannot draw water from this well, it is for the Brahmins!

Chika: I know...I know it feels bad.

Mika: In any case, why are they so stuck up around rules? If Mo landed there by mistake, why couldn't they just allow her to pick stuff?

Chika: Yeah, I understand. That would have saved her the embarrassment.

Mika: More like a public insult.

Chika: Hmm.

Mika: Mrs. Pratap also had her head in the clouds. Couldn't she have informed Mo in advance? In any case, everyone is teaching her something or the other...as if she is some uneducated, uncouth coming from the hinterlands!

Chika: Yeah, maybe Mrs. Pratap missed sensitizing Mo. But you'll agree, in this Soldierland, Mo *is* an ignorant outsider. She must loosen up, have a smaller ego.

Mika: Yeah sure, size of ego has to be commensurate with the husband's rank. So our dear Mo is eligible for an earthworm's ego!

Chika: Chill now. Aren't we hungry?

Both Chika and Mika made sense. Both cared for my well-being. Instead of feeling conflicted, I suddenly felt supported by their presence. There was no resolution, yet the heaviness slowly lifted....

12

Home Is Where the Heart Is

Namkum, 17th of July 1997

We had been cooped up in the guestroom for two months with no news on housing allotment. Captain rank accommodations were available aplenty, but piddly lieutenants were not eligible for them. Not just my boss, even the army seemed to disapprove of marrying early.

One evening, instead of the bike he had been using for some time, Suraj got back on a scooter with a profound presence—even a Greek God standing next to her would look pitiable! "This has been a loyal companion of all young officers of our unit," Suraj thumped the seat of the peeling white Vespa.

"Don't bang so hard. The poor thing will fall apart," I warned, earnestly.

"Don't go by the humble looks, she's solid as a rock! This is 'Dugdugi'...Major Asif's first love—been with him since he joined the unit. Still serving with pride."

I laughed at Suraj's admiration for Dugdugi not knowing that we would have to rely on the ancient relic for local travel. "We don't have a jonga at our disposal, Mo. Till the time we buy a bike, Dugdugi will ferry us around. In fact, she is waiting to take you somewhere special. Are you ready?" Suraj's eye had a glint. It had been raining on and off and dusk wasn't far. The idea of an adventure ride on Dugdugi didn't sound inviting. My lukewarm response prompted Suraj to hand out a piece of paper with a flourish.

It was a housing allotment letter from MES (Military Engineering Services). Finally! We would be able to move out of the Mess…and into our own house. I squealed with joy and asked him how soon we could go see the place. "Now! We can check it out right now. In fact, that's why I got her," Suraj patted Dugdugi.

Two things stood out about Dugdugi. One, she was extremely self aware. Knowing her age related challenges, she refused to move beyond a certain speed. Two, she was a big show off. She wanted the world to stop and admire her fitness in that ripe old age. This, she ensured by making big noise.

So that beautiful evening, on an absolutely empty road, we moved at a formidable pace of 20 km/hour creating sound waves like a helicopter. Going by the giggles and waves from the locals, it was obvious that we did provide some entertainment to their otherwise mundane existence!

It was beginning to get dark by the time we reached our destination—a neighbouring cantonment called Khojatoli, which NSR had refused to move into. Wide roads and freshly painted houses welcomed us. "As you can see, this little cantonment is still getting established. Incidentally, Mo, there is only one Lieutenant's accommodation in the entire brigade. Thank your stars that no other officer agreed for child marriage." Suraj was obviously teasing me for a reaction but my eyes were busy scanning the houses…trying to figure which one could be ours.

In the fast descending darkness, an isolated house at the far end of the lane caught my eye. It seemed like a square cardboard box, placed in the middle of nowhere. There was no sign of civilization beyond it…only vast, open space with wild grass. As we moved towards it, I started praying, "Please God, not that one!" Well, God was busy elsewhere: Dugdugi stopped right in front of the dreaded one!

"Gosh, Suraj! This is so remote! What if there are wild animals hiding in the tall grass all around?" I whispered.

"Just pigs, big ones."

"You mean wild boar?" I panicked.

"Come on, Mo, are these the Savannah Grasslands?" Suraj laughed aloud. He put his arm around me and guided my stiff body towards the house, "Just the usual swines, relax. I saw them this morning when I came to see the accommodation. Trust me, this place looks much better during the day. And once they put street lights in this corner, even the nights would be fine."

We had just reached the gate when all hell broke loose. A big pack of dogs resting in the garden got agitated when we approached their territory. Their barks made me want to get away on Dugdugi; running would stand a better chance though! Magically producing a torch, Suraj pointed the beam towards the dogs. A few of them backed off while a few stood firm, baring their teeth. "Are these wild dogs?" I was clutching his sleeve. Ignoring my question, Suraj threw stones at the remaining dogs and they disappeared behind the house. "Come, let's go inside. Your home is waiting for you, girl."

At that moment, I preferred to spend the rest of my life in the Mess instead!

I acted enthusiastic until we stepped inside. The house looked straight out of a horror movie with dust and cobwebs all around.

"The MES guys haven't started the electricity supply yet. The allotment happened just this morning." Suraj declared.

"Then what was the hurry to come here in this darkness?" I wondered aloud.

"The hurry was for you, Mo. Weren't you waiting eagerly for a house?"

Mika made a sudden appearance, 'Of course you were waiting for the house; but does that mean he'll bring you here in pitch dark, with spiders and mosquitoes ready to feast on you?' I shushed her, projecting more positivity than I felt. "I know, I know. Let's go around." So we went about the delightful task of checking out our very first home in the light of a small torch, wading through dust and cobwebs and enjoying the welcome music played by a band of mozzies.

Coming back to the Mess room never felt better!

The house had been built a few years ago but had never been occupied. We seemed to have created a history of sorts! Once the MES handed over the house, it was time to go. In the meantime, Major Rana had also managed to get an accommodation in Namkum and NSR was over the moon!

We both set out on different paths, happy about our time together.

Suraj was right. The place looked hugely different in daylight. The vast expanse of grasslands in shades of yellow and green was quite picturesque and the clear, azure sky completed the effect. One could see an outline of hills beyond the greens and Suraj told me that a highway ran between the grasslands and the hills. For a city girl who had never stayed so close to Mother Nature, it was exhilarating to take in the fresh air.

The sparkling clean house felt fresh and inviting! I took an instant liking especially because of the cross ventilation and bright light dancing through the day. For someone whose temperament heavily relied on the Sun, this was like a free supply of mood elevators. And if I needed more Sun, I could always walk around the garden.

Come dusk, this beautiful set up would transform. Without sufficient lighting on the streets, the house would go under a blanket of darkness and feel eerie. Mosquitoes would arrive, and so would the dogs—behaving like stubborn tenants refusing to vacate properties they inhabited for years. As soon as it got dark, they would assemble right under our bedroom window, and get busy fighting. Often, we would throw water at them to buy some peace.

These nocturnal challenges notwithstanding, Suraj and I were ecstatic in our cosy love nest...even though we didn't get enough time together. The whole routine of morning PT (Physical Training)...office...evening games, and late evening meetings would keep him away for long hours. But, compared to the Mess, I was able to deal with his absence much better since I loved the house and had a few responsibilities—kitchen garden being my latest fancy. Set up with the help of a gifted gardener, it soon started supplying a variety of vegetables. Another attraction was the huge swing in our backyard—propped against its comfortable cushions, I would read for hours on end.

I was amazed at the ease with which I had slipped into the role of a homemaker, even though I missed the excitement of a job and making my own money. When the void became bothersome, I would remind myself of the love and peace in my life and vow to enjoy while it lasted. After all, Suraj would go away to a field posting in a couple of years.

Come to think of it, the army does teach you to live in the moment!

Was I becoming wise? Or dull and boring? Chika and Mika could never agree.

13

Learning the Ropes

Khojatoli, 5th of August 1997

All the hype around Dugdugi's fitness was just that… HYPE!

She started giving trouble and after a few attempts at repair, Suraj handed her back to Maj. Asif. The office wasn't close by and I wondered how he would commute. "I'll cycle to office. It's no big deal. I might reach faster, you know!" With the two additional trips for PT and Games, his daily commute would add up to 30 kms. My concern got a matter of fact response, "No choice, *yaara*. We don't have ready cash to buy a motorbike. I have applied for withdrawal from my PF. Till then, cycle it is."

What a simple, uncomplicated approach to life! "How can you stay so relaxed and unruffled all the time?" I wondered aloud.

Suraj replied in a hushed tone "On the very first day of our military training, we're given a magic potion."

"Very funny," I rolled eyes.

This was becoming a pattern—whenever I got worked up about something, Suraj would deflect it with a silly response. Irritating at times, but always effective.

And so, Suraj started cycling to work. No cribbing, no complaints. On the third day, he returned with a smile, "You're not the only one unhappy about my cycling routine, even my Senior JCO is."

"What's that?"

"JCO stands for Junior Commissioned Officer. Troops have a separate hierarchy, just like the officers. JCOs are the most tenured among troops. Karnal Singh, the gentleman I'm talking about, must be in his late forties. He spoke to me today. Apparently, he and my troops do not like the fact that their officer ferries around on a cycle. These men care for us so deeply."

The meaning of 'caring so deeply' became clear in the evening, when the JCO paid us a surprise visit. Sitting awkwardly at the edge of the sofa, Karnal Singh pulled out a bundle of cloth and slowly untied it. We couldn't believe what we saw—stacks of cash, tied up together!

"Please use this to buy a bike of your choice, sir."

"Where did you get this money from?" Suraj was zapped.

"I had asked for three months' salary since I will be going on *chhutti* in some time. This money was just lying with me; better to put it to some use."

Suraj protested. "Nahi, *saab.* I can't take this from you. What if my PF money gets delayed?"

The JCO was equally adamant. *"Koi naa, saab, paisa kitthe jayega, aa hi jayega. Aur jo na aaya toh dekh laange...tab ki tab."*

What he was saying was—instead of worrying about the future, let's focus on solving the current problem. Despite the convincing, Suraj didn't budge. The JCO, in turn, refused to accept Suraj's refusal. Eventually, after a lot of push and pull, Suraj relented and Karnal Singh relaxed with a smile, most others would wear on recovering money!

I was touched. Never before had I seen such devotion, so much love for a superior. What must've prompted him to go out of his way to help Suraj...without even being asked! Where do these army guys get this camaraderie? How do they get over the barriers of caste, creed and religion to bond so deeply?

Our first big asset—a shiny, black Bullet arrived the very next day.

Now this is the curious thing about cultures—much like relationships, some things work for you, some don't. While Chika was mesmerized by the camaraderie and bonding, Mika felt suffocated by the stiff protocol. Caught in between, I was doing my best to adapt, without questioning things. So a sudden, rare invitation to voice my opinion stumped me.

Brigadier Kalra, our new brigade commander, had called a separate meeting with the ladies of our unit. He started, "Good afternoon. My name is Brigadier Swaraaj Kalra. I am not quite what my name suggests! My better half Kumud, has done a fabulous job of ensuring that I don't insist on having things my way. In our partnership, her role is at least 50 percent, if not more. And over these years, I have realized that it actually helps the family." We smiled at Mrs. Kumud Kalra, dressed in an off-white chiffon saree with a blazing pink sleeveless blouse. With hair tied up in a neat bun and her solitaires on clear display, she was all elegance and class. Brig. Kalra continued, "Why am I sharing this with you? Well, because I want each of you to play an active role in managing our brigade family."

Bowled over by the charming couple, I listened with interest. "Kumud and her team did some fantastic welfare work in our last posting. It's best she led this conversation here on." The mic went to Mrs. Kalra who said that she would be delighted to share her experiences. But first, she wanted to hear us. Mrs. Pratap spoke about different initiatives being carried out for the welfare of our troops and their families—focusing on hygiene, health, education and sports. NSR and a few others helpfully chipped in.

To my horror, Brigadier Kalra pointed towards me, "Why don't we hear from the young lady too?" Most ill prepared, I squirmed at the sight of the travelling mic.

"Mrs. Pratap has already shared details, I have nothing more to add," I spoke like a person in a witness box.

The gentleman smiled, "My question for you is different, young lady. I presume you got married recently?" I nodded. "And you come from a civilian background?" Another nod. Not wanting to make a mistake, I tried to get away with nods. Unfortunately, no further.

"What is your take on AWWA (Army Wives Welfare Association)?"

"Well, I have attended just a few AWWA meetings. So, it's too early for an opinion."

"Sure. But in those meetings, you must have noticed things, observed the families of our troops. Isn't it?" he persisted.

"Yes. But as I said, it is too early for an opinion." I refused to budge. Mrs. Kalra, who had been observing the conversation, took over at that point and encouraged me to share some of my observations. She said that a fresh perspective would perhaps help them improve things.

I shouldn't have dropped my guard. I shouldn't have!

But I fell prey to her earnestness, "Ma'am, I have been to three AWWA meetings and I somehow felt that the families were not really involved. Our agenda is their welfare, but their involvement in the process is quite minimal. Like last time, there was some activity on stitching and sewing. I thought they already knew a lot and were waiting for things to get over so they could have their chai-pakoda and go back home." I closed with a wide smile but sadly, I was the only one who found the joke funny.

Breaking the silence, Brig. Kalra asked, "So, what can we do to improve the situation?"

I thought hard, "Our intent is to help our troops lead a better life. Could we do something to understand their requirements better, so there is no gap between our offering and their need?"

Nobody attempted to answer my question. Brigadier Kalra was polite, "Thank you, Mrs. Shastri. That was an interesting take indeed."

The rest of the discussion was about what other brigades were doing and what else we could do. My point about finding out the real need of the 'target audience' didn't seem to have made a dent.

Never mind! I enjoyed my coffee and snacks and headed back home.

The next afternoon, when Suraj returned from work, he didn't look like himself. "What happened in yesterday's meeting with Brigadier Kalra?" he asked as soon as I opened the door. I started telling him about the interaction and how he and Mrs. Kalra were so friendly and approachable. "That's fine, Mohana. What did YOU say in the meeting?" he impatiently cut me off.

"Yeah, I was coming to that, Suraj. He asked my opinion about AWWA and I told him."

Cutting me off yet again, Suraj hissed, "What do you really know about AWWA to start criticizing?" Suraj was clearly upset and since he rarely got angry, I was taken aback.

"Did I say something wrong? Why are you angry at me?"

"Why am I angry? The 2IC (Second in command) summoned me for a proper dressing down! He spoke specifically of your behaviour…and since I was completely clueless about yesterday, I couldn't say a word."

"I was not hiding anything from you, Suraj! I didn't tell you about the meeting because I didn't think it was important… I didn't even know that things had gone wrong."

"Well, let me clarify—not just wrong, things have gone terribly wrong. Mrs. Pratap and your dear NSR did not like your comments. The advice they have sent for you is: You are new to the unit and know nothing about the workings here. KEEP YOUR TRAP SHUT."

Wasn't this exactly what I had told them? That I was new, that I had not seen enough, that it would not be right on my part to make any observations? Why then did they insist I speak up?

Ashamed to put Suraj through such embarrassment, Chika took me to task. 'Have you learnt nothing from your corporate experience? Don't you know that when people ask for fresh ideas, they are not really expecting any pearls of wisdom…certainly not from inexperienced idiots like you. They just want you to play along and talk about the exciting learning curve you are on. That's all.'

Mika was stumped. While she believed that I'd done no wrong, she was upset that Suraj got cornered.

"Ok. Let's eat first. I'm famished," he said, dryly. I got up and served lunch made using the first batch of tomatoes from our garden. The excitement was obviously lost now.

Neither of us spoke—Suraj, I guess needed time to cool off; I for sure needed time to recover from the blow!

Suraj rested for a while and then left for games without a word. His behaviour was bothering me more than the meeting fiasco. I had never seen him so mad. When he came back, I was not sure if I should continue with our tradition of evening tea on the *jhula*. To my surprise, he picked up the tray and walked to the garden, with a trace of a smile. That was enough to make me breathe and get back to my ways. "Looks like somebody has cooled off," I enquired with an impish smile.

Suraj grinned. "Now you know why I wear my hair so short! This fellow cools down faster," he tapped his head.

He wore a soft expression, "I'm sorry, *yaara*. I just blew off without hearing you. I was knocked out by the rebuke. Can you tell me what exactly happened?"

I took a deep breath, and narrated everything in minute detail. "I should have known better than to open my mouth, Suraj. I tried so hard to not get into trouble…and still here I am! And I'm sorry you were marched up to your seniors because of me," my voice was soaked in guilt.

"Listen, Mo, it's not like I had to march up in front of everyone. The 2IC shared displeasure at the way you had put across your opinions. He said these things need to be handled more tactfully, especially when we don't know anything about the new commander or his wife."

"The Kalras came across as super cool. Did they object to what I said?"

"The 2IC didn't mention it. Perhaps our own people got embarrassed in front of the guests."

Hmm. I thought about Mrs. Pratap. My two cents must've spoilt her effort to project her work.

Suraj continued, "Let's take this as a learning experience and move on. No fretting." I didn't respond. He gently touched my hand, "So, what are you thinking?"

My voice trembled with emotion, "You. I'm worried about you, Suraj. NSR once told me that an army officer's career depends a lot on how his wife contributes to the system. What if this episode damages your prospects?"

"Of course, it will. I might retire as a lieutenant!" Suraj dropped his shoulders in mock disappointment. "Come on, Mo, don't take away everything from us officers. Ladies sure play a role but I doubt they can make or break careers. Think of the decorated officers from our unit. Did they make it big because of their gallantry or because of the social skills of their wives?" I smiled at the example. "This is how I see it, *yaara.* If I am a bad officer, you can't do much to help me grow. Similarly, if I am an exceptional officer, I will shine, no matter what. Chill now."

"So how should I behave, Suraj? What do you want me to do in such situations?" Suraj thought for a bit before responding, "After yesterday's experience, you can be a little more careful; especially around seniors."

After a brief pause, he said exactly what I wanted him to…something that would make me love him even more, "Let's get one thing clear. I don't want you to suffocate yourself, just to fit in. I fell in love with you for who you are and I want to spend my life with the same person. A little tact is all I ask for."

This wasn't just music, but pure Sufi music to my ears. And I allowed it to relax me…

Army life is so much about being battle ready, that a good part of the peace tenure is spent in trainings, ranging from a few days to a few months. Suraj got assigned to a two-week training, but after the Satnam incident during Ghaatak, I was worried about injuries. That's when Suraj introduced me to an old army saying: *No news is good news*. "If you don't hear anything about me, it means I am fine. Till the day someone comes to you with some news, you should chill."

The first few days were a breeze. Chika was totally focused on staying busy and happy and did not allow me to miss him much. *Hurrah! I have a grip over myself...I have a grip on the role (of an army wife)...I have found an untapped source of strength within!* These fanciful thoughts helped me battle loneliness and boredom, and protect my new found poise.

On the fifth day, my Zen-like calmness suffered a huge setback when electricity disappeared around mid-morning. One hour became two...two became five...then seven...and it was evening. While I was busy praying for power to be restored, our *bhaiyya* showed some presence of mind. He got me a couple of candles from his room, knowing well that surviving with a small torch would be tough.

Soon it was pitch dark. Without Suraj and without electricity, the house began to scare me. I kept sitting on the bed, listening to the ever increasing noise of mosquitoes. As expected, the dogs assembled, but in a sombre mood. No fighting, no barking. Only howling—loud, prolonged, mournful cries. One followed the other and soon, the entire pack was wailing, joined by a few in the neighbourhood. As a kid, I had heard that dogs howl either when they see a ghost or when something ominous is about to happen. Their cries spooked me out but I was so numb with fear, that I couldn't bring myself to move to another room.

Sitting on the bed, I watched the last candle become smaller and smaller and when it eventually died out, I felt as if my life force was lost. I don't remember when and how I dozed off in that same position.

I woke up with heavy eyes and a stiff body. But guess what? The world was bright and beautiful with the Sun gliding up in the sky. On the long desolate lane, I spotted *bhaiyya* bringing milk and fresh veggies. Enjoying the morning breeze on the *jhula,* I sipped my tea and hoped that electricity would be restored soon.

Wishful thinking! Hours turned into days with no clarity on when the misery would end—some issue with the main supply line to Khojatoli, which people were trying to fix. After the AWWA episode, it was best to avoid NSR for some time. In any case, her advice was to be resilient and reach out only when things got out of hand. With Shaheen and Anu away, there was nobody I was comfortable reaching out to.

As days passed, I started drowning in despair! I could still manage the hot and sultry days, but come evening, my world would go under doom and gloom, as if I operated on solar energy. Once my own reflection in the mirror almost gave me a cardiac arrest. I looked nothing less than a witch—candle in hand, unruly coils around my head, deep pits under my eyes. Looking at the mirror closely, I felt pity for myself. Mika, who had been subdued for some time, was saddened by what I had done to myself.

She broke her silence with lava, 'Congratulations on going back to the Stone Age! You have an amazing life… just a few extra candles make you rich.'

It was four in the evening. The thought of dusk made me hollow and sad. Chika was drained from the daunting task of cheering me up. I had been living all alone and without power for nine days now... Just then, I saw the fan spinning. And this time, I was not imagining! Holy Christ! The power had indeed been restored!

I had survived the APOCALYPSE and how!

14

ON CLOUD NINE

Khojatoli, 10th of November 1997

Having survived those nine dreadful days, I had come a long way from the initial period in the Officers' Mess. Still, there was much to achieve. Just to bring clarity, I wrote down my goals:

1. Keep your esteem and confidence intact (despite the powerless position you are in).
2. Don't be so needy—constantly longing for Suraj's presence is a sign of weakness.
3. Learn from the unique cantonment life.

There was just one problem—I didn't know how to make these happen. Eventually, I decided to believe in the Bollywood dialogue: *Jab manzil ka pataa ho, raaste khud ba khud ban jaate hain.*

And hoped that the path to reaching my destination would present itself....

Perched on the *jhula,* Suraj and I were enjoying the evening tea and the shades of blue and orange in the sky. I imagined Suraj sporting longer hair. For someone who fancied men with long, dishevelled hair, it was tough to make do with a tennis ball! Why do army men wear their hair so short? Agreed, a messy, 'just out of bed' look wouldn't go with the uniform. But does it really need to be such a short crop, that styling is completely ruled out?

And in that blissful moment of frivolity, Suraj announced, "I need to pack for a week, *yaara*. Leaving day after tomorrow." Silence did the talking from my side. "Won't you ask me where I'll be going?"

"What's there to ask? You must be going for some training to some location nearby. But since the training will go into the night, you won't be able to return. I know the script."

"No, you don't," Suraj had mischief in his eyes. "I am going to Delhi…for an exercise organized by the Army Headquarters." After a pause, he added, "And you are coming with me." I saw his grinning face and jumped at him for a hug. "Please, please, Mrs. Shastri. We haven't reached Delhi yet. We are still in Khojatoli where people are taking evening walks. Please don't do anything that will result in another march up to the 2IC." I took my hands off him as though he were someone else's husband!

"That was below the belt." I was still raw from the faux pas with Brigadier Kalra.

"I actually love below the belt…just not on this *jhula*." Suraj clearly had plans for the evening.

But I had other concerns, "Loving below the belt and actually getting below the belt are two different things. I wonder how Col. Pratap gets a whiff of our plans and packs off his runner for timely interruption."

Suraj quickly piled the empty cups on the tray, "Come, this time, we have to beat that runner."

I moved in right behind him. The Delhi trip had to be celebrated after all!

As our train chugged into the Delhi station, my heart started beating faster. Stepping out of the bogie, I walked straight into a glitzy new world. Compared to the planet I was coming from, this place was buzzing with people, noise, commotion, and energy. Bright lights created a festive feel and I realized how much I had missed the city life.

The excitement lasted till we reached the Delhi Cantt where officers from across the country had come for the exercise. Thanks to some miscommunication about the accommodation, 5–6 officer families landed at the same guest house. After the initial confusion and disappointment, one of the senior officers in the group took charge. He instructed the staff to arrange milk for the younger kids and dinner for the rest of us. Then he started an impromptu address, "Good evening, ladies. As you can see, we are in a bit of a situation here—six families and a two-bedroom accommodation! It's almost 9 pm, any alternate arrangements would be possible only tomorrow. It's just a matter of a few hours and we will manage with what we have."

Sensing our discomfort, he continued, "Let's freshen up, get to know each other and have a good meal together! Then the ladies and kids can use the beds and those two sofas in that corner."

"And what about you...and other officers?" someone enquired.

"Oh, don't worry about us. We are trained to sleep on rocks."

And just like that, the problem was solved. I had almost started believing Suraj's story about the magic potion—what else can explain that not one, not two...all these officers stay so steady and chilled out!

As planned, we had a dinner of daal tadka, aloo gobhi, and roti (staple at every Mess, I was beginning to figure) and then everyone found a nook to rest. Six families had become one—people offering a towel or a bed sheet or some leftover fruit to the others; a group of strangers bound together by the Olive Green thread!

The next morning, the officers left early for the event. So my day was spent in the company of women and kids, perfectly at ease with each other. Kids laughed and played while the women chatted up about their lives, the postings they had seen, plans for educating their kids etc. Not one of them complained about the condition of the accommodation or about being holed up with rank strangers! I had read about *joie de vivre*...was beginning to understand it now. Just take each day as it comes, make the most of what you have and stay happy because you and your dear ones are alive!

I truly wanted to embrace this spirit as a way of life.

By evening, we were allotted a different accommodation—a plush apartment, with Col. Pratap as our neighbour. He had flown in that morning and on hearing about the issue with our accommodation, he immediately used his contacts to bail us out. "Really nice of Col. Pratap, this place is so comfortable." I lay on the bed, enjoying the coolness of the AC and feeling genuine gratitude towards Col. Pratap. Suraj wasn't so amused.

"He's right next door, Mo. That doesn't augur well," he said suppressing a yawn.

"What does that mean?" I was perplexed.

"You will know in some time. Hope I am wrong."

A knock at 7 am started clarifying things, when Col. Pratap called for Suraj. Throwing a 'Do you get it now?' look, Suraj left. Still foggy, I went back to sleep. The husband returned, finished his morning chores, got dressed, had breakfast and was gone for the day, leaving me to fend for myself in this unknown place.

A helper got my breakfast and informed that our meals will be served in the room itself. I seemed to have gone back to the Mess room at Namkum—stay indoors, read books and wait for the husband. One big improvement was a livelier room and a bed five generations younger than *Laxman Jhula*.

I was beginning to see the positives, thank God!

Around 5:30 pm, Suraj appeared. "No questions. Just get ready. We need to leave in 10 minutes." Out in a jiffy, Suraj began to grin as we walked into the next lane. "This was to dodge the CO. Had we stayed on, he would have called me for a discussion and then the evening would be spent in his lovely company." We laughed at ourselves—school kids trying to evade the principal. The evening was going to be fun!

Inspecting the expanse of the huge trees, I asked, "Is this the biggest cantonment in India?"

"I think Kanpur is the biggest, though the Delhi Cantt is big enough to have a separate railway station."

"Interesting! How many cantonments have you seen so far, Suraj?"

"Not many, perhaps five or six. But such exercises help us travel and see what a glorious and huge organization the Army is."

I could sense the pride in his voice. I added with a nod, "Even I would love to travel with you and see new places."

There was a certain sense of freedom being away from the unit. Protocol and the rules of the game were the same, still, just being part of a bigger universe created a sense of liberation.

If the railway station had given me a festive feel, Gopinath Bazaar had the combined effect of Diwali, Christmas, and New Year! For others, it might be any other day in any other market; but for me, it was a celebration of life. We roamed around the market, enjoyed some spicy, hot corn on the cob with Thums Up, bought a few knick knacks and walked back to the apartment...deliriously happy and content with life.

No sooner had we reached the apartment than the door got knocked. "Why am I not surprised? Now he's going to get even with me for dodging him in the evening. This might take long, Mo. You eat."

Suraj returned quite late. "Do you now understand why I was not happy staying right next to the CO? Expect this routine every evening."

"But why? What did he want to discuss?"

"Strategy. We are here for a simulation exercise on war strategies. Every day we'll be given different situations. Col. Pratap wanted to discuss today's performance and plan for tomorrow. You can't fault him, it's a competitive exercise, and he wants us to put our best foot forward."

So over the next week, a walk to Gopinath Bazaar became the most exciting part of my day.

A lot of my friends from business school were working in Delhi. After marriage, I had lost all contact with them and didn't know how to reach out. Hand on heart, I didn't even want to meet them. What if it disturbed my peace of mind? Stories about their jobs, their achievements were likely to unleash Mika!

Also, I didn't want them to see me in my current situation. I had quit my professional life so early and was happily settled in matrimony. They had known me as a go getter...someone who wanted to make it big. Now to see me as 'Mrs. Suraj Shastri—specialized at waiting for the husband' would be such an anti climax.

I was not ashamed of the decision to quit my job, but I lacked the conviction to defend it to others.

In an effort to keep myself occupied, I tried my hands at sketching…even painting! Quite a frustrating experience because I had neither talent nor any real interest. Just a desperate attempt to pass time.

I was getting sick of this routine. Wait…wait…and… wait for Suraj! Was this the sole purpose of my existence? Wherever we went, was this all I was going to do? Why wasn't there anything to engage me completely?

Enough was enough. I had to take charge and do something worthwhile. I decided to share my plight with Suraj, who knew nothing about the restlessness building up in me.

On the train journey back home, I took Suraj through a few secret lanes in my head, which had been painstakingly hidden from him. I spoke of boredom and a desire to do something exciting. On purpose, I stayed away from the darkest by-lanes occupied by more serious issues like lack of self worth.

Suraj didn't say much, but he was in deep thought.

Interesting how this business of sharing works…you feel lighter and the burden sort of shifts to the other person.

15

A Dog with Two Tails!

Khojatoli, 2nd of December 1997

To get me busy, Suraj explored teaching opportunities at the Army School in Namkum. Lady luck was smiling, because the school was hiring and selection interviews were lined up in the coming week. I was told that seven ladies from different units had applied for two positions. Some of them had prior teaching experience which obviously made their candidature much stronger. But I was determined to give my best shot, and since I couldn't have arranged for a BEd or teaching experience in a week, I decided to focus on the looks department instead! It was time to practise what I had learnt in the course on Impression Management during MBA.

D-day dawned, from the available options, an elegant Calcutta handloom saree made the best sartorial choice. It had a soothing mango yellow body with tiny white maple leaves woven all over. I paired it with a well-tailored sleeveless blouse which would show off my firm shoulders, ready for the responsibility of shaping young lives. Never mind the nip in the air! Taking inspiration from Mrs. Kalra, I tied my hair in a high bun, just like her. Quite satisfied with the reflection in the mirror, I observed, "If this look cannot make up for your lack of credentials Mohana Shastri, nothing can. Go for it now!"

Suraj was busy and I was thankfully spared the bike ride which would have ruined my copycat hairdo. Soon after reaching the destination, my heart started playing the drums. All the elegance that I thought I radiated seemed to melt away. What do I know about teaching to walk in for an interview all dressed up?

I was guided to a serene room full of books, which helped me recover from the sudden panic attack. After a while, someone escorted me to another room, where I was welcomed by two officers—Col. Sahoo and Col. Shalivaan. "Please be comfortable, ma'am. We will start shortly," said Col. Sahoo, politely. Both the officers were immaculate in their OGs and I was glad that I had taken the effort to come formally dressed.

The room had a sophisticated feel, thanks to a plush carpet and gleaming woodwork. I took in the decor, replete with awards and trophies, signifying a culture of achievement. Just then, a side door opened and in walked Mrs. Kumud Kalra. The original and the first copy were startled to see each other; Mrs. Kalra, in her original bun recovered first. If the two colonels in the room were amused to see identical makes of the same prototype, they didn't show it. "Ah! Mohana Shastri! I am so delighted to meet you again," chirped Mrs. Kalra.

"Same here. Mrs. Kalra, it's a pleasure."

She looked at both the officers and said, "Would you like a quick stretch break before we start with Mohana? She is a fascinating person and I'm sure we're going to love this interaction."

"I didn't know you would be here, ma'am, else I would not have copied your style," I admitted.

She smiled generously, "Come on now, I haven't patented it. You've never tried this before?"

"No, ma'am, I really liked your signature style, so tried it out for the first time today."

"You've done a great job for a first timer. Just relax and focus on the interview." I could sense the knots in my shoulders melt away, as the Colonels walked back in.

As expected, the questions were mostly about why I had applied for this job when I had a completely different professional background. I had thought this through and had decided to keep it simple and straightforward. In all my earnestness, I spoke about my love for children and how I had been engaged in home tuitions since I was in class XI. I loved teaching and from what I had gathered, even the kids enjoyed learning with me. Col. Sahoo asked me to name one thing that I'd do differently compared to my own school teachers. "I would be less prescriptive and encourage the kids to participate more."

Another interesting question was about the role of a pre-primary teacher. "A pre-primary teacher introduces kids to learning, competition, and performance. It's her responsibility to make the experience fun and enjoyable, so kids feel drawn to the school," I spoke with passion. The response triggered some smiles and I wasn't sure if I had struck the right note.

Before closing, I also highlighted the fact that I was increasingly restless without a professional life. So this job was in no way just a means to pass time. I admitted that due to lack of relevant experience, I might make mistakes but also assured them of being a quick learner. Such was my excitement for the job, that when asked how soon I could join, I said with surety, "Tomorrow? The school must have closed by now, else I could have joined right away."

Just when we were winding up, came the question that knocked the daylights out of me. "Why don't you apply for BEd?" As far as I was concerned, whatever education had to be had, had been had. I had a Masters in Business

Administration which had landed me one of the best jobs on campus. Compared to friends and peers from other career streams, I had done reasonably well. All that pride and sense of accomplishment went poof, like a balloon burst with a needle.

Mrs. Kalra elaborated, "See, now that you are married to an infantry officer, you'll typically get posted to remote locations with limited employment opportunities. Since you are so keen on a professional life, isn't it best to opt for BEd? You can make a steady career in army schools."

I knew better than to give her a glimpse of the turmoil in my head! I promised to think about her suggestion, and left after thanking the panel for the opportunity to interact with them. Once inside the jonga, dropping all pretence, I held my head. Dear God, by marrying Suraj, hadn't I completely ruined my career? I would need to start over again. And BEd! Why? Yes, I liked kids, but no—teaching in a school was not my dream. Doing it for the rest of my life, that too for lack of choice, felt suffocating.

Mika wanted me to share everything with Suraj. But what was the point in sending him on a guilt trip? So I kept things to myself. Chika had to do a lot of talking to calm me down. 'One step at a time—let's see what happens about this job. We will figure out the rest later. After this posting, you can take up a job in Mumbai. Why worry about it now?'

What would I do without Chika!

'Set yourself free,' laughed the savage Mika.

One afternoon, I saw a folded paper stuck on the fridge and asked Suraj what it was. "No idea. Must be the Mess bill," he said laying lunch.

"But who put it here?" I unfolded the paper, expecting a small bill tucked inside. Instead, I saw an appointment letter from the school, signed by Col. Sahoo. The joining date was three days later. God knows when Suraj had put it on the fridge! He was perhaps expecting me to do a triple sault or something because he was visibly disappointed at my lukewarm reaction.

"What happened? Not happy?" He walked towards me with a big smile and held me in a bear hug.

"I'm very happy, Suraj. Just a bit surprised, didn't really expect it."

Continuing to hold me close, Suraj said, "Neither did I. Obviously, we both underestimated you. The 2IC handed me this letter today, saying Mrs. Kalra was really impressed with your confidence. I am told you spoke very well in the interview. So so proud of you, girl."

As I stood clinging to him, I still felt unsettled about the BEd thing which I hadn't shared with Suraj. Chika feared that if I started talking, I would bare it all—how badly I missed my job, my exciting life at the office, how I felt inadequate enough to not call my friends, how my confidence was crushed in this land of protocol and hierarchy. And how unhappy this was making me!

How long would I be able to deny this scary truth?

The Shaktiman aka 3 ton was my transport to the school. This was going to be my first day as a professional after a break of eight months, first day as a school teacher ... and my first trip in a truck! The kids greeted me with wide smiles, some with missing teeth. Moving some school bags, I managed to find a place on the wooden plank. The mighty truck—meant to transport weapons, equipment, and soldiers—modified into a makeshift school bus, kept stopping every few minutes for kids to get in. Children of officers as well as ORs (other ranks) studied and travelled together, making enough noise to wake up the dead. They would scream 'yahoo' at unsuspecting passersby and dissolve into peals of laughter at their startled expressions! Amazed at their ability to talk and laugh nonstop, I had obviously forgotten my own childhood, which I was about to relive with these little devils.

After reaching the school, everyone jumped out and ran towards the school building. Except me, the lone adult—the last one to get down, much like senior citizens, who deplane only after everyone gets off in a blistering hurry.

Col. Sahoo informed that Mrs. Kalra, the acting principal, would be coming in shortly and introduced me to the other teachers. He then gave me a tour of the tiny set-up, housing classes from pre-primary to Class V.

Just then, a shiny, black flag car came in and Col. Sahoo announced, "There she is." In contrast to my simple orange salwar kameez, Mrs. Kalra looked stunning in a deep maroon silk saree with a black patola border. "I have to go to Ranchi for an event. I squeezed out a little time just for you, my dear," she smiled. "Of course Col. Sahoo could have managed this as well, but I thought it was important to welcome you."

"That's really nice of you, Mrs. Kalra" I said, genuinely touched.

"Come, let's have coffee in the office. Do join us, Col. Sahoo."

"Mohana, you will be interacting with Col. Sahoo for day-to-day administrative matters. He was the one to back you despite you lacking both qualification and experience. He liked your confidence and felt that you will be able to inspire this quality in our kids. For me, it was something totally different. I must tell you that when we first met, I found your remarks a bit brash, but I was also struck by your honesty. You were ready to question the system because you felt strongly about the welfare of our people. This resonates with me, Mohana, even I genuinely want to help our troops. And one way to do this is by shaping up their kids, which I believe you can do well."

I nodded, assuring her that I won't let her down. "The kids of ORs (Other Ranks) should be treated the same as the officer kids. No discrimination in our classes." I was immediately reminded of the samosa denied to me and wanted to ask—what about discrimination among the ladies?

Luckily, life experiences had wisened me enough to avoid such a blasphemy.

Mrs. Kalra took me to the pre-primary section, which was overflowing with kids. "Poor Somya has been having a harrowing time managing these troublemakers. She is overjoyed to see you, I'm sure," Mrs. Kalra put an arm around the class teacher. Her next statement amazed me, "Pick out 20 kids for your class, Mohana."

"How do I select kids? On what basis?" I frowned.

"Just take a pick. This is your first stint as a teacher, we want to extend special favours to you."

I looked at the kids who stared back at me with mixed expressions of awe, anxiety, and excitement. When it comes to selection, you need to be crystal clear about what you are looking for. In case of children, 'cuddlability' is a key factor...well, at least in my limited, subjective opinion. One by one, I started picking students while the two women looked on with amusement.

Just then my eyes fell on a boy who I thought, was too big to be in pre-primary, but his mannerisms rendered him too small for a higher grade. He sat with a wide smile and looked at me awestruck. Then he lifted both his eyebrows as if to ask 'What do you think?' Goodness gracious! Was he a giant kid or an undersized grown up? Freaked out, I moved on to the next child when this fellow announced, "*Hum bhi jaaoonga. Hum nayi teacher ke saath jaaoonga*!" I looked at Mrs. Kalra for help but she just shrugged her shoulders and said, "He likes you, let him come." As Tiny Giant got up, almost roaring with laughter, I felt unsure about this whole idea of teaching. As I picked a few others, Somya protested, "She's taking away all the chubby ones!"

Mrs. Kalra gave out a hearty laugh. "Yes, I agree. Just look at the group she has picked out for herself." Honestly, even Tiny Giant was quite cute, but I somehow had an eerie feeling about him. "You've picked six students of your choice, Mohana. Take them to the adjoining class. I'll send the rest after consulting Somya."

And so I led my gang to the new class followed by Mrs. Kalra, who asked me to step out for a chat. "That was just for fun, Mohana. As you know, we primarily have children from two regiments—Bihar and Sikh. I just wanted to have an even distribution, so kids learn to interact with each other in Hindi. Otherwise, they stick to their native language. Somya will take you through our goals for pre-primary, mostly fun-based learning. I'll be excited to see you bring in your own flavour. Good luck, my dear!"

Getting back to the class, I realized that 'Tiny Giant' or TG, the self-appointed class monitor, had decided to have a drawing period. For lack of a better idea, I played along and as soon as I said yes, everyone took out their slates and small boxes with pieces of chalk. "Teacher *ji, aap kuchh banaiye na,*" TG slipped in a request.

The more I was trying to avoid him, the more he was getting in my way. Holding my nerve, I went to the board, *"Kya banaaun? Phool ya pahaad?"*

Before anyone could respond, came TG's demand, *"Sher!* Teacher *ji, humein sher bahut pasand hai. Aap badaa sa sher banaaiye na."*

Damn! How the hell does one draw a tiger? The only part I could draw was the tail! *"Banaiye na,* teacher *ji"* TG prodded. Was he ragging me? Was this a setup of some kind—a bigger kid planted just for some laughs at my expense? Were the folks from our unit playing another prank? I froze, though in my heart I knew TG was just a kid and there was no reason to be afraid of him.

Other kids had started making noise and I had to take charge of the situation. So I forced myself to turn around and ask them, *"Kitne bachhon ko sher banana aata hai?"* Only TG raised his hand. "Very good. *Aapka naam kya hai, beta?"* I asked with a thumping heart.

"Himansu. *Humre papa 16 Bihar mein driver hain."*

"Oh. Very nice, Himanshu! *Aap yahaan aake board pe sher banaa sakte ho?"*

"Kaahe, teacher ji? Aap nahi na bana sakti hain?"

Rascal! I had little choice but to concede defeat, *"Haan, Himanshu. Aap hi sikha do."* So he went up to the board and started drawing while I asked the others to draw something of their choice. Some got busy with their slates while others chose to ignore me and stare into nothingness. By snack break, Himanshu had indeed created a tiger like creature on the board.

I hurried out to the staffroom for some tea and hoped to get some tips from Somya on handling Himanshu. She burst out laughing, "I knew this was coming, Mohana. You should have seen your face when Himanshu volunteered to be in your class." Sipping some tea, she added, "He's the sweetest soul you can hope to meet. He's just five, but because of some medical condition, he is so huge and obese. He is an inquisitive child, Mohana, you'll get around understanding him and his Bihari." This, plus some tea and biscuits worked wonders and I went back to my class ready to take on Himanshu and whatever challenges he planned to throw at me.

The rest of the day was spent making each child speak three sentences about their drawing. This exercise revealed the steep road ahead—I could not understand 70 percent of what the kids spoke. Both Punjabi and Bihari, heavily laced with a rural accent, were not what one hears in Hindi movies. Out of twenty students, just four could speak Hindi and only one little girl called Cherry could speak English. She was the only child from an officer's family and I was amazed at how humble and grounded she was.

The collective power of their vocal cords was felt when the bell rang. Celebrating freedom, they ran out of the class without even throwing me a glance! I walked back to the Shaktiman, thinking about my first day at work which was a cauldron of flavours—fun, excitement, challenge, friendship, love. . .and yes, a bit of anxiety as well. I looked at Himanshu who was walking proudly next to me, his trademark smile in place and I laughed at the way I got bullied by him.

The bus took its own sweet time dropping kids off and by the time I reached home, all I could think of was food. Alas! I had not cooked anything in the morning and there was nothing in the fridge either. Damn! No leftovers, thanks to my meticulous food management. No restaurant, small eatery or even a grocer within a radius of 7 km!

When I was scavenging the fridge, I heard Suraj's bike ride into our compound. I just hoped he wouldn't be in a mood to tease or irritate me because the hungry tigress...err lioness (enough tigers for the day) would bite his head off.

"Hello, Prof! How was your first day at the university?" The man had started on a wrong foot, God help him now. Muttering under my breath, I kept opening jars with begging eyes. "What are you doing there, Mo, when the food is waiting for you here?" Did he just say FOOD? I ran towards the dining table where my knight was laying out fresh food. "I got this packed from the Mess on my way back," Suraj said nonchalantly, oblivious to my delirium.

"I am so hungry, I could eat saw dust," I said, opening the roti packet as quickly as I could.

"You never know, this might be just that. They made it in less than 15 minutes."

The food was divine. Enjoying every bite, we had a quiet meal and then hit the bed for some relaxation. It felt so good to lie down...as though I had earned the privilege! I closed my eyes and relished the beauty of the moment.

"Tell me, *yaara,* how was it?" Suraj asked.

"Can you draw a tiger?" I countered. And thus began my narration, getting both of us rolling on the bed with laughter.

I settled into my job rather quickly and with each passing day, began enjoying the experience even more. Thanks to the orange attire I had worn on the first day, I now had a new identity—'orange teacher'. By the second week, my students started waiting for me in the playground. Soon after reaching, the bunch of kids from the bus would run towards the school and another bunch...my kids would run towards the gate to receive me. All my fingers would get grabbed by little hands and the rest would cling to my clothes...sometimes almost toppling me over. And still, the ones who wouldn't get a claim over me, would walk along, pouting. During such moments, I wished I had a long tail for these little monkeys to hold on to, so our noisy procession could walk straight.

Over time, I figured out a way to deal with Himanshu and the rest of the kids—just involve them more and more. Quiz them, give tasks, get them to speak in front of the class and when it came to drawing, just hand over the board to one of them! The weather was nice and we spent a considerable time outdoors. Since nobody questioned me, I assumed that Mrs. Kalra was fine with my approach.

My first pay cheque did pinch a bit because it was a pittance compared to what I used to make in my previous job. But what the heck! Who ever got paid purely for having fun? In fact, instead of paying me, if they charged me for the exciting time I had at the school, that would be totally justified.

Teaching was turning out to be way better than I had imagined. Our life had got into a rhythm—prepare breakfast and lunch while Suraj went for morning PT. Leave together, come back for lunch, rest a bit. Then Suraj would leave for games and I for my walk, followed by tea on the *jhula,* some reading/writing/cooking before an early dinner and day over! I loved the routine.

Professional life was very peaceful, unlike the corporate politics that I had witnessed in my very first job. Mrs. Kalra was usually busy and we had the freedom to do things our way. We were a small group of nine teachers who bonded really well. I was the youngest in age and experience, but we were treated equal. They often quizzed me on how I could create such a strong bond with my kids so soon. And this was true...my kids doted on me like they had known me all their lives. And I loved them back just the same.

Suraj knew the names of my kids...especially my favourite ones—Sonali, Himanshu, and Ramandeep. Each of them was special but Sonali was particularly dear to me. She was a tribal kid from rural Bihar, getting schooled for the first time. Naturally, she was way behind others when it came to identifying colours, writing alphabets etc. But she had a sharp brain and her tiny frame was a powerhouse of confidence. Once, we were planning for a cultural event and Sonali was the first one to raise her hand when I asked for volunteers to play *Bharat Maata*. I explained the importance of the role and told her that she will need a special costume. As a habit, she said yes to everything. So I started teasing her...

"Sonali, Bharat Maata banegi?"

"Ji, teacher ji."

"Make-up laga ke aayegi?"

"Ji, teacher ji."

"Baal bhi khol ke aayegi?"

"Ji, teacher ji."

"Aur kapda kya pehnegi?"

"Humka papa ka lungi."

I burst into a fit of laughter, joined by her. Such was the innocence of these kids that I stopped missing my corporate job in no time!

16

Sunshine and Roses

Khojatoli, 25th of Jan 1998

Life had transformed in many ways. One, the school had taken away the emptiness and given a sense of purpose to my life. Two, Suraj had been around for the most part. No special duties, no trainings, no travel, and no inspection. So life was quite monotonous and routine, thank God!

Ever since Col. Pratap made it to the Brigadier rank, he was a changed man. His pet peeves like stretched work hours, long meetings in the evenings, brainstorming sessions on Sunday mornings etc. became a thing of the past. Everyone prayed for a delay in his posting so we could enjoy this bliss for some time.

To add to the sunshine, Shaheen was back! "The break was nice with Ammi's pampering, but home is home. So, how have you been, Mo? Asif tells me that these days, you either speak of the vegetables in your garden or the kids in your class!" she pulled my leg. "No worries, both are my favourite topics so I won't get bored."

"School is a party. I can speak some Punjabi and Bihari now, not sure what I've been able to teach!" We laughed and chatted up, savouring some homemade mathris with tea. "So, how's the social scene? Have you visited all the officers of the unit?" I nodded. "And have you invited everyone back?" I gave her a blank look. "You haven't? Goodness,

Mo, how come your favourite Mrs. Rana hasn't educated you about this?"

"First of all, she is not my favourite. You are! And second, what 'education' am I missing here?"

"Well, you need to invite everyone home."

"You mean everyone together?" I got nervous.

"Silly, may be 2–3 families at a time. After visiting them, shouldn't you reciprocate?"

"I never thought of this, I should have," I confessed.

"Never mind, you can start now."

"Great! So why don't you and Maj. Asif join us for dinner tomorrow?"

"No, my dear, first invite the CO and other senior officers of the unit."

And so started my journey of throwing formal dinners....

The first batch of invitees consisted of the families of the CO and the 2IC. Menu was everything I was good at, which incidentally wasn't much: tomato soup, stuffed bhindi, pomegranate raita, corn chaat, jeera rice, and dal. Kheer for dessert. This was the best I could do. Our guests were perhaps expecting more; they kept appreciating the simple '*ghar ka khana*' and after a point, I wasn't sure if it was a compliment or a complaint!

After dinner, when the CO asked for fresh-mint, Suraj and I exchanged a baffled look. We had forgotten about it completely! I ran inside to get the face saver—some Poppins, which I usually stocked up on. All the guests examined the last course with raised eyebrows and out of politeness, picked up a candy each and popped it in their mouths, just like the name suggests. There was a hearty laugh with words like 'after a long time, had forgotten this taste' etc. which was nothing to worry about.

The next day was Sunday and being part of the Sikh regiment, everyone visited the Gurudwara Sahab in the morning. It was customary for the officer families to later spend some time together, often making impromptu plans for the day. While some such plan was being worked out, Anu nudged me with a wink, "Heard you made the CO pop." How the hell does news travel so fast!

"There was nothing, *yaar*. He asked for some fresh mint and I couldn't come up with anything else," I offered earnestly.

"Shhh! You don't need to explain anything to me. Am just wondering how you will silence your dear Mrs. Rana." It's then that I realized that NSR had been acting a bit stiff since the morning.

Aaah! I had shamed her yet again!

Next Saturday, the second batch of guests arrived, including the Ranas. Menu remained the same since that was all I felt confident about. One improvement—after-mint was served with pride this time.

The next morning, I was uptight at the Gurudwara Sahab but thankfully, no feedback. The impromptu plan led some of us to Ranchi for lunch. While we were deciding on the order, NSR said in jest, "Order anything but tomato soup and stuffed bhindi. Mohana makes it the best and you will get to taste it soon." Everyone burst out laughing. She patted my arm affectionately, "Relax, kiddo, just some leg pulling."

Later, when we got some exclusive time, she said, "Don't worry, your cooking was fantastic. Just that we all are hard core non-vegetarians. So apart from bhindi and arhar daal, some chicken on the menu would have been nice." Noticing my confusion, she added, "See, nobody talks about these things. But since you and I share a special equation, I believe we can be more open."

Chika immediately donned the protégé hat and looked at her with puppy eyes. "We have discussed this—food plays a huge role in binding us...which is why people spend a lot of time and effort in serving the best food to guests. At least, this is what I have seen and learnt in the army. So use your cooking talent well. Learn new dishes, different cuisines... non-vegetarian delicacies."

"But I have never cooked non-veg."

She gave me an understanding nod and then added softly, "I'll leave that to you. I have seen strict vegetarians serve meat and have also seen teetotallers refusing alcohol in their homes. To each his own."

That was (non-vegetarian) food for thought!

For once, Chika and Mika agreed and urged me to take the challenge head on. Not only was my next menu different, the chicken dish was a big hit. Mohana Shastri had arrived and how!

Little did I know that the bubble was about to burst.

After a winning run with hosting, there was just one invite left—Major Murthy and family who had recently re-joined the unit after a longish course. He had a reputation for being diligent and focused, with little appetite for trivia. He also had peculiar eating habits which we should have known. Ignorance isn't always bliss, as we found out that evening.

Maj. Murthy arrived on time, accompanied by his parents, wife, and two young kids. Capt. Bagga was the other invited guest, who got stares from Maj. Murthy for coming late. I had made sufficient preparation with an assortment of starters, main course followed by a dessert. Just as I started asking people about their choice of drink, Maj. Murthy cut me in, "It's already 8 o'clock, ma'am. My parents prefer to sleep early. It's best to have dinner right away."

"Sure, some quick starters?"

"Ma'am, can I request you to skip that as well? These kids fill up on starters and don't eat their meals well."

"Oh, ok. As you suggest," I forced a smile and went to the kitchen. I had kept the starters ready and now I would have to leave them aside and warm the main course. So be it.

I was serving soup when Maj. Murthy scooped up the rice tray. "Umm, this smells good, ma'am." Finally, he said something to help me relax, I thought to myself. The very next moment, I froze. While everyone else started with soup, Maj. Murthy had emptied all the rice on to his plate and then added a liberal portion of dal to it. "Can I have some ghee"? Suraj got it from the kitchen while I stood transfixed! Adding a dollop, Maj. Murthy attacked the mountain on his plate.

"Can I have some rice, please?" his father asked. Holy cow! I wanted to say, 'Most of the rice I made is on your son's plate. Why don't you guys share?' Instead, I said, "Sure" and disappeared into the kitchen. Just a bowlful, as I scraped out the last grain! Just then, Suraj walked in, "All ok, Mo?"

"Nothing is ok, Suraj. Maj. Murthy took most of the rice. This is all that is left." I showed him the bowl.

"Why did you not make enough?" Suraj blurted out and immediately bit his tongue, "Sorry, I didn't mean it that way, Mo."

"There were starters and rotis...the rice was made accordingly," I said, nervously. "What do we do now?" My mind had gone blank.

"I'll take this out, in the meantime, you make some fresh rice," suggested the dodo who obviously knew nothing more than making tea.

"Have you seen the rice we get in ration? Just cleaning it takes half an hour!" I hissed. "You go and tell them the truth. I'm too embarrassed to come out now."

"Hey, hey, hey! Relax, relax, relax!" I breathed through my mouth to calm myself and Suraj continued, "Listen, Mo. We have to do this together. We will go out and tell them the truth. Big deal, *yaar*. Come, my tiger!"

When we finally emerged, Capt. Bagga had served rotis and perhaps sensitized everyone about the situation. Because the moment I said something about rice, everyone started assuring me that they didn't want any. "We South Indians eat rice all the time. Rotis is what we crave," said Maj. Murthy's father. "You must teach me how to make such soft rotis, Mohana," said his wife. "I love tava rotis," exclaimed the daughter. Amid this brouhaha about rotis, Maj. Murthy tucked away his dal-rice with a sheepish smile. Dessert got served immediately thereafter and one of the most embarrassing evenings of my life was over. Phew!

Capt. Bagga burst out laughing as soon as the Murthys left. "I'm never going to forget your face, ma'am," he announced, helping himself to another serving of the dessert. We had developed a nice, comfortable relationship and Capt. Bagga was a frequent visitor.

"Yeah sure, go on. Rub some salt in," I jeered.

"Oh come on, ma'am, this is just 'having fun'. 'Salt rubbing' will happen the day I report this to Mrs. Rana," he flashed a devilish smile.

"Oh no, I won't be able to handle her. Please, Capt. Bagga, you can't do this to me" I begged.

"Only on one condition, ma'am, you must invite me whenever you make this dessert, reminds me of my mother."

NSR was so right—food does bring people closer, deepening the bond of friendship.

Sometimes, this bonding became a bit much though. Bachelor officers would often hop over unannounced, but I would refuse to wear my apron. "Sorry, guys, I have done enough cooking for a lifetime. Dal rice is all I can make now."

"No problem, ma'am. We will take some for Murthy sir as well!" they would retort.

Unit life was really like family...one could never keep secrets.

Just when life couldn't be better, came the news—the CO had nominated Suraj for a two-week course in 'Adventure water sports' because 'young couples deserve some fun'. Sure, but what about school? I had barely started, could I apply for a break? "You can go on unpaid leave. I doubt if it would be hard and fast like your corporate job. You are teaching pre-primary kids, they can be taken care for two weeks. Right?"

When the leave application reached Col. Sahoo, he called me for a discussion. "Mrs. Shastri, you cannot take this job so lightly. We have taken a lot of risk by hiring an inexperienced person like you. Even before settling in, you want a break?"

I didn't know how to defend myself because that's exactly how I felt. Still I tried, "I concur with you, Col.

Sahoo and I really appreciate this opportunity. I would not have applied for leave had this not been a special course, coming through our CO's recommendation. I'll be back in two weeks."

He disagreed, "The course is near Bhuj, travel will take four days. Plus, you will have to report one day prior. Twenty days—not possible, Mrs. Shastri."

My mouth went dry and I almost pleaded, "Please, Col. Sahoo. Just this one time, I won't ask for any more leave."

He forced a smile and said, "That's what you think, Mrs. Shastri. Your husband is a Lieutenant, right? Young officers have a lot to learn. You will be surprised with the number of courses he will need to attend in different parts of the country…duration varying from a few weeks to a few months. Will you not want to accompany him?" He added with a frown, "Actually, we missed considering this before appointing you. And I am not blaming you, it's the phase of life both of you are in. While I understand your situation, I cannot grant you any leave."

And so I left his room with a heavy heart and a confused head! What do I do? Suraj was both surprised and disappointed. "I thought they would be more understanding." Noticing my sad face, he added, "Listen, Mo, don't be so upset. You take your decision. We will have some explaining to do…though with Brig. Pratap, you know how difficult this can get," he wiped his brow.

I wanted my job and was ready to speak to Brig. Pratap myself. Just then I remembered Col. Sahoo's statement about multiple courses lined up for Suraj. "Tell me something, Suraj, is it true that you will travel to different places for training?"

He nodded, "That's right. Have a lot of courses lined up over the next few years. In fact, RSO (Regimental Signalling

Officer) might happen anytime now. Most courses have family quarters, so you will have the option of accompanying me to some great places. I'm quite excited."

So was I! I wanted to travel with Suraj and experience the many facets of army life, which is why I had quit my job in Mumbai. But these kids were like family, it would break my heart to leave them. Staying with them would mean staying away from Suraj. Did I really want that?

Chika encouraged me to think logically, 'Look, Mo, in a year's time, the unit would get posted in the field. Suraj will be away for at least two years. That would be the right time to focus on a job. For now, try to make the most of your time together.'

Mika did not like the idea of playing a second fiddle while giving preference to Suraj's job. But her voice was meek and I chose to ignore it at that point.

It was heartbreaking to say goodbye, especially to Sonali, Himanshu, and Raman. Just like their sweet memories, I knew that the pain of separation would stay in my heart forever.

17

THE UNIVERSITY OF LIFE

Lakhpat, 5th of April 1998

As the train moved, my excitement rose, "This trip is going to be fun. Adventure sports, that too in the sea! I wonder what exactly they will make us do." Suraj, on the other hand, stayed calm as ever. Come hail, storm or a fun vacation, Lieutenant Shastri's serenity stayed untouched. This was becoming a 'boon or bane' dilemma—should I love his composure in pressure situations or resent his 'lack of excitability'? Like now, when I wanted him to match my enthusiasm, he was sitting like a log.

"Come on, Suraj, I am so thrilled about the trip and you are behaving as if we do this every day."

He smiled, "I haven't been to many courses, so not sure what to expect. Let's see how they balance the learning agenda and the fun element."

That made sense but I guarded my enthusiasm fiercely, "I'm so looking forward to being by the sea side. If nothing, just walking on the beach and sipping coconut water will be nice."

"Sure, now listen up. Our next train from Rourkela will take us to Bhuj in 40 hours, if there are no delays."

"Whaaaat? Forty hours! How will we pass time?"

"Well, my plan is crystal clear—sleep."

"What about me?" I protested.

"That's not my problem." I knew he was teasing me, but still, it was best to pick some books at Rourkela.

True to his word, Suraj slept an awful lot, with a compelling argument in his defence, "Get up at five every morning for PT and tell me if you care for anything more than sleeping." Not wanting to take up the challenge, I wisely shifted my focus to reading.

Nevertheless, the journey was memorable where apart from sleeping and reading, we played chess, chatted up, got down whenever the train stopped, picked up some more eats. After 40 long hours when we finally reached Bhuj, Suraj was fairly rejuvenated and I was decidedly overstuffed!

Off the train, on to a *fauji* bus to take us to Lakhpat, a small coastal town where the training was to be conducted. The three-hour drive in the sweltering heat seemed longer than the 40 hours in the train. Vegetation grew sparse as we entered Kutch and almost resembled a desert by the time we reached Lakhpat. Crossing the dusty, ghost town with dilapidated houses, we noticed the ruins of the Lakhpat Fort guarded by an irregular wall. Finally, army tents in a huge open area...and the gleaming ocean at a distance!

After three days of travel, we had finally reached our destination.

Suraj went straight to report arrival, while I was escorted to the guestroom. I stood dumbstruck as Maggar Singh, our helper, deposited the luggage in a corner. The first thing that caught my eye was the asbestos sheets, in place of a ceiling. At 2 o'clock in the afternoon, with the sun right overhead, they seemed to spew fire! The most unbelievable part was the absence of a fan, which made the room feel like a furnace as soon as I closed the door.

It was a fairly big room with a double bed, a small steel table accompanied by two folding steel chairs. That's it. The spotless white walls of the room reflected bright light coming from the windows which incidentally, were devoid of curtains. The Indian style toilet was stained and stinking.

I wasn't prepared for this and the thought of spending two weeks in this torture cell, made me want to cry. However, Chika reminded me of the 'army wife' label on my head which didn't allow for luxuries like getting rattled with these small frustrations. Sitting at the edge of the bed, I eagerly awaited Suraj, food, and a better room. Couldn't decide which one was more important!

Suraj came in, saw the room, blew a whistle and to my horror, uttered one word that took away the wind from my sail: "Interesting." Clearly, he didn't find the place as bad. Damn! Just then, Maggar walked in with food, which was quite unlike what we had seen in the *fauji* Messes—looks as well as taste. Beggars can't be choosers and ignoring the excess flour on the rotis, I broke one and gave it a dip in the daal, which was so spicy that my ears felt hot at once. The *sabzi* was worse—undercooked and bland.

I checked Suraj's reaction—again very different from mine. "I'm reminded of the food in the barracks, though our cooks are way better." Not wanting to be seen as a fuss pot, I dusted off the excess flour discreetly. Thanks to the watery curd, I somehow gulped down the lunch.

"Looks like there is no Officers' Mess here. We will be eating the same food as the *jawaans*. Some 100 of them are here for the course. We have a briefing at 4 pm. I'll take a quick nap before that." And the guy just conked off! No cribbing about the heat, no surprise or complaint about the missing fan or the dirty toilet. What had crushed me in five seconds was completely lost on him.

By the time Suraj came back from the briefing, it was six. The setting sun had coloured the sky pink and a gentle breeze had cooled down the place as well as my head. Keeping the door open, I was sitting on the small steel chair enjoying the breeze when Suraj said, "Get ready, Mo, we are going to the beach!" I jumped into action, only to be disappointed at the sight of the secluded, rocky beach. 'Coconut water has to wait,' I silently noted. However, the long walk and the quiet time together were nice. Coming back to the room was not easy, especially the thought of dinner was a positive put off.

"Can we sit outside? The room is quite stuffy."

I was sure Suraj would agree. Instead he said, "It's quite dark outside, better to stay indoors."

"Worried of ghosts?" I teased.

"Scorpions," he corrected with nonchalance.

"What?" I jumped out of my skin.

"Yes, dear wife, here starts your adventure!"

"What do you mean?" I asked, nervously.

"The first thing we heard in today's briefing was that this place is infested with scorpions. They are nocturnal. So be careful if you use the toilet at night. And, most importantly, shoes are their favourite hideout. So wear them only after checking for any creepy crawlies hiding inside."

"And how does one do that?"

"Quite simple, just bump the shoe upside down on the ground. Anything inside will fall off. You just use the same shoe to kill it then." He looked amused.

"What if there are two scorpions inside the shoe—while one falls off, the other one might crawl on your hand and bite?"

"Hmm...nobody thought of such complexities. Let's plan it. Every morning, we will do this shoe exercise together so that when one of us hits the shoe on the ground, the other stays guard with another one." Suraj was obviously enjoying my expressions.

"But how will we find the first clear shoe?"

Laughing hard, Suraj patted my head affectionately, "Don't worry, kiddo, I am trained to handle such exigencies. I can stamp its sting barefoot if it comes to that."

The room was cool and pleasant because of the sea breeze, but now my heart was gripped with fear.

The first night was uneventful, not the next. I was woken up with the rustle of plastic. Initially, the sound was low and intermittent; gradually it became louder and continuous, as though someone was rubbing a plastic bag between their fingers. I couldn't think through my groggy mind at first, but then I got it. Since there was no shoe rack, the entire pile of shoes, along with the plastic covers we got them in, was lying in a corner. The scorpions must have gotten inside one of the plastic bags. But why were they making so much noise?

I woke up Suraj and asked him to check on the noise without getting off the bed. He mumbled, "How, Mo? I'm not trained to fly! Why don't we just sleep and handle this in the morning?" Unwilling to do anything myself, I grudgingly lay down. Just then, the noise became too big to ignore, as if the plastic was approaching us.

Before I could protest, Suraj jumped towards the table and picked up his flashlight. In its glare, we saw a white plastic bag dancing all over the room. "This can't be a scorpion," Suraj whispered. He went towards it and peeped inside, "Boy! You've to see this, Mo." A giant toad with dark, bumpy skin sat inside. Unable to get out of the plastic bag, the poor fellow was desperately hopping around with it. Suraj released it outside and went back to sleep within no time.

I snuggled up to the man who had earned enormous respect with this act of bravado!

For the next two days, I played the role of a 'good army wife' to perfection. The simplest solution for the toilet was to clean it myself, which I did. So one problem was immediately taken care of. But food? And the unbearable heat? Even though I didn't complain, my mind kept thinking about a solution, which was nowhere in sight.

By the third day, the mask of congeniality started melting off. More than the food, the heat was getting to me. Suraj would go in the morning for some water training leaving me behind to roast in the furnace. How the heck was I supposed to sit in that crazy heat all day? Finally, I asked Suraj to do something about it and when he spoke to the officer in charge about the issue, he got the most surprising response. In an organization where the well-being of fellow officers is paramount, this gentleman was clearly an outlier. Instead of trying to fix the problem, Mr. Indifference plainly told us that the table fan in our room had been sent for repair, so we would have to manage without one! This meant that fanning with a notebook was the only way to survive. I focused my attention on food. Was it possible to buy some eatables? The nearest town was 70 km away and it hardly stored any good grocery. "So, where does the kitchen ration come from?"

"My guess would be Bhuj."

"Can I go to Bhuj and buy some stuff?"

"I doubt that would be possible, Mo, but let me check." Turned out, a vehicle was coming from Bhuj the next morning. A survival plan was hatched then and there, "Can you arrange for some bread and jam for me?"

Mr. Indifference finally took pity and made sure that I had a reason to smile...and means to survive. Finally, my tummy was at peace but my heart wasn't. I was missing the school and my kids and regretting the decision to quit. And hey! Wasn't this supposed to be a vacation? Hadn't the CO personally arranged this 'fun outing'? Till now, all we'd seen in the name of fun and excitement was a hopping toad! And apart from wetting my feet during the evening walks, I hadn't seen any water.

A volcano of frustration started building inside me and before it burst out, Maj. Iqbal Singh Sodhi, the Godsend, arrived. He was posted in Bhuj and had come to check on the course. The first thing he did after reaching Lakhpat was to come over to meet us, and was surprised to see that we had been surviving without curtains, or even a fan! Mr. Indifference was immediately called and seriously reprimanded for not having taken care of the guests. Within the next hour, Major Sodhi got us one of the table fans from his room and also arranged for makeshift curtains to be put up. At once, the room was liveable, life was beautiful, and the vacation looked promising!

"Why don't you join us for tea this evening? I'd love you to meet my wife and our young boys." Gladly accepting the invitation, I was thrilled at the thought of having kids around. Maj. Sodhi cleared his throat, "Ma'am, just want to let you know, both our sons are special kids. Sometimes people get disturbed with their condition, hence want to prepare you in advance."

We visited their accommodation in the evening, not knowing what to expect. Mrs. Sodhi was singing to the boys—both of whom were strapped to their wheelchairs, their heads drooped to a side. Maj. Sodhi first introduced us to his wife Amrit and then the kids—Samar Singh and Balvir Singh. I was amazed that both parents kept things casual, like a normal household. "Samy is a big boy. He's 11 and Ballu will be 9 next month. Isn't it, buddy?" he patted Ballu's face, wiped his drool with a bib and then kissed their heads one by one. Both boys remained unresponsive.

Amrit told us that the kids were tired after the travel and needed to be tucked in the bed. Both parents pushed the wheelchairs to the bedroom while Suraj and I sat numb.

Major Sodhi closed the bedroom door and came and sat with us. He perhaps saw that both of us were moved. He smiled and spoke in a matter-of-fact tone, "Doctors believe that both of them cannot understand much. And maybe they are right. Since Samy and Ballu cannot speak, we will never know how much they comprehend. But to us, they mean the world."

We nodded. "Are they undergoing any treatment?" I blurted out a stupid question.

"I wish! Unfortunately, ma'am, there is no cure. After years of searching for a miracle, we have accepted that this is how they were born and this is how they will live. *Wahe Guru di marzi*." He gestured towards the sky. There was an awkward pause. "It's not been easy as parents. The reality torments us every single day, but we have learnt to deal with it. Amrit and I focus on what we can do rather than what we cannot. You'll see, both Samy and Ballu enjoy music, food, outings, so we try to create these experiences for them. Which is why we got them in this heat, even though Amrit is allergic to the Sun," he smiled.

Major Sodhi's cheerful demeanour lessened the pain and helplessness that was weighing us down. Amrit joined and enjoying the evening tea, we made plans for the vacation.

Both Suraj and I were stirred by the profound experience—cruel face of life and invincible human spirit, sitting in one frame. The impact was both humbling and empowering.

I realized how trivial my challenges were—extra flour on rotis...boredom...absence of curtains? What was I even complaining about, when these parents had accepted their fate with such aplomb.

Each day with the Sodhis was a lesson in life. I was awed by the devotion and love parents can have for their children. Equally fascinating was the partnership between the couple and how they supported each other in everything. Most of all, their indomitable spirit to enjoy life!

Major Sodhi was an encyclopaedia on jokes and had something ready for every occasion. Amrit, on the other hand, was an expert at creating jokes and finding humour in the blandest situations. Her laughter was contagious, and invariably, we would be cracking up at the silliest of things. Both were awfully fond of cooking and to my delight, they set up a small kitchen in which they would rustle up a new dish to celebrate each sunset.

One evening, we were seated outside their room, enjoying the breeze. Samy and Ballu were relishing their favourite fish fry, grunting when they wanted more. I watched the parents feed the young boys as if they were little babies.

All of a sudden, Maggar Singh, our help, came running at breakneck speed. Before any of us could react, he dived under the table and came out holding a dead scorpion by its sting! The monstrous, black insect seemed capable of real harm, but for the vigilant eyes of Maggar. I never even realized he kept a watch on us while we were busy making merry.

A nice bowl of fish fry was an apt reward, which he accepted with a shy smile, only after a lot of coaxing!

Alas! It turned out that there wouldn't be any adventure activity for me. Water sport was only for the men in uniform, as part of their training. Lakhpat, being a border area, is mostly managed by the BSF (Border Security Force) and this training was a joint exercise between the BSF and the Army to protect our waters.

Since we were just a few kilometres from the international border, choppers and water vessels would be constantly patrolling. I also learnt that what I thought to be the Arabian Sea was in fact the Kori Creek. I asked Maj. Iqbal if we could have a ride in the creek and he immediately spoke to his BSF counterpart and got us the permission. The next morning, decked up in life jackets, we climbed a motor boat. When a BSF boat with armed personnel moved alongside ours, a sense of adventure kicked in!

After the boat ride, we visited a BSF post, where their commandant welcomed us with puri, sabzi and some fresh buttermilk. A visit to the Lakhpat Fort and the local Gurudwara completed the day for us.

Next morning, Ballu woke up with high fever and not wanting to take any chance in that secluded place, Major Sodhi and family left for Bhuj, filling us with a sense of void. I thanked them for everything they did for us. I also wanted to tell them that I was inspired by their positivity and selfless love but I lost my voice to emotions.

After two days, we also said goodbye to the dusty, hot place which had surprisingly gifted us lessons for a lifetime.

Since our train was for the next day, Suraj had booked us a guestroom in the Bhuj Cantt. As we reached their Mess for lunch, we were joined by one Capt. Debashish, also staying in the Mess quarters. Just ten minutes with him was a put off. It was difficult to decide what was more irritating—his snobbish attitude or the fake accent he seemed to have picked during a recently concluded UN mission. Suraj, true to his character, politely listened to all the bragging, whereas I was just short of rolling my eyes. After lunch, he refused the custard and instead asked for some fresh fruit. When the Mess staff got some bananas, he asked for a small plate, a fork and a butter knife.

I watched in awe as Capt. Debashish peeled the banana with the knife, cut it into thin slices and then gingerly picked them with the fork. And then he educated us that this, in fact, was the right way of eating the fruit. Only the uncouth ate it like monkeys!

Back in our room, I laughed at the banana eating ceremony and Suraj shocked me by saying that in a formal set up, that was indeed the right thing to do. "You haven't seen the *fauji* etiquette. Wait till you attend a formal, ceremonial dinner."

"I'll surely fall in the monkey category," I chirped.

Suraj gave me a good look, "Chimpanzee."

The afternoon heat was terrible and my sweaty, sticky body was making me irritable. I went for a shower but the tap hissed, spat muddy water in spurts and then died down. I stared at the brownish water lying in the bucket and despite the desperation for a wash, couldn't bring myself to use it.

Frustrated, I went out to crib to Suraj, but he had already fallen asleep. Dear Lord! What do I do with this man? Nothing ever bothered him! He was at peace everywhere and ready to fall asleep in less than three minutes! His serene, baby-like face frustrated me even more at my inability to be like him.

Irritated, I started pacing up and down the room, my mind hell bent on finding a solution. What good was I if I couldn't even manage basics like hygiene. And then I got a bright idea—ladies restroom at the Mess! We just had lunch at the Mess, so the staff knew me. I could always explain if anyone questioned. And so, delirious at having cracked the problem independently, I marched out with a few clothes and toiletries.

It felt odd because there wasn't a trace of a human being in that huge place. I went straight to the bathroom which had a big bucket filled with sparkling clear water...just what I needed. I enjoyed a delicious shower, washed some essentials, wrapped my wet hair in a towel, and stepped out. A Mess staffer was standing outside, guess he must've heard the sound of running water. He seemed a bit stunned, so I politely explained the situation and trotted back to the room.

By the time Suraj woke up, I was all set for some local shopping. "Wow! Someone is looking fresh as daisy! Did you go to some parlour nearby?" Enjoying the appreciation in his eye, I playfully threw my damp hair on his face and said, "Yes, and the Mess hawaldar gave me a nice hair wash!" Suraj just raised his eyebrow, so I explained, "Chill man. I just went to the Mess for a shower."

"Whhhhhaaaatttt? What did you do?" his eyes were wide open now.

"*Arrey*, there was no water in this bathroom and I badly needed a wash. You were fast asleep. So I just went there and had a nice shower."

Suraj looked too zapped to respond. Finally he said, "Didn't anyone stop you? Did anyone see you there?"

I shrugged my shoulders, "There was nobody there. While coming out, I met the staff and explained. Why? What happened?"

"You shouldn't have used the Mess for a shower, Mo" Suraj looked agitated.

"Oh no, did I go wrong?" I panicked.

"Of course! A Mess is used for socializing, dining, community activities. It is not appropriate to use it for personal chores like bathing. I just hope this doesn't get reported." He said in a tired voice. Oh God! I'd been stupid again. Would Suraj be marched up once more?

Thankfully, he recovered quickly, "Anyway, what has happened has happened. We can't change it now. Give me some time to freshen up, then we will go."

How was he going to freshen up without water? Just then, I heard the sound of water falling in the bucket. Either they released water around this time, or the Mess guy had got the problem fixed. Either way, I looked like a fool!

The next day, our train was at 3 pm, so we had sufficient time to laze around.

Capt. Debashish was having breakfast when we reached the Mess. His attitude seemed even more condescending and he refused to indulge in a polite conversation. After finishing the breakfast in stiff silence, he asked Suraj to join him in the library for a word in 'private' while I went back to the room.

Soon, Suraj walked in, seething in anger! "I wish you had asked me before going to the Mess for your beauty bath. But no! You love taking impulsive decisions and I've to face the flak!"

I immediately knew what had happened and asked in a meek voice, "Capt. Debashish spoke about yesterday?"

Suraj gave me a dirty stare and went quiet, as if unable to find the right words. Then, without looking at me, he started, "Yes. He raised a strong objection to the Mess being used for personal washing. He blamed me for not educating you about Mess etiquette."

Mika took over the reins in self defence. "I'm sorry to put you through this, Suraj. But what business does that snooty fellow have talking about my Mess etiquette?"

Suraj jumped in, rather unexpectedly, "Wow, Mohana! First you commit the stupidest mistakes and then you criticize others! What he said is jolly well his job because he is the Mess secretary. If anything inappropriate in the Mess is brought to his notice, he has to take it up." Whoa, instead of supporting me, my husband was siding with that bozo.

Mika formulated a quick strategy—'Attack to defend'. "Nice! I like how quick the jury has delivered the verdict—Mohana's behaviour was 'inappropriate'. What about dry taps? Is that appropriate? I'll tell you how weird this place is—eating banana with a fork and knife is sophistication. But basics like personal hygiene? Well, that can wait. I don't get the rules of this place."

"Yes, Mohana, this precisely IS the problem. You refuse to get the rules. We have had innumerable conversations about this, but no, you have to question every norm, try to crack the logic behind every rule. Why? Why can't you just accept things the way they are? If you resist everything at every step, it will just cause pain to both of us."

Damn! This, after everything I had done to settle in. I refused to take the blame lying down. "I understand there are rules and I'm not someone to question them all the time. You know that. So, let's not exaggerate. The point is, as the Mess secretary, Capt. Debashish is also responsible for the comfort of his guests. Why is nobody talking about that?" Suraj didn't respond right away so I continued, "We need to stand up and speak for ourselves. Otherwise people will keep trampling all over us."

Suraj shook his head in disbelief, "What are you saying now? Who is trampling over you?"

I had been holding back for months but in the heat of the moment, off went the cork and out flew the bottled-up lava. "Everyone, *yaar*! We have been putting our heads down in front of practically everybody. When the 2IC questioned you about my comments on AWWA, you should have stood up for me. I didn't go running around telling them what I thought. They cornered me and when I comply, they get offended! Why? Mohana's inappropriate behaviour! NSR of course has a list of my misdoings. And now, this pompous Debashish. When he attacked my behaviour, why didn't you question the circumstances that led to it? Why should we be so compliant...so submissive all the time? You didn't even fight for a fan, when Maj. Sodhi could arrange it in no time."

Suraj just let out a long sigh of exasperation, and said in a tired voice, "I was talking about embracing this culture, Mohana, to understand how things work here. Instead, you're questioning my decisions! I don't know what to say."

"Well, I have a lot to say, things which I had been holding back far too long. I want to tell you, Suraj that

I feel let down by you. I feel you choose to be compliant because it's convenient. In Lakhpat, instead of expecting me to survive without a fan, you should have questioned the people in charge—why did they publicize it as a 'fun with family' course when the most basic facilities were missing. You chose to take no action because it's easier to silence me than to wake up the system!"

Silence.

But I wasn't done, "Also, I feel totally unappreciated. You didn't give me any idea about life after marriage. Agreed, you had no inkling yourself. But I don't remember a single day when you were worried about me. Namkum, Delhi, Lakhpat—everywhere you would just wear your uniform and leave. Without a thought about how I would spend my day. You just take me for granted!" My voice was beginning to crack but I didn't give up, "I alone know how difficult some days have been...almost nailing me in a pit. Every single time, I have dragged myself out of it and put myself together. Why? Because I wanted to make you happy...make *us* happy. And all I get back from you is the blame of not being able to adjust."

Suraj spoke from another zone, "I'm trying to make a small point but you seem to be blaming me for ruining your life."

We were clearly on different planets, not ready for a discussion. "You know what, Suraj, maybe you have a point here, which I can't see right now. I'm really frustrated and annoyed." Short of breath, I held my head. As an afterthought, I added, "I need a break. I haven't seen my family after marriage. I want to go spend time with them." Suraj seemed a bit surprised at this sudden idea; but even he must be equally miffed with me. For, he agreed instantly.

"Our train stops at Baroda. You can get down there. I'll arrange an onward ticket for you."

Huh? I hadn't expected him to grab the offer with both hands. And while I was initially stumped at his tearing hurry to dump me at Baroda, it actually made sense. Instead of the long commute from Namkum, travel from Baroda was much easier. Also, the place was known to me since I used to work there.

Logic and my bruised ego made me take up the offer right away. "Yes, Baroda sounds great. Don't bother about the ticket. I'll figure."

Everything happened in a jiffy and now, as our train approached the Baroda station, I had mixed feelings. Chika felt horrible about the way I had blamed Suraj for everything, while Mika was ecstatic about going home to my parents. Lt. Suraj Shastri nursed no such dilemma. Anger was the only emotion in his system. He had not spoken a word all afternoon, and now when it was time for me to get off the train, I had this strong urge to hold on to him till he said, "Don't go."

Much to my disappointment, the sulk pot kept sulking. I gave him a quick hug and holding my hurt ego, got off the train. Suraj deposited my bags on the platform and went back inside. The real impact of my decision hit me when the train began moving. I froze as the train sped past me till the last bogie bid adieu. Dear me! This was for real—Suraj had moved on without a care and I was standing all alone at the station.

Finally, a wave of exhilaration ran through my body as I picked up my luggage—no escorts, no help. Just me managing my own business. Freedom at last!

'I can go to the waiting room for a shower. Nobody will judge me,' I laughed in my head.

The heavy luggage weighed down my body but I floated out of the station with a buoyant spirit!

18

An Unexpected Twist

Indore, 23rd of April 1998

Oh, what a homecoming it was! To be back with my parents and in the house I had always known as home—a world where I belonged! Where I was loved unconditionally and allowed to be myself. Why do girls need to relocate to another universe after marriage? And then endlessly try fitting in!

Bitterness for Suraj ran deeper than I knew. I refused to even think about him, and if a defiant thought slipped in, Mika would hiss, 'Let him fend for himself, he'll know your worth.'

Honestly, once reconnected with my roots, I simply didn't feel like going back to him.

Suraj

I am so annoyed with Mohana. She went ballistic in Bhuj. Instead of admitting her mistake, she went on and on about how I had let her down. I am the one facing flak for her actions and she's the one complaining. Ridiculous! What was the need to give her expert opinion on the AWWA? Agreed, they asked her but isn't there something called common sense? What's the use of these fancy professional degrees without worldly wisdom?

And then the bath in the Mess. I rest a bit and madam does the unthinkable. Again, I am the one who cuts a sorry face and has to apologize. Forget gratitude, Mohana calls me servile! If Major Sodhi could get the fan, why couldn't you? *Arrey* Sodhi sir has 15 years of experience, I have three! Where is the comparison?

I'm glad she's not here. We both need some time away from each other.

I am not asking her to come back.

Mohana

I couldn't believe my luck!

Suraj called to inform about a two-month-long exercise that would require him to stay with the troops, so it was best for me to stay put. Yay!

I was determined to make the most of this freedom—spend time with family, go out with friends, roam the streets and make merry! Anything to get back the chirpy, carefree Mohana, who had got lost somewhere.

Suraj

I heard about ITC (Intensive Training Cycle) this morning, and called Mo to tell her that I would be with the troops for at least two months. I thought she would be disappointed and crib about being away for so long. Instead, she sounded ecstatic!

I found it a bit odd but couldn't bring myself to say much. As it is, I'm very uncomfortable expressing emotions.

Things haven't been good between us after the fight at Bhuj. Mo seems to be holding a grudge...that's not her.

Perhaps dumping her at Baroda was a bit much. I was confident that she would manage her way around, but still, I should've been more considerate. Call it anger, lapse of judgement or plain ego, I did behave stupidly.

If Mo was around, I would hold her and whisper a sorry. But broaching these complicated issues on the phone is beyond me!

I don't like this strain. Hope we can put this behind us.

Mohana

Meeting Neil was pure coincidence.

I had planned an evening catch up with Sumi, my closest childhood buddy, who worked in an ad agency. I was leafing through a magazine at her office reception, when a deep voice called out, "Hey! Is that you Mohana?" I looked up at a cheery face with smiling eyes, though I couldn't place him immediately. "Now don't say you don't recognize me, I may have put on a few pounds at the most!" laughed the guy with an easy, relaxed demeanour. As we shook hands, my brain raced for a recall. He had a dusky complexion and long, dishevelled hair—just my type. "You just broke my heart," he made a face. Then added, "Let me introduce myself—Neil Basu, same business school." Oh yes, of course! I knew him even though we hadn't interacted much.

"Sorry about this, Neil. I am coming from another world you know...and seem to have forgotten a lot about this one," I spoke honestly.

"Really? Which galaxy have you shifted to?" He grinned.

"Umm well, I married an army officer…have been with him in a small place in Bihar for the past one year. And you are right, that's practically like living on another planet."

"Whoa, army officer! Wish I had the courage to wear the uniform. I'm such a city dog, scared at the thought of living in a tent."

"Well, they do a lot more than living in tents." I felt a sudden pride for the forces.

"I'm sure. In fact, I would love to hear more."

Just then, Sumi joined us after wrapping up the day's work. "Mo!" she screamed into my ears, crushing me in a bear hug. "I've missed you so much, you idiot." She laughed and planted a kiss on my cheek. Noticing Neil, she scoffed, "Don't you have anything apart from hammering us all day?" Neil just stood scratching his head; smiling at Sumi. She introduced us, "Meet Neil, one of our toughest clients. Thanks to his ever changing ideas, we keep chasing our own tails."

"I know, I know, I know," Neil held up both his hands, "Guilty as charged. But come on now, Sumi, we have done some fantastic work together, haven't we?"

Sumi made a face, "Fantastic I don't know, but yes, we did manage to finish some work together." I loved their friendly banter. "So can I enjoy the evening with my friend or do we have to tolerate you just because you are a key client?" Sumi could be such a pain!

Neil's response was surprisingly polite, "I wouldn't like to suffer any more insults in front of Mohana. You guys carry on."

Decades of friendship ensured that Sumi and I just knew where to go. Reaching our favourite joint, we ordered our special pav bhaji and milkshakes and then settled for a giggly evening together.

"How do you know Neil?" Sumi asked, casually.

"Well, he used to be my senior in business school. He was quite bright, if I remember right."

Away from Neil, Sumi behaved differently. "He is. Super creative. That is why he pushes us hard for original ideas." Sipping on the thick, yummy chikoo shake, she continued, "In fact, to be honest, Neil has taught me a lot about my work. I was getting away with very basic stuff before he came on the scene. My ego wouldn't allow me to admit this to him, though," she winked.

"You were ruthless, Sumi, cracking those rude jokes with a client!"

"He is a sport, *yaar*, that's why I take my chances. If I weren't engaged, I would have fallen for him in the very first meeting," she sighed. "Anyway, you tell me, Mrs. Mohana Shastri, how is married life treating you?"

So I started with my stories, enjoying how Sumi's eyes grew bigger every now and then. We went so hysterical with the *jaamun* tree story that people around started giving us nasty looks.

Oh, the joy of 'being'...without the worry of protocol!

"Hey! This is Neil. I got your number from Sumi." I was pleasantly surprised to hear that deep voice and immediately accepted Neil's offer to meet for coffee.

"You look nice," Neil welcomed me with a friendly hug. I was wearing a simple white kurti with a pair of denims; so the compliment was surprising.

"What? You like my *Kolhapuri chappals*?" I teased him.

Smiling, he gestured me to sit. "Marriage hasn't changed you one bit."

"Ha! So you think. Marriage in fact has impacted me in very many ways. But here in my home town, with my old friends, I insist on being the same old Mohana." If there was a hint of bitterness in my voice, Neil thankfully didn't notice.

"Great! That makes it easy for me as well. In fact, I was not even sure about calling you."

"I'm glad you did. Chill now."

Neil was so friendly and effortless in conversation, that it seemed we were old friends. He asked me about life after B school but I told him I was more interested in his story. "I was always fascinated by media and was lucky to get through a national daily. Was part of their sales team based out of Mumbai…moved here a few months ago to handle branding for this region."

"Why? Why would you move to a smaller city after working in Mumbai?" I enquired with a raised eyebrow.

"Are you a criminal lawyer? I've never felt so defensive about my decision" Neil laughed. I loved the way his unruly hair fell on his forehead. "No actually, it's a valid question, Mohana. After handling sales for almost three years, I was looking for something new. Our company was exploring the idea of publishing in regional languages and wanted to study a few regions. Central India is a big potential market and I got picked for this project. So here I am, in the beautiful city of Indore…checking the market's response to our ideas. That's how I got to know your friend Sumi."

"How interesting! So are you your own boss?" I was intrigued by the professional world I was once a part of.

"Well, pretty much. My boss sits out of Mumbai and makes sure she breathes down my neck once in a while, just to make her presence felt," he mouthed the last words in a whisper. "But by and large, there is a lot of freedom in our organization. That's how they have been able to retain someone like me," Neil pursed his lips.

"So what happens once your project is over?"

"Well, I'll have a few options. I can go back to Mumbai and try for a good role with the marketing team. Or maybe take over some regional responsibilities and stay put here... for a few years. Though I'm not sure if small town life will work for a spoilt metro fella like me," Neil scrunched his nose. What an expressive face he had, always adding an element of drama!

"What's so difficult about small-town life?"

"Well, the biggest challenge is finding my type of people."

I was intrigued, "And what's your type?"

"Now, don't take offence, I know this is your home town. But I have spent most of my life in London and Mumbai. My choices around music, food, books...life in general are hugely different. While people here are warm and hospitable, I haven't been able to make friends. Conversations don't go beyond a point, if you know what I mean."

My mind was frantically comparing our life with Neil's... almost feeling sorry for the lack of freedom we had. "What happened? Lost in some thought?" Neil snapped his fingers in front of my face.

"I'm actually quite envious of you, Neil. Just look at the choices you have—where to live, which job, what role. And you can change a location just because you can't make friends. Gosh, you're spoilt silly." The last part came out rather strongly.

"Are you angry about that?" he looked confused.

"I'm sorry, Neil. I didn't mean to get it out like that. Can we talk about something else?" The angst in my voice hadn't gone unnoticed.

"Is there something bothering you, Mohana? Can I help?"

How sweet was this guy! Barely had we met and he seemed so genuinely concerned. But I stopped myself from pouring out the venom. I wasn't going to complain about my life to everyone I met. "It's nothing. Thanks for asking, Neil," I said with a smile, brushing off the cobwebs in my head.

After an enjoyable coffee and conversation, I drove back home in Paa's car, humming a happy tune!

Suraj

Asif sir has given me complete charge of ITC (Intensive Training Cycle) for our company. This is his signature style—give big responsibilities to his juniors and then enjoy their struggle. The run is rough, but we eventually thank him for the massive learning.

I've been living in a tent for almost a month, orchestrating the training of 120 odd soldiers. Right from preparing the training calendar to conducting lessons, I have to manage it all. After Ghaatak, endurance training, night firing etc. is not so tough. Nevertheless, it keeps me terribly occupied.

We are camping some 50 km from Namkum so access to phone is ruled out, which is why I haven't been able to call Mo in all these weeks. If Asif sir sends a replacement, the first place I'd visit is the phone booth at Namkum. I'm beginning to miss Mo, feel like speaking to her!

Wonder how she is doing.

Mohana

"Sorry if I'm hounding you, Mohana, but weekends are dreadful in a new place. I was getting bored sitting alone."

"Did you ask Sumi?" I blurted.

"Um well, I have a professional relationship with her. I don't want this to become a story in her office," Neil didn't mince words. "But if you are in, I can check if we all can meet later in the day?" he asked hopefully. There was no reason to refuse.

We all reached almost at the same time, looking fresh and relaxed. We had chosen a terrace restaurant, famous for its Italian cuisine. The lovely evening breeze and the choice of music created a perfect ambience.

"I've never had the pleasure of being with two gorgeous girls for dinner. Pardon me if I'm tongue tied this evening," Neil announced as soon as we settled down.

"Good for us! We will be spared of your expert opinion on everything," Sumi retorted. When I glared at her, she laughed, "What? Why are you giving me that tough look? You don't even know the guy."

"And she won't get to know me any better today, because this evening will be about you, Mohana. Very few people have been able to earn Sumi's love and respect the way you have. I want to know the secret." Sumi and I exchanged unsure glances not knowing which one of us Neil was taking a dig at!

As the evening progressed with pasta, risotto and some lovely Sangria, Neil stayed true to his word and focused his attention towards me. I didn't mind the arc lights one bit. While Sumi helped me dole out some childhood stories, she too listened in rapt attention once I started talking about my life as an army wife. They were intrigued by the tough life in the forces and the spirit to serve.

But, at that moment, I wanted them to look beyond the halo and help me with my own struggles. I was torn between Mika's need to preserve the real Mohana and Chika's expectation to adjust better.

In the end, my own confusion stopped me from opening up to them.

In two months, apart from catching up with friends, I also did some random assignments that brought me some moolah—revealing how much my confidence and esteem depended on financial independence. For a girl who had done odd jobs all through her school and college, this realization should have come earlier. Better late than never!

Neil and I hadn't met in a long time since he was frequently off to Mumbai. When I heard his excited voice on the phone, I realized how nice it felt. Grinning from ear to ear, I said, "Very well, Neil. I have been doing some amazing things in the last few weeks, would love to tell you."

"Sure. That's why I called. We must meet up. We have something to celebrate."

"What? What? What? Tell me, tell me, tell me."

Neil laughed, "Well Mohana, thanks to the phenomenal response in this region, we are launching our Hindi newspaper soon. And I will head sales."

"But how will you survive the small town folks?" I chaffed.

"Actually, Mohana, your reaction that day got me thinking. You were right, I am spoilt for choice. I decided to not overindulge myself and applied for the position. Just heard that I've made it."

I was astonished that something I said out of spite could inspire a positive change!

"Wow, that's some news! Where are we celebrating?"

"Well, I was thinking of inviting you and Sumi for lunch this Sunday. Can you come to my place around noon?"

His place? I was a bit surprised. "What's the point of coming to your place and ordering from outside? Shouldn't we just meet at a good joint?"

After a pause, Neil replied, "How easily you make assumptions. I am rather skilled in the kitchen department, my lady."

I apologized, "So sorry, Neil. I don't know too many men who can cook. As a matter of fact, I know none! Can't wait for your treat."

"Great, would you prefer Chinese, Italian or Indian?"

Good heavens! Was this man for real? "Anything is fine, Neil, I am already impressed."

"Oh, Come on now, don't tell me you're so easy to impress," he pulled my leg. "All right then, it's decided... Sunday afternoon, my place."

At the last minute, we thought of a gift for Neil. Sumi promised to pick something and join me straight at Neil's place.

Having been to bachelor pads before, I was expecting a barren, dusty place suitably decorated with beer bottles and odd clothes stuffed in corners. Instead, I was welcomed into a house that looked fresh as a daisy. The living room had basic cane furniture with some colourful cushions adding brightness. Pristine white curtains danced around the windows. There was a small dining table in a corner with an ethnic runner in tribal print. The walls were bare, but hey, there were a few potted plants in the room! "Where have you hidden your wife? This cannot be a bachelor pad!"

Neil gave a full throated laugh, "So much for breaking my back cleaning the house to welcome you guys."

He offered a tour of his house and we reached the kitchen. "Come on now, this can't be a day's effort." I said admiring the neatly arranged kitchen shelf. My kitchen wasn't half as clean or organized.

"Ok, ok. You got me there. I do have an OCD (Obsessive Compulsive Disorder) for cleanliness." With mischief on his face, he added, "My mom's gene was too strong for my father...the poor man has to deal with two fanatics now!"

I liked his sense of humour. "So is this how your house looks all the time?"

Another laugh. "Well, yes. My mom comes every few weeks and adds a small piece here or there. That's the only change honestly."

Super impressed, I settled on the sofa, while Neil donned the host's hat and asked if I would like some wine. A welcome thought, but somehow Chika was uncomfortable at the thought of sipping wine with Neil, with nobody else around. When had I become so conservative? Does marriage do this to girls...or was it the *fauji* conditioning? Either way, Neil sensed my hesitation and offered me some juice instead. There was a sudden awkwardness and I prayed for Sumi to arrive soon.

"So tell me, Mohana, you did work for some time after MBA. How was the experience?"

"It was fabulous! It was one of the best companies on campus and I truly enjoyed my stint—just about a year."

"Then why did you quit so soon?" Neil enquired.

"Well, postings in the Infantry alternate between field and family stations every two years. So when Suraj got a family posting, we chose to get married right away, else, it would have been a long wait for us. It's been a year now and just like the corporate stint, married life has been a learning experience." I closed with a smile, hoping for the doorbell to ring, Neil to lose interest, something in the kitchen to start burning...anything to stop the conversation which had moved from my job to my marriage. Unfortunately, nothing came to my rescue.

Neil stayed silent and his expression helped me relax and carry on. "The culture of the services is very different from the way I have been brought up, Neil. I am used to a carefree life. Plus right from my childhood, my parents gave me the freedom to take decisions and live life on my terms. Being in a place that exacts certain behaviours...is stifling. There are days when I want to break free." Neil nodded as if to say 'I understand'.

A good listener always manages to get people talking. And Neil was an expert. His inquisitive eyes gently prodded me on. "The hardships are not easy, Neil. Just like you, I am also an urban product...not used to loneliness, or living without basic comforts like electricity...that too for days at a stretch! It gets to me, I plunge in a pit...especially during evenings."

"So, is it the same in all cantonments?" Neil interrupted me for the first time.

"I hope not! Most people in the unit say that this is an exception, as it's a new cantonment. They've enjoyed a glorious life in more established set ups."

Neil added, "So life can be much better going forward." Unfortunately, I didn't share his enthusiasm. He sensed it, "Something else is bothering you." Boy, he could read my mind!

"I want to be financially independent, Neil. I miss my job! I worked so hard to get into an MBA program...harder still to do well in the job. All those efforts have come to nought! I hate not being able to work," I finally spoke those words! By now, I was relaxed enough (with Neil) and charged up enough (with my emotions) to bare my heart. Mika had taken the driving seat. "I've been doing a lot of thinking...and have realized that my sense of worth comes from what I do. When I was in a job, my confidence was going through the roof, it's not the same now. You know, I was in Delhi some months back but didn't reach out to any of my batch mates. They would all be doing great things in their career whereas I've been growing tomatoes!" Neil seemed to open his mouth to say something but decided against it. Good for me, I continued, "In one year's time, I feel obsolete. Like the world has moved ahead on different trains and I'm still at the platform."

"And Khojatoli—the cantonment where we live is still coming up. No telephone lines. Some senior officers have *fauji* phones which give them the luxury of calling other *faujis* through a mini telephone exchange. Earthworms like us don't have even this comfort!"

Neil looked amused, "Earthworm?"

I gave out a long breath, "The army is extremely hierarchical...and I understand the need. But when you are at the bottom of the heap, you do feel like an insect."

"Then call yourself a caterpillar at least! You'll grow into a beautiful butterfly soon."

"Tadpole?" I asked and we both laughed.

It was amazing the way Neil and I connected. In fact, I was more comfortable sharing my problems with him than with Sumi or Maa, perhaps because, both were staunch Suraj supporters. Neil had no such biases—positive or negative.

Nobody was answering the phone at Sumi's place and there was no way to know her whereabouts. After trying a few times, we just assumed she was stuck somewhere. "I'll go over to her place on my way back; let's dig in now," I eyed the aromatic food. The fare was simple, but lip smackingly delicious—steamed rice with Thai veg curry, grilled fish and a salad. I loved the food and the relaxed energy with which it was served. For me, NSR's watch had taken the joy out of hosting; Neil's chilled out attitude was something to learn from. When I pointed this out to him, he simply said, "Socializing is supposed to be an enjoyable experience. In any case, this lunch is an effort to know you, Mohana, not to impress you. So why would I get worked up?"

Profound!

"Ok, tell me something, what do you like about the army life?"

"Plenty of things...but their spirit, camaraderie, and discipline top my list. And we have some of the most wonderful people in our unit itself." I thought of Shaheen and Maj. Asif, my most favourite people in the unit. Then there was Captain Bagga...and the forever travelling Anu. Not to forget NSR, who despite her quirks, was a very nice person.

"The issue is with me, Neil, I am not able to fit in," suddenly Chika took over.

"Now don't be so harsh with yourself," Neil said, softly. "It's such a different life...I can imagine how tough it must be; more so for someone as enterprising as you! From what I understand, Mohana, you have done a phenomenal job. In your place, I couldn't have handled the situation half as gracefully," our eyes met and I knew he meant what he said.

That was the first time someone had supported me, told me that whatever I was doing was not easy and that I had done a great job. Why didn't Suraj ever say this? In fact, he often made me feel otherwise, that I wasn't trying enough.

I had carefully avoided bringing up Suraj in the discussion; mostly because I was still miffed with him. Mika had been running the 'Shut Suraj out' campaign exceptionally well. If Neil could sense a brewing tension, he was sensitive enough to not bring it up.

What was supposed to be a celebration with Sumi and Neil, turned out to be a quiet afternoon of enriching conversations. I left feeling light and wondered if there is a bigger gift than being heard and understood!

My bond with Neil had strengthened, not realizing the turmoil this was going to create.

Suraj

This morning, Asif sir gave us a surprise visit. He said the JCO (Junior Commissioned Officer) had complained that my planning was lame and hence he wanted to check things personally. But I know that he just wanted to give me a break because he asked me to take it easy for a couple of days.

The jonga brought me to Namkum and the first thing I did was to call up Mo. She felt very distant. She enquired about the course, my health, if the food was good, if the tent was comfortable. All the right questions, but something was missing.

Maybe she was busy or preoccupied with something. But if that be the case, I would expect her to tell me, because that's how straightforward she is. I couldn't get a pulse of things today. I should have just asked her directly. Instead, I acted cool and asked her to have fun.

12 pm: I'm quite restless after the tepid conversation with Mo.

Plus the house feels empty and morose without her. With her nonstop silliness and laughter, Mo used to add so much life to it.

2:30 pm: It's barely been a few hours, and I'm already bored. How did this girl manage to live alone for weeks at a stretch!

5 pm: I've spent the day thinking about Mo and our fight in Bhuj. In anger, both of us said hurtful things. I can still feel the sting of her words, 'You choose to be compliant because it's convenient. It's easier to silence me than to wake the system up.'

6 pm: Did she call me spineless? Why would she do that, she knows how the system works!

7 pm: Let me call Mo again.

7:30 pm: Coming to Namkum was futile...Mo's not home...out for dinner with friends.

10:30 pm: Would she be back home?

11 pm: I'm annoyed with Mo. She's having a gala time with friends, while I'm languishing alone.

11:30 pm: Wonder how Mo survived that Mess room when I was busy with Ghaatak. It was dreadful, but I didn't encourage her complaints because I wanted her to learn the army way of life. We are taught to be mentally strong and I was trying the same with her.

12 am: Wish Mo was with me right now. I want to touch her…hold her…kiss her…make love to her. I'm on fire thinking about her soft, smooth skin and how her body feels against mine.

12:30 am: It's best to go back to the camp and get busy. No point staying home and playing mind games.

6:30 am: I'm glad I started early. Found a 3 ton taking supplies to the training location. Is there a bigger stress buster than driving this monster!

Mohana

Poor Sumi! That day, she got late buying a gift for Neil. While running down the stairs, she slipped and fell, broke an ankle and lay in bed with her leg in a cast. I filled her in on the visit to Neil's place. "I hope you're not falling in love with Neil!" Sumi jolted me out of the blue. Chika was already in the 'See, I warned you' mode, making it difficult to focus on Sumi.

"*Arrey*! You're just going on and on about him, so I thought of checking," she grinned.

I recovered, "Grow up, Sumi. We are not in school anymore."

"Agreed, but we are still human. And it's natural to get attracted… Neil definitely seems smitten by you. I thought I'll check your side too."

I sat frozen, Sumi reached out for my hand and apologized, "Sorry, Mo, if you felt bad, I was just joking *yaar*."

I forced myself to say, "Your jokes suck as always! Should I get some books on improving sense of humour?" We rolled our eyes and hugged.

I left with a pounding heart and a chaotic mind. Sumi had innocuously voiced my own fear. Was I falling in love with Neil?

I had been thinking about him an awful lot.

I truly enjoyed spending time with him.

I loved the attention I got from him.

I loved to hear about his work.

The instant connect that I had felt when we met at Sumi's office had now grown into a deep bond of understanding.

I had shared my deepest insecurities because I could be myself with him, since he wouldn't judge.

Did all this amount to a crush? Infatuation? Love?

I didn't want an answer. I didn't want a lecture on moral science from Chika. And most of all, I didn't want to feel guilty about Suraj, who in any case had been too busy to call. We had barely spoken a few times in all these months. Agreed, I was not home when he had called last week, but he could have tried again.

Still riled because of my unresolved issues with him, I decided to listen to Mika and enjoy my last few weeks in civilization.

Neil had received an official announcement of his promotion that morning. And he wanted to celebrate. This time, the venue was a garden restaurant away from the city.

When I was getting ready for the evening, Maa casually asked about the plan. She didn't seem happy to hear Neil's name every now and then. But she was the last person to interfere in anybody's matters. Ignoring her frown, I went back to doing my hair. An outdoor setting demanded that I secured it well. So leaving aside the ones framing my face, I picked the rest of my hair and put it up in a loose bun on top of my head. Loved the chic, messy look just as much as the freedom to dress my way, without a care.

Mika whispered, 'You dress up hot. Ok?' I pulled out a flattering black dress that I'd bought in college. Fitting in without trouble made me pat my back! Not usually the type to indulge in make-up, that day I felt a strong desire to doll up. Alas! I didn't have too many products in my kit, but I decided to use whatever I had—a peach lipstick, eye liner, a hint of blush, and some mascara. Boy! The girl in the mirror certainly wasn't Mrs. Mohana Shastri.

Feeling like a Christmas tree, I mustered all my strength to walk out of the house, reminding Maa that I would be late getting back home.

As I walked into the beautiful garden setting, I felt several eyes on me. Neil looked up from a corner table, our eyes met and his expression changed. He stood up to welcome me, watched me walk up to him and gave me a gentle hug. He seemed to have lost his voice, his eyes spoke loudly though. We sat down, hoping for the awkwardness to melt away soon. "Whoa, Mohana! You should have warned me. I get disoriented by too much prettiness," he finally found his voice.

"Stop it, Neil. I am neither used to so much attention nor all this dressing up. I went a bit overboard *na*?"

"Oh, come on now! You're perfectly dressed for a beautiful evening. Just give my eyes some time to adjust to this ravishing you!"

I wore an awkward smile, while Chika cursed me for the mascara.

Neil's new role was the obvious icebreaker. I just had to broach the topic and he started talking about how he was both excited and nervous about handling such a huge responsibility. His authenticity was something I admired immensely.

Just then, a big group walked in and some of the men waved at Neil. "That's a very big client of ours. The entire team seems to be out for dinner. Mo, if you don't mind, I'll say a quick hi to them."

Neil walked casually towards the group while I wondered—did he just call me 'Mo'? Only my closest friends did that. It felt special, as if Mo was an official declaration of closeness. I observed Neil—how he shook hands and cracked jokes with his clients. Such an easy charmer, and what a great life lay ahead of him. At such a young age, he was already a regional head. In a few years, he would be back in Mumbai handling a national portfolio. Being in media, he would have such a glamorous life—meet new people, visit exciting events, travel to different countries. The works!

Mika took the driving seat, "Had you not rushed into marrying Suraj, perhaps you could be a part of this happening life; and have an exciting career too." Chika was belligerent, "You are a much married woman, Mohana... married to your best buddy and yet you are helplessly falling for Neil!" My head was in a spin. Mika bounced back, "What about Neil? Is he just fond of you or is there more? Shouldn't you find out?" Chika was tired, "All right.

Go ahead. Make a fool of yourself. What if he doesn't think of you as special? What if he is spending time with you just because he doesn't have friends? Hasn't he mentioned this you?"

The riot of emotions must've shown on my face. For Neil sensed it at once. "Are you ok, Mo?"

I needed all my strength to not let him read my mind. "Yeah, yeah. I'm perfectly fine. Was just getting bored sitting alone," I made an excuse.

"So sorry to keep you waiting… Couldn't avoid them."

Neil did most of the talking that evening. Thankfully, in his excitement, he didn't notice that I was busy fighting a battle in my head.

The hotel was by far the most luxurious I'd ever been to. We were in a spacious room bathed in the soft, yellow light of a bed side lamp. The glow was just enough for us to trace each other's silhouettes as we stood facing each other. Without warning, he pulled me in. I was a bit startled but quickly settled in a sweet embrace, enjoying the musical notes of his heartbeat. This truly felt like the best place in the world; because he had to literally tear himself away to study my face.

"Have you grown prettier or have I not given you a good look before?" Being clumsy with compliments, and too unsettled to meet his eyes, I wanted to go back to the embrace. Only if he would allow that!

He pinned me a few inches from his face, "Hey, look into my eyes. They're more engaging than my throat!" Who cracks such silly jokes during intimate moments? I wish I were stronger; I wanted to hold his gaze and play hard to get. Instead, I became a molten mass. 'Be a tease, be a tease…oh please be a tease', a weak voice whispered in my head but shame on me! I was unable to even open my eyes. Oh God! I needed to be touched so badly.

He sensed my need, but instead of ending the torture, he did what I had wanted to do all along—become a tease. So he just held my face in both his hands, and witnessed my misery. When he traced my lips with his thumb, I couldn't muffle a soft moan. Gosh! He was driving me crazy. By now, my lips were literally pleading to be kissed and my hands were caressing his firm back. Tiny tremors of need were moving from my body onto his.

Finally, ending my suffering, he closed in and when his lips met mine, all other senses ceased to exist. Oh! How much I had waited for this moment. Tender kisses soon turned urgent and demanding. I was already hot with passion, and when his hands started to express themselves, I went wild. "I need you so badly…" I whispered between uneven breaths.

"Really? I thought your interest has shifted," his tone suddenly became bitter. I jerked open my eyes to look at him, Oh no! That was Suraj! He knew about Neil. Crap!

At that very moment, my alarm went off, yanking me out of the most sensual dream ever! I sat up with a jolt, feeling hollow. Suraj! Oh God, he seemed more rugged and desirable than ever. I felt such a strong pang for him that I curled up in a foetal position and started sobbing. Tears of longing, love, guilt and shame…all came crashing…like a roof had given way!

What had I been thinking? How could I get attracted to Neil when I was so much in love with Suraj?

Is it possible to love two people at the same time?

19

Breakthrough

Indore, 25th of July 1998

I reached the kitchen to find Maa making tea. I knew she had an inkling about things with Neil. Given her magical sensing power, would she know that I was completely unsettled because of a sensual dream?

"Here, have your tea, Moni. You don't seem to have slept well." She gave me a questioning look.

"No, Maa, in fact I overslept." I muttered, hiding behind the newspaper. Without a word, she sat opposite, sipping her tea. "Any plans for today?" she asked after a while.

"Umm, no…" I continued to avoid eye contact.

"Moni, do you mind applying some oil in my hair?"

Ah! This was her master plan to trap me. Maa knew I would never refuse her. "Come, let's go to our usual spot," she patted my shoulder. So we both went to her room and she settled on the carpet while I sat on her bed. When Maa rested her back on my legs, I felt cornered for questions about Neil.

Instead, she said, "Avanti is here."

Avanti was my cousin settled in the US. She was a child counsellor, pursuing a doctorate in child psychology. "For good," Maa added.

"What do you mean?" I was perplexed.

"Even I don't know much, Moni. She said something about her husband not being well and hence they decided to come back. We will find out."

While applying oil, I noticed more greys than I'd seen the last time and the thought of Maa growing old saddened my heart. "You stay home, Moni. Avanti will be here after lunch."

I agreed and gave a big sigh of relief since the topic of Neil didn't even come up. I had been unnecessarily worried.

Guilty conscience!

"Maasima, I'm so glad to see you!" Avanti hugged Maa. Both of them were close—something that made me jealous as a kid. Maa's elder sister, that is Avanti's mother struggled with numerous health problems and was frequently in and out of hospitals. Maa, the kind and affectionate soul that she is, not just tended to her ailing sister, but also cared for Avanti. So in our growing up years, Avanti would often be at our place, with Paa managing her pick-ups and drops without a complaint. In that positive and loving environment, my sense of jealousy couldn't thrive and I learnt to accept Avanti as our own.

Avanti came straight to the point, "I know you are eager for details. I didn't share earlier because things were not clear." Maa's back immediately stiffened, so did mine. "The news is not good, Maasima. Prakhar has been diagnosed with something known as Muscular Dystrophy, a rare disease where muscles become weak and progressively degenerate," Avanti spoke in a matter-of-fact tone. Maa and I held our breaths. "It started a few months back when Prakhar had difficulty getting off the bed. After running a battery of tests and taking multiple opinions, the diagnosis was confirmed."

An eerie silence enveloped us. Even Maa seemed too shocked to say anything. Eventually she asked, "How is Prakhar coping?"

Avanti kept staring at the floor, "As of now, it's not too bad: some trouble breathing and a little stiffening of muscles. We're hopeful that the medication and exercises will arrest or at least slow down the damage. But the disease is progressive and..." I sensed a slight quiver in Avanti's voice. Suddenly, she burst into tears and Maa instinctively gathered her in her arms while I looked away, blinking back the stinging moisture in my eyes.

"Maasima, I am so scared," Avanti muttered between sobs. "The last few weeks were horrible. Prakhar couldn't take this well. He started directing his anger at me—yelling, blaming me for ignoring him. Not knowing how to handle the situation, we decided to move back. Here, he has a big support system—parents, brothers, childhood buddies."

Maa was in deep thought, "Fear often triggers the most unusual behaviour. Prakhar's entire world has turned upside down; the anger spells must be a panic reaction." Avanti nodded and put her head on Maa's shoulders. They looked adorable: two beautiful souls wrapped in empathy and love.

"What about your doctorate?" Maa suddenly remembered. Avanti straightened up and wiped her face. "I don't think I'll be able to pursue it. Prakhar needs all my attention right now." Then almost as an afterthought, she added, "But there is a selfish voice that instigates me to not give up on my dreams."

Crap! Chika Mika in Avanti's head too!

"After working so hard to build a career, it's tough to give up everything. But if this is where life has brought me, I need to rethink my dreams."

Maa patted her knee, "Sure, but be kind to yourself too; it's not been easy on you either."

"Thanks, Maasima. Your words always work like a balm. Once we settle in, I'll start exploring work opportunities here."

Maa smiled, "Who knows, all the medical help, yoga, and family support might result in a miracle. Life can always spring surprises. We need to give it a chance and do our best."

Avanti's face lit up at once. Such a powerful thing—hope!

After Avanti left, I tried correlating my own story with hers. Compared to her, my challenges were insignificant. And yet I was thinking of an escape route—Neil. The thought made me feel small. And vile! Then I remembered Maa's advice to Avanti—*show some kindness to yourself*. So, instead of beating myself up, I decided to understand what was going on. What was it with Neil? Did I really love him? Were Suraj and I drifting away JUST because of him? There was no denying the fact that I was attracted to Neil. But more than Neil, I was attracted to the idea of a life with him. He was a great guy, and we did connect beautifully. But hey, wasn't the prospect of a comfortable life where I could have things my way the biggest draw?

With Suraj, things were different—I didn't need to evaluate my feelings. The dream and its impact on me had ruled out any doubt whatsoever of my love for him. Then what was pushing me away from him? Diving into the complex web of thoughts and emotions, I came out with one finding—despite going against my grain to create a happy, loving world, Suraj didn't seem to appreciate my effort.

'But this grouse is baseless, Mo. In your quest to be strong and resilient, you kept your battles to yourself. How on earth is Suraj supposed to appreciate you or support you if he doesn't know the effort you've put in?' Chika observed.

This was true. Barring the outburst at Bhuj, when had I let myself out?

Mika, however, wouldn't have any of it, 'Oh please! Just look at the way he's treated Mo after marriage—expecting her to think, feel, and behave just like him. Doesn't he get the simple logic that he's he and she's she! He is the one who wanted to join the forces...he is the one who underwent a training to get into their mould. With neither of these being true for Mo, how can she operate just like him?' Chika kept quiet. 'Also your point about Suraj not knowing Mo's feelings is moot. What happened in the Debashish episode? Even after Mo shared her feelings, did Suraj stand by her? Isn't she allowed to have a different point of view? Why should she always indulge him when it's NEVER the other way around!'

'Come on now, who are you kidding here?' Chika erupted in Suraj's defence. 'As a matter of fact, Suraj has ALWAYS indulged Mohana. He may not be vocal about his emotions like Bollywood heroes...but aren't actions louder than words?' Mika remained unimpressed, so Chika built her case, 'Remember the corn incident?'

Without having to think hard, the memory flashed like it happened yesterday.

That evening, we had invited the CO and his family for the first time. Anxious about hosting a formal, elaborate dinner and unsure of my cooking, I was an edgy bull! Suraj, my unsuspecting victim, walked into the kitchen and volunteered help. The intent was great but where were the skills to execute any task? I would rather he left me alone.

But no, he insisted on helping and so finally, I asked him to take out the boiled corn on the cob from the pressure cooker and remove the kernels, while I got busy with something else.

Half an hour later, Suraj deposited a bowl full of perfectly peeled corn. I thanked him and was about to resume my chopping when I saw his thumb...a swollen, shiny, red blob...ready to burst. He tried to hide it in vain. On much insistence, he revealed that the corn was boiling hot and he had used his thumb to peel it. When asked why he hadn't waited for the corn to cool down, he had calmly replied, "I thought you needed it urgently. You were already so stressed, Mo, I didn't want to trouble you more." My heart had melted then, just as it was melting now.

This was my Suraj—innocent like a five year old...stupid in fact!

And here I was, holding a grudge against him... forgetting all his small acts of love.

The situation was rather interesting: Chika had a point; Mika had a point too.

If they refused to see eye to eye, how on earth was I going to make Suraj understand my perspective? Before anything else, the fight between Chika and Mika had to be resolved.

Chika was invited to give examples of Suraj's love for me. She produced a laundry list. Small things like roasting rotis while I rolled them out, sneaking an extra *laddoo* in my plate during a religious ceremony, encouraging me to buy stuff when he hardly ever spent on himself, making my favourite ginger tea, using the small mirror in the bathroom every time I captured the dressing table, never complaining about my cooking even after a disastrous experiment, riding his bike slow because of my fear of speed...the list could go on and on.

Mika had no choice but to give in. "Ok, ok. I agree that Suraj cares for Mo very deeply. But that doesn't make him perfect. He could still have issues that cannot be ignored. Right?"

Mika's list had only big ticket items, a few of which had already been discussed—Suraj's passivity in the AWWA, missing fan, and Debashish episodes, where he overlooked the flaws in the system, and expected me to comply. This wasn't all. Mika then shared some new and startling observations: 'Why didn't Suraj explain my predicament at the school to Brig. Pratap and choose to go alone? Instead, he silently observed me take the painful decision of quitting. Agreed, there were other courses lined up and sooner or later, I'd have to quit. But why did he allow it to be sooner than later? In Lakhpat, he didn't seem bothered by the fact that I would spend the entire day in that furnace! I was trying to be Mother India, but shouldn't he have taken a more empathetic stand?'

Chika considered the argument. 'These are valid questions. I always thought you instigated Mo to be selfish. But this is standing up for oneself, I get you.'

For the first time, Chika was being respectful towards Mika. Lapping up the opportunity, Mika added, 'Mo's effort of adjusting to a new life must be recognized. Also, it's important to know why Suraj is so docile!'

Chika agreed and the meet ended with a resolution—dialogue with Suraj. But unlike Bhuj, I needed to play my cards carefully.

Suraj

Mo's peppy voice brought instant relief, my girl was herself again! She said she had been doing a lot of thinking and apologized for the nasty things she had said in anger. True to her nature, she got emotional remembering a lot of things I did for her. Calling them 'small acts of love', Mo said she was lucky to have me.

Just when I thought things were rosy, she pulled out a surprise.

Mohana

Discussing touchy topics is never easy. Suraj was stunned when I told him that I wanted to share some of my observations, laying out Mika's arguments.

"Where are you going with this?" suddenly his voice was tense.

"I am not getting anywhere, Suraj. I just want you to help me understand your behaviour," I tried to infuse some calm.

"What is there to understand?"

"Listen, Suraj, instead of making my own assumptions, I want to understand your point of view. Why did you silently concede to Brig. Pratap's wish? Why did you not lodge a complaint against the shoddy guest room at Lakhpat? Why did you not give a push back to Capt. Debashish on the Mess facilities? To all these questions, I can simply assume that you don't care about me. But I don't want to jump to any stupid conclusion, Suraj. I know you love me, care for me. Then what explains your passivity and inaction?"

"Again you're calling me spineless."

"What do you mean 'again'? I never called you spineless and I'm still not calling you any names. All I'm asking for is a conversation about your behaviour."

Suraj was livid, "Wow! Mohana madam demands an official explanation for Lt. Suraj Shastri's questionable behaviour—heartless, spineless, ruthless and God knows what else. I have no explanation to offer. You are free to think whatever."

BANG!

He slammed the phone.

There was no hope of Suraj calling back. His way of dealing with the hurt would be sulking.

Sulkpot!

Suraj

Mo didn't intend to hurt me, I know that. But her questions were so pointed and offensive. I banged the phone because I just didn't know how to deal with her!

Not wanting to spend the evening by myself, I planned a catch up with Bagga sir at the Officers' Mess. We'd not got drunk in a long time. He was stuck with the CO so I had little option but to enjoy my own company till he arrived. Solitude and beer got me thinking. Honesty was one of the qualities I appreciated the most in Mo. Then instead of appreciating the fact that she had been honest and open about her feelings, why was I so upset? Each of her argument was spot on. What was the explanation for my behaviour? Why didn't I stand by her?

I couldn't decode my own actions.

By the time Bagga sir walked in, I was high and deeply pensive. I am intensely private and normally don't discuss my issues with others. But that day, I let the guard down. Over the next few hours, we discussed a lot about our lives—our backgrounds, our upbringing and how it still impacts the way we operate.

When I hit the bed that night, I felt I'd solved the puzzle.

Mohana

I was beginning to question the whole idea of an 'open conversation with Suraj'! He had not called in a week and I didn't know whether to reach out to him through Shaheen or allow more time and space.

My ticket was booked for the next week but with the tumult between us, I had mixed feelings.

That's when it arrived. A lemon yellow postal envelope with my name scribbled in Suraj's illegible scrawl. Oh goodness, it flashed a memory of hundreds of his letters, safely tucked away in a suitcase. Just like old times, I rushed to the privacy of my room to immerse myself in his words. And boy! Wasn't I bowled over?

Mo, my dearest!

Why are you so lovable?

Why are you so beautiful?

Why are you so far away?

And why are you so damn right?

You have this irritating habit of breaking into a bhangra after winning small arguments, some of which are not even worthy of a celebration. I am no different. Though I don't break into a jig, I do love to prove you wrong.

But not this time, yaara. Today I am happy about the fact that I was wrong...and you were right. Last night, Bagga sir and

I caught up over drinks. I think it was the combined effect of your words, booze, and Bagga sir's wisdom that helped me crack the code. I'll explain everything in detail when you're back. For now, you'll have to make do with this short explanation:

Much as I was enraged with your questions, I could neither deny nor answer any of them. Last night, when Bagga sir mentioned something about family values and how they define us, I had a Eureka moment!

You've heard about my grandfather and the terror he created while he was alive. All my childhood, I saw mom and dad, helpless in his dominating presence. 'Complying' was the only way to avoid his wrath, and we kids were encouraged to do the same. In my growing up years, not once did I disobey or challenge him (even though we disagreed on a lot of things) and guess what? My parents always appreciated this...my ability to acquiesce!

Grandpa has been gone for more than a decade; but last night, I realized that he continues to live in my head...and have a strong hold on my psyche. It shows in the way I associate with authority figures: I don't ever question them or disagree; I just comply. And since the army culture also values this attitude of aligning with superiors, this was never a problem.

Until a small goat locked horns with me! You got me thinking if I should have behaved differently. In fact, I asked Bagga sir what he would have done in the 'missing fan' episode. He said he wouldn't have tolerated such inefficiencies. Exactly what you had said, Mo!

Have been thinking about this...the grooves in my soul, my being...I am sure they run deep. Can I fix this? Well, I can try. I'm no longer a powerless five year old, conditioned to taking the path of least resistance. As an officer of the Indian Army, while I have to adhere to the command of my seniors, I do have a standing of my own.

Love the sound of those words...feels like a breakthrough, worthy of a bhangra!

You are such a free bird, Mo. I can understand how tough it must be for you to adapt to this new life. You've tried hard and I respect you for that.

Life in the army will be the same. But I promise you, Mo, life with me will be different. I invite you to come and experience it for yourself.

How long do I need to wait? I'm so hungry for you!

Suraj

I was overwhelmed!

Suraj had not only figured out such a deep rooted issue, but also promised to work on it. What wisdom and what an amazing spirit to grow!

Just for fun, I sent him a response:

Dodo! When you can write so beautifully, what happens in person? Anyway, I've figured the best way to communicate with you—we are installing letter boxes in all the rooms!

The last few days at Indore were reserved for my parents. I just didn't feel like leaving the nest and spent my time doing small chores around the house.

Maa knew that I knew what she knew...about Neil. An epitome of sensitivity, she never broached the topic. One evening, while enjoying tea with her, I thought of putting her doubts to rest...just in case she was still troubled. "You know, Maa, this vacation has taught me an important lesson—marriage is about choosing the right person and then creating the best possible life with them. You can't imagine a picture-perfect life and then fit in someone who can help you create it."

Maa smiled. I eased—knowing how much this meant to me.

I boarded the train, tingling with the excitement of going back to Suraj. At the same time, it was not easy to leave behind a world I loved so fiercely.

After that beautiful evening in the garden restaurant, Neil and I hadn't met. He had to go to Mumbai and even I had woken up to reality. We did have a good chat on the phone where I thanked him for his support during the 'lost and confused' phase of my life. I didn't want to offer details unless asked. But Neil, the thorough gentleman, didn't probe. Wishing me well, he said, "Everything happens for a reason, Mo. You got clarity about your personal life; and I was able to take some important career decisions. This is not the end of the road. We're friends and we will stay in touch."

I was ecstatic when he came to see me off at the station, along with a limping Sumi. Just like the others, he too hugged me and when our eyes met, there was no awkwardness. Neil had not shared his feelings, and now I would never know.

But I knew that the sparkle in his eyes was intact. Just as his desire to live a full and happy life.

20

TURNING OVER A NEW LEAF

Khojatoli, 7th of August 1998

After two months of outdoor life, Suraj looked even more desirable! But the long train journey had left me desperate for a shower. I rushed in for a quick wash but the man kept knocking on the door asking me to either come out or let him in. "I have missed you like mad, Mo, can't stay away any longer!" I felt just the same.

All was good in our small world.

Suraj had picked up his rank and was now a Captain in the Indian Army. Ahem! Remembering the tadpole joke, I felt my tail shrinking!

Unit life resumed with a visit to *Gurudwara Sahab* from where, we scooted off to Ranchi for an early lunch and movie. With so much to share, I wanted to give the movie a miss. "No way, guys are raving about this new girl Aishwarya Rai. I've got to watch her today." I felt cheated! He was keen on some Bollywood babe instead of time with his wife, who'd been away for months. Chika scoffed, 'After your escapades with Neil, who should be feeling cheated?' I considered telling Suraj about Neil, but what would we achieve out of it? So I brushed the idea aside, at least for then.

Over dinner, Suraj's eyes sparkled with mischief, "A new officer is joining the unit tomorrow. He has been assigned to me. Let's have some fun, Mo." I got it immediately—payback time! And we hatched a plan to fool Second Lieutenant Rajan Vaidya.

Determined to play my part to perfection, I wore a plain salwar kameez, a low bun and the sternest expression. As planned, Suraj brought the unsuspecting victim to the Officers' Mess to meet me. "Good afternoon, ma'am," Suraj clicked his heels, gave a salute and introduced me, "This is Dr. Mohana...our resident doctor, who does an exceptional job of keeping us in shape. You'll need her fitness certificate before starting induction."

The youngster did the same salute routine and announced, "Second Lieutenant Rajan Vaidya reporting on duty, ma'am." About 5 ft 5" and barely 50 kgs, his uniform was his only proof of being an army officer. What a baby, my heart melted!

Driven to perform no less than Meryl Streep, I thundered, "Good afternoon, Lieutenant Vaidya. What is wrong with you?"

"Nothing, ma'am, why do you ask?" the kiddo glanced at Suraj, who refused to partake in the conversation.

"Have you seen yourself in the mirror? You look like a refugee from some drought hit place," I said with a straight face.

Rajan broke into a shy smile and muttered, "I've always been lean, ma'am."

"Lean? I call it malnourished! How did you get through the Academy? Were you not underweight?"

"I have heavy bones, ma'am. And I am stronger than my physique suggests."

"So, do we get into arm wrestling to check your strength?" He looked helplessly at us, not knowing how to handle my unreasonable aggression. I continued my attack, "Even without examining, I can tell that you do not qualify this unit's fitness requirements. How will you win the respect of the troops with this scrawny physique?"

Clearing his throat, baby face tried to explain, "Ma'am, I am not underweight. The Academy is so rigorous, we all lose weight there. I will be much better in a few months."

"Then let your medicals wait. Captain Shastri, what is your opinion?"

"Well ma'am, Lieutenant Vaidya might be a bit underweight, as you say, but his fitness is not to be questioned. In fact, he was the best cross-country runner from his batch."

Rajan looked at Suraj with lovelorn eyes and a thankful smile. "Hmm ok. Only if you insist, Capt. Shastri. All right then, Lieutenant Vaidya, let's start the examination. Please strip." Rajan's smile changed into shock and his eyes jerked open.

"Here, ma'am? In the library?"

"Then where? You want to strip in the Mess hall?" The hapless soul took off his cap, shirt and was undoing his belt when Suraj stopped him—unable to put up with any more nonsense.

A rainbow of emotions ran through Rajan's face when he came to know about my identity. He looked so adorable, I couldn't stop myself from hugging him. He reminded me of my younger brother in many ways. Goofball!

Over lunch, I told Rajan, "Hey listen! Sorry for being so vicious. I got a bit carried away. But I'll make up for this, ok? I'll treat you to the best homecooked meal ever."

"Sure, ma'am, that indeed will be the best gift. My mom is an awesome cook and I really miss her food."

"So come home today itself. We will have dinner together," I said, affectionately.

"Sorry, Mo, this will have to wait. Rajan will move to the company barracks to stay with the troops for some time."

"I see. How long?" I was curious.

"Well, maybe a few months. Asif sir will decide."

Later, when I asked Suraj about this, he explained that this is a standard practice of inducting officers in the unit. "Troops are the biggest part of any unit, with just a handful of officers leading hundreds of them. Very often, officers are higher in rank but younger in age. Take Rajan for instance. You've been calling him a baby yourself. How will he command the respect of his troops?"

"The rank on his shoulder will help him," I replied.

Suraj shook his head in disagreement, "Well, respect comes after acceptance. To get the men to accept us, all officers spend their initial months in the barracks—interact with them, understand their life here, talk about their life back home, have a drink in the evening, eat the same food, use the same toilets, have a similar routine as them. This breaks the ice and we form a bond for a lifetime."

Such unique practices!

It was a pleasant surprise to see Rajan at a Mess party. Despite being the junior most officer of the unit, he seemed relaxed enough to joke around with the senior lot. His self assurance spoke a lot about him.

Just then, I saw him walk towards me with a naughty smile, "Good evening, ma'am! How are you? Am I looking any better?"

"A tad better!" I grinned.

When Capt. Bagga heard us recounting the incident, he was visibly disappointed, "Ma'am, you must understand that I have landed here because of my father. I was born to act and will definitely go to Bollywood after retirement. Till then, this powerhouse of talent must be nurtured!"

He took a bow; we rolled our eyes!

Shaheen would constantly pamper me with her signature sweets which were par excellence. Major Asif often called her Colonel Halwai Singh and would joke about setting up a business after retirement. "I will procure the material, Colonel *saab* will make the sweets and Mohana ma'am will manage the marketing...perfect business plan."

"Mo would singlehandedly consume whatever is unsold...which is a good incentive to not sell!" Suraj would add, leaving us in splits.

Thanks to my sweet tooth, exercise became compulsory. The same cantonment that once petrified me, was familiar territory now. I would go for long walks in the morning and would sometimes see the school bus en route. Kids and I would excitedly wave at each other and my heart would flutter at the thought of joining back.

Not everything was hunky dory though!

Hierarchy among the women had always left me disillusioned. One day, NSR paid me a surprise visit, "I wanted to share something I've noticed, Mohana." Her words sucked the life force out of me. Limp, I listened, "After discussing so much about protocol, it's sad that I've to bring it up again. Maj. Asif is way too senior to Suraj for you to treat Shaheen as your buddy. Both of you are close, I know, but when you are with others, you must honour the protocol. In a Mess party or in ladies' meet, especially in front of the brigade ladies, it's better to address her as Mrs. Siddiqui. You must have observed that even I don't address the first lady by her name, even though we are good friends. This is the army tradition, of respecting seniority."

I couldn't respond to NSR at all. What she was suggesting was downright coercive!

Instead, I ran to Shaheen at the first opportunity. "Whether I call you Shaheen or Mrs. Siddiqui is between us, right? How can someone else meddle in our affairs?"

She pressed both my cheeks between her palms and said, "Here is one active volcano, always ready to erupt! Come let's douse you with some cold coffee."

Shaheen had this brilliant ability to diffuse tension, but this time, the anger brewing inside me was not to be put out with cold coffee. "So should I become a puppet and start dancing to different tunes?" I asked, bitterly.

"I don't think anyone is wanting to make a puppet out of you, Mo. In fact, it's not even about you or me, it's about following a tradition."

In a voice quivering with emotion, I protested, "This tradition is so restrictive, Shaheen, it makes me feel small and stupid…and worthless!" I wiped a defiant tear, "There is no sense of identity for me. I've been trying so hard to fit in…but these things just throw me off balance."

Shaheen stayed silent for a while. Then in a calm voice, she asked, "Do you know the roots of this tradition?" I shrugged my shoulders. "Even I'm not sure, but this is what I've heard. In olden days, every war would take away a huge number of soldiers. Their women and children would be left behind, at the mercy of the society. To protect them, and each other, women started creating support systems for the widows and families of dead and injured soldiers. Automatically, senior women who were more experienced assumed powerful roles and thus a parallel hierarchy among the ladies started emerging. A tradition that started for a noble cause kept evolving and assuming different forms over time."

"What you shared makes sense, Shaheen. But look at us today—our context has completely changed. Shouldn't traditions change with time?"

"I believe they have. Army etiquettes used to be way more rigid earlier. But I get your point." She looked at me affectionately, "You are an amazing girl, Mo—confident and fiercely independent. People like you change the world. It's just a matter of time before you will create a different culture in this unit itself! But are you in that position today?" I just pursed my lips. "We all need to choose our battles, Mo... and choose them wisely. Think about this."

This was Shaheen, my friend and mentor, who gave such valuable life lessons over everyday coffee conversations!

Suraj's *sahaayak* got married and returned with a box of sweets. Gifting some cash, I asked him to buy his wife something of her choice. "I don't know when I'll meet her, she's in the village," he said, longingly. With a shy smile, he pulled out a photo album—the young couple looking embarrassed in every frame.

"She's so young, and so are you Maggar! Why did you get married so early?"

"It's not early, *memsaabji*. We are childhood sweethearts, married after a long wait. Any more delay and her family would have married her off elsewhere."

I asked if he missed her. His expression hardened and he stunned me with his response, "Who wouldn't? But this is the army. Here, we have to control our emotions. Married accommodation for the *jawaans* is limited and we are allowed to get our families over only for a few months. Right now, the waiting list is so long, not possible during this posting. Next will be field tenure where families are not allowed." Taking a deep breath, he added, "We can't allow ourselves to get emotional."

At 23, Maggar Singh and thousands of young soldiers like him would be forced to stay away from their new wives. What sacrifice, even on part of those girls.

And nobody seems to think much of it; *faujis* are somehow not entitled to emotions or physical needs like the rest of the world!

To keep restlessness at bay, I got busy and how! Right from cooking, gardening…to exercising, walking…to making artificial flowers and soft toys, I was doing it all. And the house paid the price! After paper flowers in every nook and corner, we now had monkeys on every curtain and Donald Ducks with colourful felt jackets inhabiting every room. These got proudly displayed because they had turned out well. The puppies weren't as lucky. God knows what was wrong with the design, my poor puppies didn't have a snout! Soon I had a battalion of flat faced puppies that looked good only from behind. They were strategically placed on the windows, giving an impression that they were peeping out.

The unit ladies had started encouraging me to 'start a family'—who will play with these toys? You should get a baby while these lovely toys are still new. When I shared this interesting thought with Suraj, he vehemently refused, "Please, Mo, have mercy on my baby! How will she ever differentiate between a dog and a rabbit after playing with this cross breed? What's it called—a Puppit?"

The man and his sick jokes!

Mulling over life since I came back, I was happy with my experimenting and learning. Earlier, I used to equate success with one's ability to earn. But now, I could sense a shift—I was asking myself what have I learnt from this experience? How has it impacted my outlook in life?

So what if I was not earning, I was learning. And growing big time!

21

JOIE DE VIVRE—THE JOY OF LIVING

Mhow, 20th of January, 1999

Finally, we were going to Mhow! After hearing fun stories about military courses, I was ready for an extended party for three months. Cherry on the cake: Mhow—an important training destination for the Indian Army, was barely an hour from my hometown Indore!

While I went to my parents' place, Suraj went straight ahead to Mhow to figure out the accommodation. When he came over the weekend to shift me and the luggage to Mhow, he had either underestimated the stuff we were carrying or overestimated the capacity of his vehicle. The man came on a bike! To top it, he wanted to borrow a couple of mattresses because the temporary accommodation allotted to us had a bare bed. When I suggested that we should engage a small loading vehicle, he almost took offence. "You're insulting my Bullet, Mo. She's one sturdy beast we can rely on. And where is the fun in routine things?"

Unbelievable as it sounds, we placed the folded mattresses on the bike and installed ourselves on top. Suraj being taller could reach the ground, whereas my legs enjoyed the freedom of dangling on both sides. A monstrous suitcase came on my lap and a backpack with kitchenware—steel vessels, plates, spoons etc. clung to Suraj's chest. My back being the only vacant room in the mansion, Maa strapped it with a bag of spare curtains, bed sheets etc. How resourceful!

When the bike started moving, my entire focus was on not slipping off the mattress. Suraj, on the other hand, was riding the bike as if he was born in a circus. Our procession moved ahead with sound effects from the jangling vessels. While 30 kms had felt invincible in the beginning, slowly I began to relax and enjoy the ride.

Mhow took my breath away. Cool, fresh breeze, lush greenery, beautiful tar roads, lovely British architecture, and smartly dressed men and women out for evening walks—sneakers, dogs, aviators et al. I had seen quite a few cantonments, but this one felt like the first world! My poor legs, bearing the weight of the heavy suitcase had gone numb but I maintained a dainty smile now that we were among our own people. Yes, I had crossed the psychological border—Soldierland was home and soldiers were family.

We crossed the magnificent gates of the Infantry School and then the MCTE (Military College of Telecommunication Engineering), both of which I later learnt, are esteemed training establishments of the Indian Army. Just then, I saw some old, battered quarters and a sense of déjà vu gripped me. When our bike turned towards them, I was mentally prepared and didn't feel my spirits sag.

I slipped off the mattress in a rather unbecoming fashion, having sat like a formaldehyde preserved frog for so long! The house looked more like a heritage site, perhaps a century old. Clasping the mattresses, I made a grand entry into our new abode—a huge living room with an interesting choice of furniture—an oversized dining table and two charpoys!

I took a tour of the house. The living room led to an open courtyard which had the washing area, toilet etc. The kitchen was on the other side such that if someone were to serve hot chapattis off the stove, they would have to sprint through the courtyard towards the dining table, lest the chapatti went cold en route.

'No cribbing!' Chika warned.

'But this is sarcasm!' Mika protested.

'Same family of emotions...not allowed.'

Reminding myself of the 'Embrace, embrace, embrace; learn, learn, learn' motto, I walked towards the kitchen. It was getting dark so I switched on the light and holy cow! There it was. The biggest rat ever...almost the size of a rabbit.

Giving out a loud scream, I ran out as if I'd seen a vampire! "There's a rat. God, it's so big. It's some animal, Suraj."

"What animal, Mo? Let's go and check." I clung to Suraj and watched the monster move around fearlessly. "I think this is a bandicoot...a rat variety living in the fields. He must've been around for some time; his confidence shows that this is his territory."

"But his territory happens to be my kitchen! What do I do?"

"Share the space. He doesn't look aggressive, won't create trouble unless threatened. I've lived with a similar character on a post." Once again, I wondered why OJT (On Job Training) was the only method to train army wives!

Suraj stepped inside the kitchen and the rat immediately made way for him. "Did you see that? He won't bother you, Mo. You'll get used to him." I reluctantly agreed and soon enough, Suraj's prediction came true—I did get used to him. He would disappear as soon as I entered the kitchen and stay away while I was there.

A thorough gentleman, just like the chivalrous men in uniform!

Life during a course was really quite hectic with the amount of studying involved—assignments, preparation, tests, and grades. Suraj seemed to be back to school! I had to figure something for myself. There were some jaw droppingly awesome libraries where I could spend my whole life. Only if I could visit them whenever I wanted…distances were huge and there was no public transport inside the cantonment, though some *fauji* buses did ply around. Suraj solved the problem the moment I mentioned it, "I'll go for my classes with somebody. You keep the bike."

"But I don't know how to ride it."

"You know how to ride a bicycle, right? So you'll figure the Bullet in no time."

That evening, I had my first biking lesson. The Bullet and I took to each other like long lost friends and remained inseparable over the next few days. The stunning roads and sparse traffic suddenly made me speed crazy. "You won't allow me to ride fast but become a *Sherni* as soon as you climb the bike!" Suraj mocked as I rode through the length and breadth of the cantonment with him as pillion.

After a few days of practice with him, I was on my own. Life had transformed phenomenally—as if I had grown wings. Never knew riding a bike could be so empowering. Thankfully, the cantonment rules ensured that I was duly hidden behind Suraj's helmet, otherwise I would make a spectacular scene riding around with crazy hair and a crazier grin!

After visiting home almost every weekend, it was time to play the host. The dilapidated house was hardly inviting, but we wanted to give Maa and Paa the unique experience of life in the services. Also, this being the first visit from family,

I really wanted to treat them special. Chika ensured that the rooms were clean and a nice spread was planned for lunch. Suraj, in the meantime, had taken Maa and Paa on a mini tour of the cantonment, leaving them suitably impressed. On reaching our place, they seemed excited and happy, hiding any disappointment at the condition of the house.

The first thing Paa wanted was *thanda paani*. That's when they got a reality check—there was no fridge! "Difficult to carry everything for three months," I explained.

"I can understand," Maa agreed. "But how do you manage without a fridge in this heat?"

"Come, I'll show you." I led them to an earthen pot draped in a wet cloth. I drew water from it and after just one sip, Paa said, "Nice! Not just cool, but also tastes better than fridge water."

"And what's in that?" Maa asked pointing towards another small pot, dressed similarly.

"That's buttermilk. Here we get a few litres of ration milk every few days. Without a fridge, it goes bad in hours. So we make buttermilk, store in this, and try to consume it before it gets spoilt. I feel like baby Krishna, having so much curd and buttermilk," Suraj blurted, ticking us.

After lunch, everyone wanted to rest. So giving the luxurious charpoys to my parents, we went to the unused extra room. It was a hot day and I had been slogging since the morning, so I immediately fell asleep on the bed sheets spread on the floor. Soon, I felt something crawling on my body, which I brushed off in my sleep. But it started crawling again, on different parts of my body. I grudgingly sat up and was aghast to see hundreds of black ants all over me and Suraj. I sprung up with a muffled scream and started brushing them off with the help of some napkins. "These black ones are harmless. Had it been the red ones, we would be dousing ourselves with buttermilk!" Suraj said dusting my hair. Searching under the bed sheet, we saw tiny cracks on the floor, through which they had descended upon us. Within minutes, they disappeared as mysteriously as they had appeared!

We all enjoyed a dormitory experience that night.

As the summer set in, the asbestos roof and the cemented floor would heat up like a furnace. The big floor fan in the living room would try hard to help; but would only end up displacing hot air. Lunchtime, which is when Suraj returned from his classes, was hell...and we still had another month of peak summer.

By now, I had picked up a thing or two about the *fauji* spirit of *joie de vivre*—celebrate and enjoy what you have. In that 'rubber hits the road' moment, we figured an ingenious way to survive the blazing heat and stay joyful.

1. Send Suraj off for classes and read a book, enjoying the morning breeze.
2. Wait for the lassiwala to deliver some chilled lassi around mid-morning. Use that energy to cook a decent lunch in the scorching kitchen.
3. Pour bucketfuls of water on the parched floor, and watch it disappear. Repeat, to ensure a moist floor for a few hours.
4. Sprinkle water on the bed.
5. Convert the floor fan into an air conditioner by draping a wet Turkish towel around it.
6. Take bath using cool water stored in a bucket. Rinse off sweat, germs, and irritability.
7. Welcome Suraj to a cool room, a dewy fresh wife, and a good lunch.

8. Relax on the moist mattress.
9. Around 5 pm, enjoy the divinity of matka kulfis, thanks to a regular vendor.
10. Go for a long walk—enjoy the cool evening breeze, highlight of the Malwa Plateau.
11. Visit the Mhow market/library or socialize.
12. Thank Lord Almighty for the small pleasures of life.

Three months were over in a jiffy, and it was time to say goodbye. An emotional me took refuge in the most peaceful place I knew—Maa's lap! She soothed my hair, "My little Moni has become quite mature."

"Why? Do I have grey hair?" I jumped.

"No, silly! Paa and I are so proud of you—how beautifully you've adjusted to this new life."

Taking a deep breath, I nuzzled into her lap.

22

Bolt from the Blue

Khojatoli, 21st of April 1999

Coming back to the unit was bitter sweet. While it was a relief to return to the comfort of our home, I missed the freedom and relaxed life of Mhow.

And just when we were settling back, came the news.

Our unit was being posted to Sopore in Kashmir. Since the unit's previous posting had also been in the valley, everyone was expecting Northeast. But the decision was quickly accepted, leaving me no option but to follow suit.

Truth be told, both Chika and Mika had lost their spark at the thought of the trouble hit valley!

MORE was in store.

"I am going to be a part of the Advance party, Mo," Suraj announced over lunch.

"What does that mean?" I asked, having never heard the term before.

"Well, when a unit gets posted out, the mobilization is done in phases, with the Advance party, moving ahead of the rest of the unit. Their job is to reach the new location and get attached to the outgoing unit." Suraj paused to check if I had understood thus far. I nodded and he continued, "So once we reach Sopore, we will work with the outgoing unit to understand the geography and local peculiarities; and finish the formalities around weapons, equipment, vehicles etc. before the main body comes in. Major Murthy will lead the Advance party. Rajan and I will be supporting him."

My heart stopped at what I heard next.

"We have to leave next week."

What a bolt from the blue! We were expecting another six months in Namkum! What was I going to do?

Seeing me distraught, Suraj assumed I was worried about the packing and assured me that a few experienced guys from his company would come and help me. Are all men as dumb or did I have a unique piece? My whole life was about to get uprooted—my home, kitchen, plants, toys, terracotta lamps…everything I had lovingly fostered was about to disappear in boxes.

And this was the easier part… What was nibbling my innards was the thought of separation! In these past two years, I had woven my life entirely around Suraj. After having lived together so intimately, having discussed and fought over big things and small, having been through the ups and downs, we had come to exist as one. All of a sudden, we were going to be thrown in two different directions. How would I survive?

Hiding my pain, I put up a brave facade. But it was just that—a facade. Every conversation, every wink, every laugh, every hug, every kiss, every touch, and every argument was a painful reminder of what I was going to miss.

We had just two days left. But I refused to shift to the Mess… wanting to cling on to the house as long as I could. The house that I had once dreaded, was tugging at my heart now. I wanted to cook another meal, have another evening tea on the *jhula*, pluck another veggie from the garden, watch some more of the grasslands and the hills beyond... greedy for every tiny experience that had felt mundane all this while.

And then, the packers landed and took charge. Chika and Mika held each other and watched with dismay, as the 'homeness' of the place was systematically destroyed. Within hours, all that was left behind was memories of our first love nest.

During my B-school days, I had made a presentation on change management. Wish I could remember something... anything that would help me manage this change better. Chika and Mika sat huddled in a corner, refusing help. I was going back to civilization, to my parents, to a new job, to a carefree life...everything that I yearned for. Why then was I so crushed...almost empty?

How can love and longing for one person overshadow everything else?

A day before leaving, everyone assembled at the Mess to send off the Advance party with best wishes. Suraj, who was going to be an acting Major in the field, was to pick up his rank—Major Suraj Shastri. But it just didn't matter. When the safety and well-being of our loved ones are under siege, everything else looks petty.

Post lunch, we had the 'Pipping' ceremony. Keeping with the army tradition, Suraj's new ranks were kept in a tall glass of liquor (mostly mixed), which he had to empty at one go, for the ranks to be put on his shoulder. Such was the impact of the drink, that Suraj started slurring right away and could barely walk straight.

As I rode the bike with a sloshed Suraj slumped against me, I felt like Jhansi ki Rani with a grossly overweight Damodar Rao on her back!

The next morning, everyone from the unit came to the train station to see us off, reminding me of NSR's favourite dialogue—"Unit is like a big family". It was heartbreaking to say goodbye to the people I was so deeply attached with. Amid the warm hugs, wishes, instructions, and endless packets of food, Shaheen and NSR kept wiping my tears, chiding me for being such a cry baby.

Namkum and its lovely people had taught me so much about life. I wish I had the voice to thank them one last time!

23

When the Going Gets Tough...

Indore, 3rd of May 1999

It had been a week since I came back to my parents' place. When I had gotten off the train at Delhi, Suraj had given me his signature tight squeeze, "Go straight to a doc for a saline drip. You might be dehydrated, after crying buckets! Some stamina you have, *yaara*!" Before a fresh batch of tears got delivered, he had climbed back into the train that would take him away from me...to Pathankot from where he would take another train to Jammu and further on.

Standing dazed at the bustling Delhi station, I had felt a pit in my tummy which seemed impossible to recover from. Thankfully, I was wrong! Chika's regular doses on resilience and positivity ensured that I was better in a week. 'You can't sit around with this forlorn face, for God's sake. You have to make up for the lost time, Mo. Get a job and put your education to good use,' she insisted.

After being out of action, I didn't know exactly where and how to start. That's when Avanti called, "Hey, Moni! Just came to know that you're back. Couldn't call earlier, Prakhar and I were attending a naturopathy camp in Kerala."

I was relieved to hear the chirpiness in her voice. "Yeah, Maa told me. How was it? And, how is Prakhar?"

"Well, the answer to both your questions is—great! The camp was specifically designed for Prakhar's condition—yoga, pranayam, therapeutic massages...the works! He feels much stronger now. They will assess his progress after six months."

"Awesome! How was it for you?" I was curious.

"Wonderful! Since those people didn't want me to hover around Prakhar, we both got some freedom from each other," she laughed. "I worked on some interesting summer camp ideas for children, which I want to discuss with you. Maybe, we can work on this together."

What a Godsend! I was excited and wanted to know more. "Give me a few days. Prakhar's father has a small property which I'm trying to convert into an office. Let me get it in shape and also firm up my thoughts."

Avanti was the no-nonsense kind, always doing something to change the world. Our educational backgrounds, personalities, attitudes...everything was so different that I was surprised she wanted to join hands with me!

A few days later, when I reached her office, she was painting one of the rooms, "Adding some colour to make this place alive. Let me order some lassi and join you in a bit," she disappeared leaving me to drench in the sweet memories of the lassi I used to have in Mhow. That was barely a month back, but felt like distant past...and Mhow, which was just an hour's drive from Indore, felt like another world! How quickly life had changed.

"Listen, Moni, I want to roll out at least one camp during this summer break. Too much to do in too little time. Would you like to help?"

"Why not, Avanti, but I don't have any formal education in this."

"You have enough experience of working with youngsters. I know you taught kids when you were a kid yourself! Plus your silly-pilly, laugh at anything personality will go well with our teenage clients. I tend to scare them off, you know," she said with a trace of a smile.

And thus, I got associated with '*Insight*'—a small firm dealing with big issues like self-esteem, body image, aspirations etc. Avanti's two-week curriculum aimed at encouraging children to open up, discuss their challenges, and get personal insights.

My job was to market the program and also conduct a few sessions. *Insight* wasn't just an opportunity to do something worthwhile, but also a getaway from my anguish for Suraj. Sopore, Suraj's location was rife with violence, and news of unrest and insurgency in the valley would curdle my blood with fear.

Staying busy was the best remedy and *Insight* was a blessing.

Avanti and I had been on whirlwind visits, creating awareness about teenage issues. We had 14 enrolments and another few would be ideal for a batch. After an event in the morning, we were waiting at a prestigious school to begin our presentation. Poor Avanti had been nursing a migraine which became worse. I asked her to go home and assured her that I would be able to handle the show. Visibly relieved, she gave me a weak smile and left.

The auditorium was filling in with students and teachers. I was gripped with a sudden bout of nervousness as I heard the co-ordinator invite me to start. I climbed the stage wearing the brightest smile. 'Even a fake smile has the power to relax you,' I'd read somewhere. And sure enough, after a slightly shaky start, I was completely in my element. Sharing some of my challenges as a kid, I asked if they had experienced anything similar. Kids opened up, and we exchanged stories, cracked silly jokes and shared our big dreams.

The session was a big success and we got 13 enrolments from it. "I knew I had partnered with a star," Avanti beamed. We now had two batches instead of one! It was time to focus on getting the camp rolling.

Suraj

Life here is precisely what is expected in a field station—stressful and uncertain. Every day is a new challenge.

We are based at Sopore, a beautiful town in the Baramulla district. At some point, it got the name of 'Apple Town' because of the flourishing apple orchards. Unfortunately, the town is marred by terrorist action now.

In the army, we always try to build trust with the locals. But given Sopore's volatile situation, Murthy sir asked me to go slow with locals, but interact aggressively with fellow *faujis*. This morning, I'd gone to the Brigade Mess to meet our fellow officers. Bumped into a course mate and heard that Shree, my buddy from the Academy, is posted in Batalik. That's awesome because I haven't met the bugger in ages! Gem of a guy—one of the most loved and respected people in the Academy.

Shree and I trained together at OTA (Officers Training Academy) and were good friends since. But we became really close during the YOs (Young Officers' Course) at Mhow. Everyone has a lot of fun doing YOs, but I had a double bonanza with Mo just an hour away!

Shree wanted to meet Mo, so we visited her B school. Over canteen chai and samosa, these two hit it off instantly!

On our way back, he said, "Sweet girl your Mo. Bastard, you better be good to her or I'll thrash you to a pulp." He always said that having a girlfriend close by is a luxury for a *fauji,* and insisted that Mo and I must spend as much time with each other as possible. For this, he did everything from lending me his bike...doing my assignments... dropping me to Mo's place and more. When I tried to thank him, he always rubbished it off saying it was just for the homecooked meal at Mo's place. The three of us hung out quite often for movies, dinners, road trips.

Once, our instructors confiscated our bikes. Coincidentally, public transporters also announced a strike the same day. It was Sunday and I told Shree that it was a pity I couldn't meet Mo. The next I knew, this rascal went and borrowed an old, dilapidated scooter from some mechanic for a few hours. After a quick grub at Mo's place, he rushed back to return it in time. We had expected the strike to be called off by late evening, which unfortunately did not happen. In the absence of public transport, I was stuck. I had to anyhow return the same night because our training drills started at 0500 hours the next morning.

With no other option, Mo drove me to Mhow in her dad's car. By the time we reached, it was 10 pm; too late for Mo to drive back on her own. Who would come to our rescue? Shree, who else! He went back to the mechanic's house, woke him up and borrowed another creaky scooter for a few hours, and our cavalcade travelled to Indore—me and Mo in the car and Shree leading the way on his scooter!

Somewhere en route, he stopped. "Chai pakodas?" So we enjoyed roadside snacks and tea at midnight, dropped Mo to her place and rode back to the barracks hoping that the scooter wouldn't break down.

That's Shree in a nutshell—a friend's friend. Heart of gold!

The last we met was two years ago, when he made a rushed visit to give us our wedding gift, and to appease Mo who was livid that he couldn't make it to the wedding.

Now that we are close by, a catch up is a must. Once the rest of the unit joins us, I'll take a few days off to go meet Shree.

Mohana

Bone tired from the launch of two simultaneous batches, we decided to take a day off.

Ready to slack the whole day, I parked myself in front of the TV. That's when I heard about it for the first time. All the channels were talking of intruders in Kashmir occupying important positions on the Indian side of the LOC (Line of Control). There was speculation about their identities as well as the response of our armed forces to this challenge. Alarm bells started ringing in my head but there was no way of calling Suraj. The arrangement between us was clear—he would call me whenever possible and as always, I would trust the 'No news is good news' mantra.

The day passed through bouts of restlessness; thankfully, in the evening, I heard that reassuring voice, "*Kaisa hai, yaara*?" When I asked him about the intruders, he downplayed the situation, "Don't be so anxious, Mo. These things keep happening. Often, it gets blown out of proportion. It's all cool here." I so wanted to believe him but the news channels had hammered a totally different picture in my head. He clarified, "Listen, I'm not really sure. But I've heard that there is some trouble in Ladakh, quite far from where I am."

"Where are you?" I asked; just to have clarity about his whereabouts.

"I'm in a lovely place, Mo. You would so love to see this: a small village surrounded by apple orchards. There are no phone lines there; so I've walked for two hours to call you, we better talk something nice."

This is the thing with Suraj—when he doesn't want to tell you something, he simply won't! I stopped my probe and started telling him about *Insight* and how much I was enjoying my work. I wanted to go on and on, he closed with a promise to call back whenever possible.

I was a cauldron of emotions: Happiness (Suraj called!), longing (oh that soothing voice), gratitude (he walked for hours just for me), anxiety (how far is Ladakh from Suraj's location), relief (he is safe), and doubt (did he tell me the truth?).

Suraj

Good to see Mo's passion for *Insight*; just hope she doesn't get too upset by the goings in the valley. I hate lying to her, but can't tell her what's going on this side.

It's been a busy week...we have been in counter insurgency operations for the last few days. Our informants led us to four militants holed up in a remote house. It took us two days just to get to the exact location, and persuade them to surrender. Finally, just when we thought everything was sorted, the rats threw a grenade. Landed just a few feet away and for a moment, I thought it was all over... the shrapnels wouldn't have left any chance of survival. We kept lying down, waiting for the grenade to explode... somehow it didn't. We immediately opened attack, taking them down. A grenade not exploding is nothing short of a miracle. Unlike Mo, I am not much of a believer. But that day when I saw that green beast roll towards us, I did say a silent prayer. Still can't believe my luck!

Mohana

Being busy was such a boon! It took my mind away from Suraj.

Situation in the valley was rapidly aggravating. To protect my sanity, I purposely avoided the TV and newspapers. If this wasn't enough, family and friends were clearly instructed not to discuss Kargil with me. *Insight* needed my full focus.

First week of the camp was over in a jiffy and the prospect of the weekend felt dreadful. Unable to resist, I switched on the news and what I saw was way beyond my darkest imagination—there was nothing but Kargil everywhere. Not only were the intruders still hiding in their secure bunkers, but their number as well as strength was much more than estimated initially. People were raising questions about their identity, many experts hinting at the mujahideens in fact being Pakistani soldiers.

In just one week, the problem seemed to have snowballed into a crisis!

Suraj

Calling Mo is not easy. So many questions: What's going on in Kargil? Who are these intruders? How did they get into our territory? How many of them? What will happen now?

Come on, I don't have the answers!

In fact, nobody has a fucking idea. Every hour, comes with an update...which makes the situation even grimmer. It seems the bastards infiltrated into our territory and occupied the posts that we vacate during the harsh and unforgiving winters. Clearly, it was a mistake to trust them blindly.

There is so much speculation. Someone was saying they number in hundreds...800 or something. That's insane! Not just well protected in bunkers, those swines also have the advantage of being at a height—can easily neutralize anyone attempting to approach them.

I just don't have a good feeling about this.

So far, our unit is still engaged in CI Ops (Counter Insurgency Operations) in Sopore, but if the situation in Ladakh worsens, we may be sent there. Even our troops want to contribute—twiddling thumbs and awaiting updates on radio sets is no fun!

Mohana

It was a big day—the final day of the summer camp!

The kids had worked hard to put up a skit showcasing teenage issues. The finale would be a panel discussion consisting a few kids, some volunteer parents, and Avanti—our expert voice. Another way of creating 'Insight'.

We had booked a banquet hall since a 100 people were expected. Avanti's grandparents were the Chief Guests and I was the anchor. Sumi and Neil, my supportive friends were coming to cheer for me, apart from Maa, Paa, and Deepu—my kid brother.

It was 1 o'clock by the time we finished the rehearsals. Famished but satisfied, we left the venue after instructing everyone to be back by 6 pm. I planned to gobble up lunch, wear a hair mask, and take a nice nap. Host duties are not easy!

When I reached home, Deepu who was visiting us for the weekend, opened the door. As I walked past him, announcing '*bhookh, bhookh*', I caught a strange look on his face...as if his jaw was hard set. I checked if he was feeling fine and noticed that he was avoiding eye contact. Just then, Maa appeared, wearing a bigger than usual smile. "Come, come, let's eat. We have been waiting for you," she said, almost grinning.

"What's wrong? You guys seem odd," I said with a frown.

"Of course, adults will feel odd, you've been living with kids for two weeks now." The jibe was characteristic of Maa, but the fake smile wasn't.

Unsure, I just said, "I'll quickly change and come. You guys start. It's already quite late." As I walked towards my room, both Chika and Mika felt that something was amiss. I had been avoiding the TV, but this suspicious behaviour made me go for it right away. The TV had been disconnected and even the remote was nowhere to be found. My suspicion grew and without changing, I went back to Maa and Deepu, who were busy laying the table. "Why is the TV in my room disconnected?" I almost shouted.

Maa was a bit taken aback but immediately recovered and said, "The maid must have done that, Moni. I'd asked her to clean your room well. Come, now let's eat." She almost pushed me in the chair but my gut feel was too strong to be ignored.

"Wait! What are you guys hiding from me? I can just sense that something is not right." More fake smiles. "See, just look at yourselves! You are acting so strange, I'm freaking out." No response. "Is Suraj ok? Did you hear something about him?" I was holding my mom's hand now. "Tell me, Maa, I'll be able to deal with it. I need to know the truth," my voice was trembling.

They exchanged glances and finally Maa said, "Something has happened…but it's not Suraj. We haven't heard anything about him." I was almost shivering with fear and even though I had bragged about my ability to deal with the truth, in reality I just wanted to run away from it. Maa held my hand and took me to the living room and switched the TV on.

And there he was! Shree or Major Alagappan Shreedharan, as the TV reporter was addressing him. Martyred that morning…Batalik sector…tremendous bravery…enemy at a height…holed up in bunkers…opened fire…injured… valour…love for the motherland…bullet on the head… salute the spirit…26 years old…loved to travel…mother, sisters…how will we retaliate…who are these intruders… loss of a young, bright officer…supreme sacrifice…nation indebted…

The words kept hitting me while I sat staring at Shree's face on the screen. In an instant, a loved friend had become a martyr, a hero and was being referred to in the past tense. There was no confusion, no false reporting, as I had hoped. All the channels were talking about him and how this loss had further escalated the Kargil conflict…or the Kargil war, with people reporting live from the 'battlefield'. What had started as a minor situation had escalated into a full-blown war…with our dear Shree being the first officer casualty.

Maa and Deepu sat with me in silence. They knew Shree so well; he would visit our place with Suraj when they were doing a course in Mhow. That's when I had made friends with a lot of Suraj's buddies. But Shree was special…such a helpful, generous soul…and so much fun…always taking the effort to stay in touch. How abruptly everything had changed. Shree was gone...never to come back!

Between grieving for Shree and fearing for Suraj, I had completely forgotten about the event. It was almost 5 pm. Forget getting ready, I had not even had my lunch. Nobody had.

'If you have learnt anything about the army spirit of staying strong in the face of adversity, now is the time to use it,' Chika prodded. Mika agreed. I washed my face and asked Maa and Deepu to come for lunch. We ate the cold food in silence and I went to my room to get ready for the evening. Never mind the hair mask or the beauty sleep, I wasn't going to make any more compromises.

Everything went like clockwork and the event was a huge success. Kids were ecstatic, parents were appreciative, Avanti was relieved, Sumi was thrilled, Neil was proud, and I was dazed.

After the guests left, Neil wanted to take everyone out for a celebratory dinner. That's when a tidal wave of despair hit me. I broke down, unable to speak. Avanti told everyone what had happened and asked them to give me time to settle down. As I sat surrounded by my dear ones, yet feeling utterly lonely, Avanti told me that Maa had informed her about this when I was getting ready.

"You know what Maasima said about you?" I looked up teary eyed.

"Never knew Moni could be so strong."

Suraj

I still can't believe it.

Shree is gone.

He fell to the bullets this morning.

I am numb.

From what I hear, he and his team were sent to sniff out the enemy locations and their strength. The terrain is horrible. Not sure if they were caught unawares, but it was a lost battle from the start. Approaching a well sheltered enemy sitting at a height…must've taken so much courage. Shree would've known his chances even before starting.

He was a buddy Goddammit! A brother I could trust blindly. How can he just cease to exist! He wanted to do so much in life…everything snubbed in a moment.

The loss is huge, but I haven't reacted at all. No tears. All I feel is anger. Anger for what happened to Shree and our men dying in Kargil. A patrol team has been captured, I hear. How dare they! We must avenge these deaths. Teach those fuckers a lesson. They cannot get away this time, shouldn't be allowed to.

Mo must be devastated. She shared such a great bond with Shree. How they loved to gang up against me like school kids! I want to comfort her, but calling her is ruled out for now. There are no STD booths here and the luxury of walking to the town is gone. We are on standby, waiting for further orders. There are specific instructions not to disclose information about our location, movement, plans etc.

Hope Mo remembers that no news is good news.

Mohana

Suraj had not called in a while. Not even after Shree's news.

Major Murthy gave a surprise call—sounding all casual, trying hard to be funny and cool. When I mentioned that

Suraj hadn't called in a long time, he said that my handsome husband was busy charming the pretty Kashmiri girls. Ridiculous! Was I in kindergarten?

Well, at least Suraj and the others from the unit were safe, wherever they were.

In order to stay sane and carry on with life, I tried hard to embrace the 'no news is good news' philosophy. Things would however go topsy-turvy, the moment the phone rang. I would abandon all pretence of being in control and run towards it with a prayer. Others in the house would do the same, just that they would wait outside the room instead of crowding around me.

Life in our household had converged around the TV. We would be hooked on to news channels hoping for a miraculous update of victory. Instead, all we saw was fireballs, smoke, and gunfire. Every evening, TV channels would air a press conference where the piling casualty figures would be announced.

To keep me going, I did everything from *Reiki*...to Positive energy...to chanting the *Mahamrityunjay Mantra*...to public prayers...to *Shree Yantra*...to *Taveez*. Anything to keep Suraj safe. And my family supported me in this madness, even though they didn't believe in most of these things.

They understood that in times like such, only the currency of hope could make me rich.

Despite positive feedback from the two batches, there was a lull at *Insight*. Avanti had decided to focus on developing some module for teachers which she wanted to run before the start of the new session. However, she would drag me for the meetings, because she believed that my people skills were precious.

I had just come back from one such meeting when the phone rang. I ran an obstacle race and made it at the third ring. Suraj—oh my God, how long had I waited to hear his voice! I wanted to sob and would have, had his voice not felt so empty and distant. He enquired about me in such a deadpan manner, that I immediately sensed that something was wrong. "What's the matter, Suraj? Are you not ok?"

There was a pause followed by a whisper. "How can I be ok, Mo? I have to take Rajan's body to his parents." Oh my dear God! This couldn't be true! "Happened this morning. Not part of Kargil, this was a separate encounter with the terrorists. This kid singlehandedly took on the attackers, can you beat it!" Suraj's voice was dripping with anger but I could feel the pain hidden deep inside. I was at a loss of words. What do you ask: what exactly happened, when it happened, why it happened? It didn't even matter anymore—Rajan, the sweet boy was no more. The skinny fellow whose fitness I had questioned had wiped out terrorists. How proud and how utterly broken was I!

"Listen, Mo, I am at the airport doing the formalities. Need to go now. I'll be flying back to Srinagar tonight itself. I will try to give you an update as soon as possible. As of now, we are on standby waiting for further orders."

My mouth went dry. My biggest fear was coming true. All along, a part of me had clung on to stories of apple orchards and Kashmiri girls. I tried to give myself some hope, "What further orders?"

Suraj snapped without warning, "Don't you know what further orders I am talking about?" He immediately apologized, "Sorry, Mo. God willing, I will be able to explain everything to you one day. Love you, need to go now."

I sat exhausted…tired of fighting my emotions, tired of acting brave, tired of being scared and tired of this hopelessness and gloom gripping me all the time. I wanted to cry…bitterly and loudly…

And I did just that.

Suraj

It helps to be numb the way I have been for some time now. I wouldn't be able to function otherwise. This loss… first Shree and now Rajan…my brother officers. We use that term for fellow officers, but these two were really like my brothers. That is the kind of love and closeness I shared with both of them.

Rajan and I had been together ever since we set out with the Advance party. Together for every meal, every briefing, every operation…including the last one. In a flash, a normal search exercise turned bloody. There was unprovoked firing from a house and Rajan standing closest took a bullet on his leg. The little fellow was made of steel! He just charged inside the house and opened fire. Took down both the fuckers; but not before they had done the damage. I'll never forget the image of Rajan dragging his blood-soaked leg inside the house.

And now he is resting inside this coffin which I have to hand over to his parents. There are heightened emotions all around. Kargil seems to have united the entire nation. I am amazed at the huge crowd at the airport…people with garlands have lined up to receive their hero. Those two weary souls must be his parents. They are making an effort to smile at me; strength of character runs in this family!

A big crowd has gathered in the narrow lane, outside Rajan's house—recognition for a brave soldier. But his parents look overwhelmed; they are grieving, not celebrating his martyrdom. Shouldn't they be given some private time with their son?

But whom do I ask? There are too many people controlling things. In fact, Rajan's parents seem sidelined. His dad tells me that the local corporator wanted a small function in Rajan's honour. The corporator, however, is nowhere to be seen and everything is on hold till his arrival.

I refuse to be a bystander and instruct the coffin to be moved into Rajan's house so that his parents and family members can spend some time with him. "Corporator sahib is on his way. We cannot make him wait," someone protests.

"Why not?" I ask a simple question. Either because of the solemn occasion or the Kargil effect, my order is followed.

For once, the OG (Olive Green) prevails over the white kurta.

Corporator sahib arrives and waits restlessly till Rajan's body is brought out. Once the body has been laid down for people to pay their respect, he grabs hold of a mic and starts ranting about how Rajan's sacrifice won't go waste. He blames the government in Delhi for Kargil and for the loss of this precious life. He announces financial help for Rajan's family and asks the crowd whom they would support—his party which stands behind the citizens or the ruling party of the country which is responsible for the 'mass murder' of army men.

Without a thought, martyrs are reduced to murder victims.

Rajan's parents sit with their heads bent, silently wiping tears. They are waiting for the drama to get over. At one point, the angry corporator refers to Rajan as Rajeev and the grieving mother raises her eyes, looks at me and shakes her head in disgust.

I'm pained to see how Rajan's death is being used for political mileage.

At that moment, I feel that my brother died for nothing. This country didn't deserve him!

It's been two days since I returned from Rajan's funeral. I'm listening to the updates on my radio set—the infiltrators have captured many strategic points on the treacherous mountains of Ladakh, Kargil, Mushko. They are armed with sophisticated weaponry—rocket launchers, HMGs (Heavy Machine Guns), missiles and even have artillery support!

I get a message from Murthy sir: the Division Headquarter has assigned us to *Operation Vijay*. Our troops need reinforcement, they have been battling the enemy, and extreme weather conditions for too long. It's time to help them. Orders are for the Advance party led by Major Murthy to start at 4 am the next day. Our target is to recapture one of the highest peaks in Kargil—Tiger Hill.

We are charged up and get busy packing. By dinnertime, our pitthus are ready, vehicles are loaded and we are all set to start. There is so much energy, that waiting till four in the morning is difficult. It's the same feeling when you wait in the green room all padded up, raring to go on the field and hit a six!

I don't want to call up anyone; but Murthy sir is insistent. "Our families have a right over us. They deserve to hear from us before we leave. With the scoundrels snugly tucked,

God knows our swim is against the tide. But we will teach them a lesson."

I call my parents. They listen in silence. My brother says, "Go for it, buddy!"

Then I call Mo. She is uncharacteristically calm. She wishes me success. She says her prayers will be with me. She asks if I've kept the picture of *Shirdi Sai Baba* in my pocket. I say yes. Any other day, I would laugh such things off. Today I don't mind, if it gives her strength and hope. I want to tell her that I love her. I also want to tell her that if I don't come back, she should find someone nice and start a new life. But I can't talk much.

Instead, I tell her about my diary in which I have written a lot of things for her. She gets the message and immediately, chokes up. Not wanting to prolong her agony, I quickly end with 'See you, *yaara*' even though I don't expect it to happen anytime soon.

Who knows, maybe never....

24

Stroke of Luck

Indore, 29th of June 1999

How punishing can helplessness be! I realized it that night. After Suraj hung up, I just didn't know what to do with myself. How can you chill in your air-conditioned room when your partner is at war? I felt guilty for the comforts around me. In the name of patriotism, all I was doing was binge watching news. Oh God, couldn't I just pop some sleeping pills and wake up only after this nightmare was over?

There was nothing to engage me.

Read? Nah.

Talk to mom? Nah.

Sumi? Nah.

Avanti? Nah.

Neil? Nah.

Shaheen/NSR/Anu? Nah, even though they had reached out to check on me.

Go for a walk? Nah. What if someone calls?

Music? Are you nuts!

Write? About what?

Writing seemed to be the only thing I was even willing to consider. Picking up a diary, I started scribbling my thoughts, then my fears and finally my dreams. I wrote about everything that I wanted to do in life and how it was going to come true. I enthusiastically visualized a beautiful and happy life with Suraj...a life of companionship, mutual respect, and lasting friendship. It felt wonderful to live in that warm bubble of imagination.

I savoured those images for a long time. How was I going to make that happen? What would be my do's and don'ts?

This required a lot of thinking and I kept working through the night. Early in the morning, when Suraj would actually be travelling towards Kargil, I went and kept the diary in the small mandir of our home. I prayed for a chance to live my dreams and honour my promises. Somehow this brought immense peace.

And hope.

It was past noon when I woke up. I had slept like a log and in a household particular about waking up early, nobody had disturbed me—small perks of having your husband at war!

I was surprised to see Deepu in the living room. "It's not even the weekend, what are you doing here?" I asked.

He got up, put his arm around me and said, "Just felt like spending some time with you. Maa has big plans for the day. Do you know?"

I was clueless. We went to the kitchen where Maa was preparing lunch. "It's almost lunchtime, Moni. Do you want tea now?" she enquired while making chapattis.

I hugged her from behind like I always did and stayed there. "No Maa, let's have lunch." I said, still cuddling her. Any other day, Maa would push me off with her shoulder because she can take this cuddling business only so much. Today was another day, and I chose to fully enjoy the fringe benefits of the Kargil war!

"By the way, what big plans is Deepu talking about?" I asked.

"We are having *Mahamrityunjay Hawan* today."

We are having what? I couldn't believe what I just heard. My parents were the last people to indulge in rituals.

"Someone said it's very powerful. People have been doing it for thousands of years to pray for the safety of their warriors. It's our turn now...nothing to lose, right?"

"Does Paa know?" I asked, cautiously.

"Of course, in fact he is the one arranging the *hawan samagri*. We will do the *pooja* and *hawan* in the evening."

I was amazed at my family. They were doing everything in their power to make me feel better. The *hawan* was performed as per instructions in the booklet. What the booklet didn't mention was the black soot that would cover everything in the room. They perhaps assumed that it would be done in the open. Never mind, for the next few hours, it kept everyone occupied with dusters and mops.

The backbreaking effort yielded two fantastic results—one, we were able to get the room back in order and two, we were so tired that everyone crashed out after dinner.

And then the phone rang.

I checked the clock: 4:45 am. Who was calling at this unearthly hour and why? My head was still groggy and muddled, but my body was already set in motion. I froze after reaching the phone and kept staring at it till Deepu came and asked if he should pick it up. I closed my eyes, took a deep breath and brought the receiver to my ears, "May I speak with Mrs. Mohana Shastri?" asked a gruff voice.

"Speaking," I whispered.

"Good morning, ma'am. I am calling from the brigade headquarters at Srinagar. I have an update on Maj. Suraj Shastri." I couldn't utter a word. "You might need to pack your bags immediately."

"Why? What happened?"

There was a pause and the gruff voice continued, "If you want to meet your husband, you will need to travel."

"Is he ok? Yes, I can travel. Should I come to Srinagar?"

"No, ma'am. You will need to go to Namkum."

What the heck was he saying? "Sorry, I don't get you. Can you please tell me clearly?" I was almost whimpering. Deepu stood next to me breathing hard.

And then I heard it…that familiar low pitched laughter. It was Suraj! How was that possible? "You are such a cry baby, Mo! Can't even prank you," he said laughing.

"Shut up! No tell me, how come you are calling?" I was hysterical! Deepu also broke into a wide grin but refused to leave my side even when I gestured him to.

"You won't believe this, *yaara*! As per instructions, we were all set to move to Ladakh. Just a few hours before we were supposed to leave, the decision was put on hold by the Div. Commander. He was not sure because the Advance party is a small number of troops with just two officers, not a complete unit. They need much stronger support. So another unit was sent instead of us. We're being sent back to Namkum. In fact, I'm calling you from Pathankot."

What an incredible turn of events! Was I imagining?

And then the wonder words, "Mo, can you come meet me at Namkum?"

"Of course, Suraj! Why would you even ask?"

"No, *yaara*, you have just started with *Insight*."

Logical thought, but I brushed it aside, "No more summer camps, so Avanti shouldn't have a problem. I just need to give her an idea of how long I'll be away."

"Listen, Mo, I can't predict anything. Not sure why we are being sent back and for how long. Could be just a few days and I might be terribly busy. So think this through. Don't ruin something you just started only for a little time with me."

While everything Suraj said appealed to my rational mind, the veto power was with the emotions. "Now you listen, Suraj. After these horrid months, I can't let anything come between us, except this irritating Deepu who is snatching the phone now."

As Deepu got into an animated conversation with Suraj, I ran towards Maa laughing like a hyena!

At such a short notice, it was impossible to get a reserved seat on any train. Air travel was prohibitively expensive for a young army man's jobless wife, who was too proud to ask for help. I begged and convinced Maa and Paa to allow me to travel in an unreserved compartment, something that none of us had experienced before.

The next evening, I made a humble appearance in the general compartment of Shipra Express, and occupied the window seat that Deepu had somehow managed to grab. He stood next to my window wearing a worried look and repeating his list of do's and don'ts. And I assured him for the hundredth time that I could take care of myself and would call home after reaching Namkum.

As the train moved, I looked at fellow passengers with whom I was going to spend the next 30 hours of my life (assuming no en route delays). The space normally occupied by four people in an AC two-tier coach, had 13 of us with a few kids sitting on the luggage rack above. Everyone was speaking at the top of their voice. I seemed to be the only one listening. The woman sitting opposite me was constantly yelling at the three kids, who were least bothered about her or anyone else who asked them to sit at one place. Like bunnies from the Duracell ad, they kept running around tirelessly. Quite aimlessly as well! The fourth kid was sleeping in the woman's lap and looked a bit unwell.

I was quite spectacular myself. Dressed in a boring biscuit brown salwar kameez, covered from top to toe, I could easily pass off as a gunny bag…which in fact was the plan. For my parents, Bihar was one of the most unsafe places in the country. After the horror stories of drivers being thrown off cars and girls getting kidnapped from trains, I couldn't blame them for the paranoia. So even though Bihar was still a day away, I had gotten in the act of blending in rather than standing out. I sat still in a corner, avoiding eye contact, hiding my face behind the cotton dupatta…only allowing my eyes to read the small book I held in my lap.

Suddenly, the woman opposite me pulled out a gunny sack, spread it right between the seats, made her naked baby stand on it and started making 'sss'…'ssss' noises. To my horror, the baby urinated right there in front of everyone and the mother carelessly pushed the wet sack under the seat. I looked around, but everyone seemed cool about what had just happened. Too jittery to protest, I forced my eyes back to the book, though my mind was in a tizzy! Only when the wet sack began to stink, did I realize what I had signed up for. Not only was I to breathe in that aromatic environment, I would also have to eat, drink, and sleep in it. In barely three hours, the stench, noise, and suffocation were getting to me. 'Hardly a price to meet Suraj,' Chika reminded, as I pulled out the parantha rolls for dinner.

I had been sitting terrified like a poodle among street mongrels...though nobody had done anything to intimidate me. Their aggression was perhaps just a way of life, but I still chose to keep to myself. By midnight, everyone was asleep, sitting in their places and I was also ready for a snooze. Just then, I realized that I needed to go! Though I had been careful about not drinking much water, the tiny sips had finally made way to my bladder. Dear me, what if there are robbers at the door? What if they use chloroform to mug people? What if there is a rapist lurking around? What if someone flicks my luggage when I'm not around? These worries kept me glued to my seat. At one point, Mika even suggested using the *susu* sack: 'Nobody would know that you've also contributed to the mess.'

Eventually, the bursting bladder made me abandon all worries and run towards the loo!

No robbers, no chloroform, and no rapists. The only assault was of the horrible toilet which would haunt me for the rest of my life!

By the next day, my body was stiff (from sitting in the same position) though the knots in my head had eased out (the guys around didn't mean harm).

Slowly but surely, I was moving towards my destination—Gomoh, a small decrepit station, a few hours from Namkum. There was a sense of familiarity about Gomoh station since Suraj and I had once spent a few hours there, waiting for some train. After evening, it had felt like the world capital of drunkards, but with Suraj by my side, I couldn't have cared less.

Things, however, were different now. The train would reach Gomoh at 1:30 in the morning, and halt for a few minutes. Instructions from Suraj were crystal clear: "You need to remember three things:

1. A few of my guys will receive you at the train itself.
2. You will not get down from the train unless you've seen them.
3. For any reason, if they are not there, let the train take you to Howrah. Someone will receive you there and bring you to Namkum."

The instructions were simple, not the situation. At 1 am, when everyone was fast asleep, I was ramrod straight, checking my watch every now and then. By 1:20, I was tiptoeing over the passengers sleeping in the aisle, my heavy suitcase in my arms. By 1:25, I was waiting at the door. By 1:30, I was looking out for Gomoh station which was nowhere in sight. Damn! The train was running late and there was no way to find out how long the wait could be. Going back to my seat meant crossing over all the people once again. So I just waited near the door and hoped that nobody was keeping an eye on me.

Finally, we reached Gomoh and my eyes started searching the platform for our *'khalsaas'*. A few men from the compartment woke up and looked at me curiously. One of them asked if I needed help, which I politely declined.

I desperately looked out again and there they were—two guys in combat uniform with the tell-tale olive green *pagdi*. They were running along the train, looking inside as frantically as I was peeping out! I waved and they rushed towards me with broad smiles.

When I heard *Sat Sri Akal, mem sahib*, I was home!

The next train took us to the Namkum station which resembled an army base. Hundreds of men in the Sikh regiment uniform were milling around. My chaperone told me that the Advance party had just come back from Sopore and were busy unloading the train. My heart fluttered!

Among the hundreds of *faujis*, I started searching for the special one who meant the world to me. All I could see was rugged *khalsaas*. Where was my chocolate boy? I scanned the crowd for a clean-shaven handsome face with a short crop. Such a specimen was nowhere to be seen.

Finally, I asked my escorts about Suraj and their mischievous smiles prompted me to look around once again. Their grins became wider and even other soldiers around us started enjoying the scene. It was obvious that Suraj was around, but where?

That's when I saw someone wave at me. His bright smile and his face seemed familiar. Oh my dear God! Was that Suraj? He had been standing just a few feet from me but I hadn't recognized him. How could I? He was dressed as one of the soldiers—black *patka* and a full-grown beard!

I narrowed my eyes and took a few moments to make sure it was him. Running into the arms of the wrong guy would be a major league *faux pas*!

Life had come full circle. We were back in the same room of the Officers' Mess, where our journey had started two years ago. So much had happened and yet, when we entered the musty room, it seemed nothing had changed!

Like a rainbow, the room was filled with different shades of needs—each as precious as the other. Need to know (what's happening—why are you guys back in Namkum?), need to relax (both of us had just come from long travel), need to freshen up, and of course the need to love—the most pressing of them all!

When Suraj held my hand, I wasn't able to meet his eyes. Few months of separation was enough to make me behave like a shy schoolgirl on her first date! Suraj thankfully wasn't plagued by any such awkwardness. Without a word, he just pulled me in his arms. Bliss! A hug can work like a balm, heal the bruises of separation in one instant. We stood savouring the moment and the soothing, reassuring warmth of our embrace.

Only when Suraj started nuzzling around my ear did I realize how rough his beard was! Even for someone who can practically live off kisses, the prospect of manoeuvring through the coarse foliage was not particularly inviting. Plus, it was tickling me and before long, I ended up giggling. "Your beard is not helping," I tried to be polite.

"How is it bothering you?" Suraj asked, defiantly.

"The texture is prickly as hay," I said.

"Sorry, ma'am, they don't distribute moisturizers and body lotions at forward posts." The war of words had started.

"Silly, you don't apply either of those on a beard. You need deep conditioning," I spoke like an expert.

"Oh yeah? When was the last time you sported a beard?"

"Well, I once dated a bearded guy." I thought my response was smart but Suraj outdid me.

"Well, then you're used to hairy smooches," he said with finality, literally sealing the argument with a kiss.

Just then, there was a knock and I was ready to bang my head on the wall. For a change, instead of whisking Suraj away from me, the Mess staff informed that the officer's briefing was at 6 pm. That meant we had the whole day to ourselves. Hurrah!

The first priority was to get rid of that beard. "You don't look like yourself, Suraj. It feels like I'm with another man," I complained.

"Oh, I thought you'll like the variety," Suraj raised an eyebrow. My guilty conscience rustled—did he know about Neil? Was he being sarcastic? "I had grown it to look like a soldier. In a hotbed of action, it's best for the officers to not get singled out. Now that you're suitably impressed with my raw appeal, let's shave it off," he twisted his moustache.

I was thrilled at the idea of helping Suraj shave, such things always have a romantic touch...well, in movies. Reality was messy and time consuming. Half way into the process, I realized that it was best to let Suraj finish the job and made a quick move to the bed. Bone tired from the journey, I was knocked off immediately.

When I woke up a few hours later, Suraj was sleeping next to me. His face had an angelic glow, now that the shrubbery was gone. The peace on his face belied the stress and violence he had seen in the last few months. I felt sorry for him and for all our soldiers who brave it out without a complaint.

Lost in thought, I didn't realize when Suraj woke up. "What are you thinking?" he asked, groggy voiced.

"Umm...nothing." Then turning towards him, I asked, "So, how do you feel?"

I was expecting words like fresh, happy or relaxed. Instead, he said, "Guilty." His eyes were glued to the ceiling, "I feel guilty, *yaara*. We were supposed to go for the Tiger Hill. And we should have. Having served there in our previous tenure, we know the area like the back of our hand. We could have helped." Taking a long breath, he continued, "But I understand the decision. Reinforcement needed was much bigger and there was no time to move the rest of our unit."

I finally asked that one question that had been bothering me, "How come the Advance party was sent back to Namkum?"

"Not sure. We'll probably hear about it in today's briefing."

He turned to face me and our eyes met…longing and love bottled up for months were ready to erupt like a volcano. There was so much to say, that we let our bodies do the talking. And they did discuss a lot!

Lovemaking may be a physical act, but it is emotions that run the show. Well, at least with me. This time, tears of gratitude ran down my face right in the thick of things. Suraj noticed. I thought he would question why my tears interfere in every department of life. Instead, he just wiped them off and kissed my moist face over and over.

He understood that I couldn't control my heart, just the way he couldn't control his head—a part of him was thinking about his buddies at the war!

25

Bliss of Togetherness

Ranchi, 3rd of July 1999

Ladies and kids from our unit had already moved out of Namkum, making the place feel strange and barren. Major Murthy met me in the Mess, "Good to see you, ma'am, you held the fort well."

I smiled, "Am here thanks to your special request to the CO."

"Any day, ma'am. The Advance party had roughed it out for a few months and a break would help. There's an Armywide freeze on *chhutti,* so families visiting us is the only option. My family is stuck with school admissions and all, but I'm glad you youngsters could meet." Such thoughtfulness and sensitivity under that tough exterior, I marvelled.

Suraj came back from the briefing with news about a mass mobilization exercise. The entire Division (more than 10,000 men) was to move to an undisclosed location over the next 8–10 days. Suraj was in-charge of the move. Since the job required a close co-ordination with the local administration, railways and the army, he was to camp at the railway station.

The next morning, we shifted to our new base, the Ranchi railway station—noisy, dusty, and bustling with people. Another first for me—living at a railway station!

After finishing some formalities, we were assigned a quarter—a waiting room converted into a makeshift home. The station master had thoughtfully got it cleaned and cleared of all unnecessary furniture except a couple of beds, a small table, and a few chairs in the living room which opened into a small area that had a shower-room, two toilets and some space for drying clothes. All good except the stench! Our drying area shared a ventilator with a public urinal. Reminded of the *susu*-sack, I wondered if I hadn't suffered enough already! "Just give it a few hours, you'll get used to it!" said Suraj, nonchalantly.

Damn his cool, no big deal attitude; once again not leaving me any chance to complain.

As expected, Suraj would be away most of the time. Often, I would see him talking to people or walking in and out of the station master's office on the opposite platform. But mostly, he would be in his makeshift office at the far end of the station. After months of being incommunicado, it was a luxury to have him somewhere around.

He would join me for meals and usually be back in the room around 8 pm. I would be alone for the most part but there was a big change in me now. Instead of cribbing about loneliness, I was thankful for every moment that we could spend together. Kargil indeed had impacted me in more ways than one.

Tired of sitting in the room, I would often step into the hustle bustle of the station. Being a train enthusiast, I enjoyed watching the movement of trains and how an incoming train always galvanized the platform into hectic activity. Equally interesting was the stillness when a train left…like the lull after an important life event.

I dreaded to think about the final day of the exercise when Suraj would board the last train and leave.

That day wasn't too far.

Our first train was getting ready. It was supposed to carry heavy vehicles and equipment, not easy to load. Rain Gods threw in an added challenge—heavy showers beating down the tin roof, creating a deafening noise.

Undeterred by the sheets of rain or the thunder and lightning, our soldiers loaded the massive equipment on the open wagons of the train. Sitting in a corner, I watched in awe as some soldiers hopped on the train while their friends bid farewell with loud calls of '*Bole Sonihal, Sat Sri Akaal!*'

After the train left, a distinct gloom descended upon a place—already covered with thick, black clouds. I felt lonely and scared, like a kid lost in the woods. I walked back to the room hoping that Suraj would not keep me waiting for long. He came almost immediately...completely drenched. "The train wasn't moving. I had to push for a *dhakka* start!" he tapped my nose and with one dazzling smile, wiped off all the darkness weighing down my soul.

Over dinner, I noticed that Suraj looked much relaxed, "The start is always tough. Now that the first train has left, I feel more confident about managing the rest. We will need about 12–15 trains altogether."

"Good job, sir! But you've got to give me some idea about where these trains are going. I refuse to accept that you have no idea about this."

Suraj ate in silence; perhaps contemplating whether/how much to share. Finally he said, "The war is becoming bigger and deadlier, *yaara*. We have lost hundreds of men. There is immense anger—how can someone just come into our territory and harm us? And will we not retaliate?"

He took a bite, "Now, what I am sharing are thoughts, not decisions. You must understand. There is a lot of action across the border near Rajasthan and Punjab. We hear that they have instructed their villages to be vacated. What does all this add up to? This time we can't be caught unawares."

I nodded and he carried on, "Hence the deployment of infantry battalions."

"So is the plan to attack or to defend?" I pushed my luck.

Suraj remained poker faced for a minute and then smiled, "See, this is the problem with answering one question. The next two are already lined up!" But I refused to cow down and bore straight into his eyes. "I honestly don't know, Mohana. These high level decisions are made at the Army Headquarters, and for obvious reasons, get communicated to us just before action. We only have to be fully prepared to execute them."

I was getting adept at hiding emotions. "Just one last question. What happens to the Ghaatak platoon? Will you really go into the enemy territory and strike?"

Pat came the response, "Most happily. Isn't that why we train so hard?"

"And what happens if you get caught and jailed?"

"Well, you'll need a passport and visa to visit me, that's all!"

When we went to bed, it had been pouring nonstop for almost seven hours. Thunder and lightning were a welcome change from the ear piercing train horns that would assault us every now and then.

Sometime past midnight, we were woken up by a loud banging on our door, as if something was terribly wrong. It set off a panic reaction and Suraj and I immediately tried to get off the bed from either side. *Phachaak!* Our legs went straight in knee deep water. "Shit! Where has this water come from?" I shrieked. Wading through it, Suraj switched on the light. Holy crap! We couldn't believe what we saw.

Brown, muddy water had flooded the room. My entire kitchen had been swept off the table—plastic plates, bowls, and glasses were floating around along with wrappers, empty packets of chips and the dirt from the tracks. I stood staring at my slippers sailing in a corner. Suraj, in the meantime, opened the door. It was the station master, completely drenched and shivering! Being a short man, the water was touching his thighs. "The whole area is flooded, sir. I was in my office trying to save my files when I remembered you. The lights in your room were off so I thought you might be asleep." He examined the bed, which was the only dry item in the room. Thanks to its tall legs, our mattress was just a little above the rising water.

Suraj had recovered from the shock by then. "Thank you, Vermaji...really nice of you to come all the way for us."

Vermaji folded both his hands in a *Namaste* and said, "No, no, sir! Please don't say that. You people are doing so much for the country; we can never thank you enough."

Suraj patted his shoulder and gestured him to relax. "So what do we do now? If the water level rises, the mattress will also get wet," Suraj looked around with a frown.

"My suggestion would be to wait and watch. But you please fold it and keep it ready. If it continues to pour like this, we will need to shift it higher. I'll see if I can send another table which can be mounted on the bed." He turned to leave but remembered something, "Hope your suitcases are safe."

That's when it hit me—all our belongings had been kept on the floor in the drying area. I instinctively held my head in my hands. "Don't worry, madam, it will be fine. You are a brave lady. I'll send across some tea for both of you." He went away after giving us a polite nod.

"Brave lady," Suraj winked.

"Brave or not, lazy lady I certainly am. Oh God, Suraj! All our clothes must be soaking wet. How will I wash them?" I fell back on the bed, legs still submerged in the muck floating around.

Luckily, the rain slowed down, saving us from the 'Mattress on table, table on bed' circus. We had the sugary tea watching the receding water level, and decided to worry about things only in the morning.

Wiping our legs and feet with a wet towel, we hit the sack as if nothing had happened.

We woke up to an entirely different visual. The water had miraculously disappeared leaving behind a thick deposit of sludge. Chocolate wrappers, cigarette butts, plastic cups, and used condoms were thrown in to add character to the slippery, brown gunk. A distinct smell of sewage wafted around and it seemed I would spend the rest of my life cleaning that mess.

Suraj had other pressing issues like the next train to worry about. Luckily, one of his uniforms had been spread out for drying. He left, promising to send someone over to help me. Ten minutes later, Vermaji was inspecting the room nodding his head. "You don't worry, madam. I've assured sir that I will get this cleaned in a few hours. You just take care of your belongings."

True to his word, Vermaji got the whole place cleaned on priority. By afternoon, two women appeared with bottles of phenyl and scrubbed the floor sparkling clean. The place, in fact, was cleaner than before and smelt so strongly of phenyl that the urinal next door was put to shame!

I now had a new job title—washerwoman. Recovering from the sight and smell of the flood was still manageable, but washing the stains off our clothes was a whole new ball game! Vermaji was hugely supportive; he got extra clotheslines put up in the living room, transforming our room into a *dhobi ghat*.

Next morning, the sound of dry clothes, fluttering under the fan filled me with a deep sense of achievement.

Over time, the last platform became '*fauji*' platform since all our trains were taking off from there. Soldiers in combat uniforms would go about their work under the curious gaze of onlookers, me included. More than what they did, I loved to observe how they did it. Be it wrapping up boxes and grain bags in tarpaulin covers or hauling massive equipment or lining up those enormous trucks on the convoy trains, everything was done with zeal and dedication. Having seen the corporate world where people are often disengaged with their jobs, I was amazed to see how tirelessly these men worked. Where did they get their motivation from? What kept them energized? How could they joke around, doing the most laborious jobs?

They would mostly avoid eye contact with me. But if that ever happened, they would politely wish and get busy with their work. The cooks were no different. An empty wagon at the side of the '*Fauji* platform' had been converted into a kitchen, where a team of cooks would prepare meals for all the soldiers deployed at the station. Heat from the massive cooking stoves would drive me away in no time, but the cooks would be on duty round the clock. We would eat the same food as the troops but unlike Lakhpat, I was not complaining about it anymore. Eating whatever is served and being thankful for it was a big life lesson taught by our soldiers.

The Kargil war had aroused the whole nation. '*Fauji* platform' on the Ranchi railway station soon became a popular tourist destination. More and more people started coming over just to get a glimpse of their heroes. With at least 2–3 trains moving out every day, people knew that they were witnessing something momentous. Speculation was rife, though the men in uniform were tight lipped!

I often saw people walk up to the soldiers for a handshake. Why just kids, everyone around seemed to have learnt the art of saluting. People would get small gifts like sweets and chocolates; though flowers and garlands were accepted more easily.

The third train of the day was getting loaded. So far, it had either been freight trains that carried grains and weapons, or open wagons that carried vehicles and big equipment. For the first time, a passenger train was getting ready. Hundreds of soldiers with *pitthus* began appearing on the platform to board the train. Simultaneously, a huge crowd started to build on the neighbouring platforms and foot over bridges. Soon people climbed the roofs of nearby buildings and trees. Emotions mounted as the train started moving amid chants of '*Bharat Mata ki jai*', applause, whistles, and salutes to the departing heroes.

From that day, this became a routine. Every train left the station amid resounding chants and applause that would continue long after the train had disappeared.

I was hosting lunch for the bachelor gang of our unit. The arrangement was a bit unconventional though—the guests were supposed to bring their own food. Plates too!

The bachelor boys came in along with a new face, Second Lieutenant Yash Sethi. "Ma'am, I've heard so many stories about you and Suraj sir. I'm so glad to meet you," the kiddo said, earnestly.

Major Bagga was in his element as always, "Thank your stars that Mohana ma'am didn't induct you in the unit! Poor Rajan wasn't as lucky." Rajan's mention changed the atmosphere in the room.

'Rajan wasn't lucky in many ways,' I thought silently.

But Major Bagga quickly changed the subject to food. "Let's eat, ma'am. We got your favourite *kadhai paneer* from Rajbhog." Rajbhog was a small restaurant in Ranchi that we used to visit quite often. I was touched. Not only did these guys remember my favourite food, they took the effort to get it for me despite their hectic schedule.

Our unit was to leave the next morning and everyone was busy with the final wrapping up. "Thank you so much, Capt. Bagga...oops you're Major Bagga now! I really appreciate your effort. Don't know when we will have a meal together again," I spoke straight from heart.

In his unabashed filmy style, he reassured me, "Don't you worry, ma'am! We will teach those worms a lesson and come back soon. Just make sure you welcome us with your *tadke wali arhar daal.*"

Just then, Suraj walked in and everyone took off at him, "The honourable railway minister has arrived! Let's show some respect or he will make us sit in the guard's cabin tomorrow!" Major Bagga quipped and we all burst out laughing. For a while, we forgot the circumstances and enjoyed the food and each other's company. Memories of some of the funny incidents brought crazy laughs and I savoured the positivity and indomitable spirit surrounding me.

But hey, wasn't I living it myself? The next day was D-day, but just like others, I was able to keep my worries aside and be in the moment!

Most of our unit had left in the morning. The next train was scheduled to depart at 5 pm. This was the final *fauji* train to leave from Ranchi, with Suraj and his team along with a few hundred soldiers on board.

I also had a long journey back home, but hopefully a comfortable one, thanks to Vermaji. He guided me to try a new route via Raipur and also booked me a seat in the AC coach. My train was at 8 pm. Our stuff was packed and I was sitting in the room waiting for Suraj. He had been out since morning, finishing the last bit of formalities. There was little hope of any time with him. Surprisingly, I was not pacing around restlessly, like I normally would, under such circumstances.

The war had taken away more than 500 of our brave men, including our dear Shree. However much we may be against war, the challenge had to be countered. And it would be selfish to wish otherwise. I decided to just stay with that thought.

Finally at about 4 pm, Suraj stepped into the room, looking tired. "I ate something, don't worry," he blurted even before I could ask.

"Tired?" I tried to sound normal.

"A bit…but quite relieved. The tiredness is from too much talking. I've interacted more in these 10 days than in my entire tenure!"

I didn't know how to respond. There was nothing to say when there was actually a world to explore. "Let me take a quick shower. Don't know how things will be once we reach."

"Can you hold me?" I managed to utter. His face softened, as if he remembered that I was not going to accompany him any further. He held me in a warm embrace and kissed my hair. I savoured the familiar scent—so distinctly Suraj—comforting, reassuring! Wish I could hold on to it somehow….

"Mo, I need to go." The words jerked me back to reality. Suraj asked if I could pack the used uniform in his luggage. I put it in a cover and packed it in my bag instead. I would have to make do with it, till I could enjoy his embrace once again.

Even before Suraj had finished his shower, a few guys came to collect his luggage. There was no time. The train was ready. Suraj came out, looked at me for a moment, reached out for a quick kiss and asked, "You coming to the train to see us off?"

I stood as a face in the crowd, my heart swelling with pride…and bursting with pain, thinking about the man I had come to love more than ever! He waved at me and gestured me to stay strong, before disappearing in the sea of uniforms.

As the train pulled out of the station, the crowd exploded in cheers and applause. People started running along with the train—shaking hands, waving goodbyes, throwing salutes and showering petals. As the train caught speed, my vision blurred. The reverberating chants of '*Bharat Mata ki jai*' kept me strong and rooted, despite my body wanting to collapse out of despair and anguish.

Slowly, the X on the last bogie disappeared. The commotion settled as the crowd started melting. Soon, only Vermaji and I stood on the platform.

"You are a brave lady, madam," he said, thankfully without looking at me.

I swallowed the lump in my throat. Giving him a glance, I wondered if he was really that short or had I grown a few inches taller!

And the Journey Continues...

The Kargil war is remembered as a military, diplomatic, and political success for India. 'Operation Vijay' launched by the Indian Army, along with 'Operation Safed Sagar' of the Indian Air Force cleared the Kargil sector of infiltration by Pakistani soldiers and militants on the Indian side of the Line of Control.

On 26th July 1999, the operation was officially declared closed after all military objectives were achieved. According to the official figures, 527 Indian soldiers were martyred and another 1,363 were wounded in the war. Keeping with its tradition of celebrating bravery, the Indian Army set up the Kargil War Memorial in Dras which has inscriptions of all the Indian soldiers who lost their lives in the war.

After the war was over, Suraj's unit was instructed to move back to Sopore in Kashmir for completing their field tenure. Like the rest of the army, they got over the pain of loss and went back to their job—protecting the motherland.

Suraj, a Major with the Indian Army, finished his term as an SSC (Short Service Commission) officer. After serving the nation for five years, he decided to move into civilian life.

The decision came as a surprise to Mohana who had expected him to proudly don the uniform all his life. When questioned, Suraj being Suraj, evaded a straightforward response and joked about the war scaring the hell out of him. In her heart, Mohana knew that her professional aspirations might've triggered the decision. Yet again, without a word, Suraj had asserted his love for her.

After an emotional goodbye to his brother officers, Suraj has joined Mohana in building a new life together. The roles have now been reversed: Mohana is the breadwinner for the family while Suraj mulls over the road ahead. Having left behind everything that he was confident and passionate about, he is gearing up for an unnerving journey of finding his feet again.

Major Asif requested for a compassionate posting to Delhi to help Shaheen undergo medical treatment. Dreaming of parenthood every single day, they stay hopeful, happy and as much in love as ever. NSR and Major Rana, Major Murthy and family, Major Bagga and all the young officers of the unit continue to travel together as one big happy family. Avanti and Prakhar are positive of the magic of natural therapies. Neil's region is consistently ranked the best in the country, thanks to his sharp, innovative marketing mind. He continues to be a friend and support to Mohana. Sumi has relocated to Australia after marriage.

As for Mohana, she cherishes Namkum and all the bittersweet experiences it offered. "Just like Pilates, the army toughened my core," she tells everyone with a smile. A small corner of her heart will always carry warmth and gratitude for everyone who was a part of her growth story.

With wings a tad stronger, she aims to fly higher.

ACKNOWLEDGEMENTS

They say it takes a village to raise a child. And I say, a book is no different! Well, at least mine used tons of help.

Born to an excited but inexperienced mother, my book-baby showed discipline issues—excess words, characters running amok, plots and sub-plots burdened with details. My village took charge of helping me raise her, and raise her well, ahem!

It is my joy and honour to thank my friends and supporters, in the order of their appearance in my writing journey.

Shibu Warrier, for patiently listening to half-baked ideas during our walks, reading each chapter as it took shape, celebrating how this baby slowly came alive. Also, for his undying faith in my abilities!

Nidhi Bhandari, for her encouragement during the nervous and unsure early days.

Swati Srivastava and **Shruti Warrier**, for pampering and indulging the new mom, assuring her that her baby was beautiful. Swati, also for the rare feat of tirelessly reading two versions of the manuscript and helping with some critical decisions on the storyboard.

Nirupama Madhwesh, for bringing in some much-needed tough love—pointing out the slack, mercilessly dismissing superfluous details, and questioning the mom on why her grip on the baby was not firm enough!

Somya Shikha Kumar, for being the gentle, loving observer who enjoyed small things about the baby, filling the timid mom with immense confidence about her parenting skills.

Maj Gen Neeraj Bali, for bringing in a rare combination of heft and cheer while looking through my work and to our many conversations around it!

Kalyani Gopalakrishnan, for diving in with a sense of purpose, and coming up with expert observations and fresh perspectives.

Samir Nakra, for being ever-so-ready to share his deep understanding of the ethos and culture of the Indian Army and helping me write some critical pieces.

Narendra Pandit, for agreeing to go through a fat manuscript, even though fiction is not his cup of tea!

Amrita Shetty, for not being the fast and furious reader that she is, and slowing down to assess a book which is not even 'her type'.

Gaurav Suri and **Aneesh Issar**, for indulging a stranger and her request for a bias-free evaluation.

Chander Suta Dogra, for guiding me around the alien land of book publishing.

My Publisher, **Dipankar Mukherjee**, for his conviction in my work, when the rest of the publishing world looked away.

My Editor, **Indrani Ganguly**, for the keen, discerning eye with which she brought a professional touch to my rookie work.

Last but not the least, **Meena Vaidya** and **Sharad Vaidya**—my precious Aai and Baba, for being the light of my life!

Nandita Warrier
Pune, 2023

ABOUT THE AUTHOR

Nandita Warrier is an Executive Coach and Leadership Facilitator, deeply invested in the idea of growth. She has spent over two decades exploring what makes people reach their fullest potential. Her work spans across the globe through her contribution to organisations like the United Nations and others.

Guided by her motto—'Intensity without being intense', Nandita loves to unpack complex issues simplistically. Her debut novel *Two Inches Taller* is one such attempt—the journey of a flawed, complex and yet endearing character, brought to life using nuanced strokes of humour and reflection.Her most recent accomplishment has been overcoming a life-long fear of dogs to become a loving parent to a naughty cocker-spaniel.

Amid the hustle and bustle of life, she shares a warm, peaceful nook with her husband and daughter, who indulge her enthusiasm for learning new things, the latest being growing her own food. Ever optimistic, Nandita remains energized towards an elusive life goal—a flat tummy.

Nandita will be thrilled to meet you here:

Twitter: @WarrierNandita

Facebook: https://www.facebook.com/nandita.warrier/

LinkedIn: https://www.linkedin.com/in/nandita-warrier-01946221/

Instagram: @nanditawarrier

Readomania

Readomania exists to nurture, curate, and bring to you content you love. We are a publishing house that takes pride in encouraging talent, new or old, and provide a wonderful platform for awesome stories.

We make this possible in multiple ways.

The first as an independent publishing house. Readomania boasts of multiple imprints across various categories—fiction, nonfiction, children, to name a few. An eclectic mix of content for its readers, when you read a Readomania title, you enter a world that's yours, supported by unique and quality narratives.

The second, as an online publishing platform for writers—a place to share stories, poems, opinions, travelogues, a way to explore your creative talent. Available as premium, as well as free-to-read content across multiple genres, the reader is spoilt for choice.

Join us in this journey, as we explore, develop, and present stories to our readers and audiences. Welcome to the world of Readomania, get ready to craft stories that enrich lives.

You can visit us at: www.readomania.com